S0-CFX-082

PENGUIN BOOKS

Steve Jackson's Sorcery!
THE CROWN OF KINGS

The grim towers of the Mampang Fortress stand before you, stark against the landscape. Evil oozes silently from its centre, poisoning all it touches with its malevolence. Somewhere within these walls the dreaded Archmage is hidden and, with him, the legendary Crown of Kings you have risked so much for. You will need all your wits about you and your magical skills will be tested to the limit as you pit your life and your strength against the unknown horrors inside!

Steve Jackson, co-founder of the highly successful Games Workshop and author of many Fighting Fantasy Gamebooks, has created this thrilling epic adventure of sword and sorcery, with an elaborate combat system, a dazzling array of spells to use and a score sheet to record your gains and losses. All *you* need is two dice, a pencil and an eraser.

Many dangers lie ahead and success is by no means certain. Powerful adversaries are ranged against you and often your only choice is to kill or be killed!

The Crown of Kings is the fourth and final part of the *Sorcery!* epic.

THE
CROWN
OF
KINGS

PENGUIN BOOKS

For Avis, Celeste, Pere and Xavier

PENGUIN BOOKS
Viking Penguin Inc., 40 West 23rd Street,
New York, New York 10010, U.S.A.
Penguin Books Ltd, Harmondsworth,
Middlesex, England
Penguin Books Australia Ltd, Ringwood,
Victoria, Australia
Penguin Books Canada Limited, 2801 John Street,
Markham, Ontario, Canada L3R 1B4
Penguin Books (N.Z.) Ltd, 182 – 190 Wairau Road,
Auckland 10, New Zealand

First published in Great Britain by Penguin Books Ltd 1985
First published in the United States of America by Penguin Books 1985

Printed in the United States of America by
R.R. Donnelley & Sons Company, Harrisonburg, Virginia
Set in Palatino

CONTENTS

INTRODUCTION

The Crown of Kings is the fourth adventure in the *Sorcery!* series, following *The Shamutanti Hills*, *Kharé – Cityport of Traps* and *The Seven Serpents*. But *Sorcery!* has been designed so that each adventure is playable in its own right, whether or not readers have been through the previous ones.

If you are new to *Sorcery!* you may prefer to start your adventure from the very beginning. The first adventure, *The Shamutanti Hills*, takes you from Analand, your homeland, out into the wilderness of Kakhabad, armed with a knowledge of magic to see you through your journey.

The Crown of Kings is, however, a complete adventure in itself. Set in the Fortress at Mampang, you must recover the Crown of Kings, which is guarded by the Archmage himself. But before you confront the evil Archmage, you must find your way into Mampang and then through the traps and terrors of the Fortress itself.

New players will find all they need to undertake the journey as warriors. But if you would prefer the magic arts to the power of the sword, you will also need *The Sorcery! Spell Book* (reprinted at the end of this adventure) to learn your magic spells before you embark. Readers who are now on the final stage of their journey will be able to skip over the rules section and plunge straight into the adventure. Their characters, equipment and experience must be carried over from the previous adventure.

THE SIMPLE AND ADVANCED GAMES

Beginners may wish to start with the simple game, ignoring the use of magic. Rules for fighting creatures with swords and other weapons are given in each adventure book, using a combat system similar to that used in Puffin's *The Warlock of Firetop Mountain*, the original Fighting Fantasy Gamebook. By rolling dice, you battle creatures with weapons only.

More experienced players will wish to progress quickly on to the advanced game, in which your fighting ability is somewhat limited but your most powerful weapon will be your knowledge of magic, a much more powerful tool. In actual fact, the advanced game is fairly simple to learn. There is no reason why beginners should not proceed with the use of magic from the start. But learning spells will take some time and practice with the Spell Book (pages 351–68), and the 'simple' option is given for players who wish to start their adventure with minimum delay.

HOW TO FIGHT THE CREATURES OF KAKHABAD

Before setting off on your journey, you must first build up your own personality profile. On pages 18 and 19 you will find an *Adventure Sheet*. This is a sort of 'current status report' which will help you keep track of your adventure. Your own SKILL, STAMINA and LUCK scores will be recorded here, and also the equipment, artefacts and treasures you will find on your journey. Since the details will change constantly, you are advised to take photocopies of the blank *Adventure Sheet* to use in future adventures, or write in pencil so that the previous adventure can be erased when you start another.

Skill, Stamina and Luck

Roll one die. If you are playing as a *warrior* (the simple game), add 6 to this number and enter the total in the SKILL box on your *Adventure Sheet*. If you are playing as a *wizard* (the advanced game), add only 4 to this number and enter the total. Wizards are worse fighters than warriors, but they more than make up for this by the use of magic spells.

Roll both dice. Add 12 to the number rolled and enter this total in the STAMINA box.

There is also a LUCK box. Roll one die, add 6 to this number and enter this total in the LUCK box.

For reasons that will be explained below, SKILL, STAMINA and LUCK scores change constantly during an adventure. You must keep an accurate record of these scores and for this reason you are advised either to write small in the boxes or to keep an eraser handy. But never rub our your *Initial* scores. Although you may be awarded additional SKILL, STAMINA and LUCK points, these totals may never exceed your *Initial* scores, except on very rare occasions, when you will be instructed on a particular page.

Your SKILL score reflects your swordsmanship and general fighting expertise; the higher the better. Your STAMINA score reflects your general constitution, your will to survive, your determination and overall fitness; the higher your STAMINA score, the longer you will be able to survive. Your LUCK score indicates how naturally lucky a person you are. Luck – and magic – are facts of life in the fantasy world you are about to explore.

Battles

You will often come across pages in the book which instruct you to fight a creature of some sort. An option to flee may be given, but if not – or if you choose to attack the creature anyway – you must resolve the battle as described below.

First record the creature's SKILL and STAMINA scores in the first vacant Monster Encounter Box on your *Adventure Sheet*. The scores for each creature are given in the book each time you have an encounter. The sequence of combat is then:

1. Roll the two dice once for the creature. Add its SKILL score. This total is the creature's Attack Strength.
2. Roll the two dice once for yourself. Add the number rolled to your current SKILL score. This total is your Attack Strength.
3. If your Attack Strength is higher than that of the creature, you have wounded it. Proceed to step 4. If the creature's Attack Strength is higher than yours, it has wounded you. Proceed to step 5. If both Attack Strength totals are the same, you have avoided each other's blows – start the next Attack Round from step 1 above.
4. You have wounded the creature, so subtract 2 points from its STAMINA score. You may use your LUCK here to do additional damage (see over).
5. The creature has wounded you, so subtract 2 points from your STAMINA score. Again, you may use LUCK at this stage (see over).
6. Make the appropriate adjustments to either the creature's or your own STAMINA score (and your LUCK score if you used LUCK – see over).
7. Begin the next Attack Round (repeat steps 1–6). This sequence continues until the STAMINA score of either you or the creature you are fighting has been reduced to zero (death).

Fighting More Than One Creature

If you come across more than one creature in a particular encounter, the instructions on that page will tell you how to handle the battle. Sometimes you will treat them as a single monster; sometimes you will fight each one in turn.

Luck

At various times during your adventure, either in battles or when you come across situations in which you could be either lucky or unlucky (details of these are given on the pages themselves), you may call on your LUCK to make the outcome more favourable. But beware! Using LUCK is a risky business and if you are *un*lucky, the results could be disastrous.

The procedure for using your LUCK is as follows: roll two dice. If the number rolled is *equal to or less than* your current LUCK score, you have been *Lucky* and the result will go in your favour. If the number rolled is *higher* than your current LUCK score, you have been *Unlucky* and you will be penalized.

This procedure is known as *Testing your Luck*. Each time you *Test your Luck*, you must subtract one point from your current LUCK score. Thus you will soon realize that the more you rely on your LUCK, the more risky this will become.

Using Luck in Battles

On certain pages of the book you will be told to *Test your Luck* and will be told the consequences of your being Lucky or Unlucky. However, in battles you always have the *option* of using your LUCK either to inflict a more serious wound on a creature you have just wounded, or to minimize the effects of a wound the creature has just inflicted on you.

If you have just wounded the creature, you may *Test your Luck* as described above. If you are Lucky, you have inflicted a severe wound and may subtract an *extra* 2 points from the creature's STAMINA score. However, if you are Unlucky, the wound was a mere graze and you must restore 1 point to the creature's STAMINA (i.e. instead of scoring the normal 2 points of damage, you have now scored only 1).

If the creature has just wounded you, you may *Test your Luck* to try to minimize the wound. If you are Lucky, you have managed to avoid the full damage of the blow. Restore 1 point of STAMINA (i.e. instead of doing 2 points of damage it has done only 1). If you are Unlucky, you have taken a more serious blow. Subtract 1 *extra* STAMINA point.

Remember that you must subtract 1 point from your own LUCK score each time you *Test your Luck*.

Restoring Skill, Stamina and Luck

Skill

Your SKILL score will not change much during your adventure. Occasionally, you may be given instructions to increase or decrease your SKILL score. A Magic Weapon may increase your SKILL, but remember that only one weapon can be used at a time! You cannot claim 2 SKILL bonuses for carrying two Magic Swords. Your SKILL score can never exceed its *Initial* value unless specifically instructed.

Stamina and Provisions

Your STAMINA score will change a lot during your adventure as you fight monsters and undertake arduous tasks. As you near your goal, your STAMINA level may be dangerously low and battles may be particularly risky, so be careful.

If *The Crown of Kings* is your first adventure, you start with enough Provisions for two meals. If you have played the previous adventures of the series, the Amount of Provisions you carry will already have been decided. You may rest and eat only when allowed by the instructions, and you may eat only one meal at a time. When you eat a meal, add points to your STAMINA score as instructed. Remember that you have a long way to go, so manage your Provisions wisely!

Remember also that your STAMINA score may never exceed its *Initial* value unless specifically instructed.

Luck

Additions to your LUCK score are awarded through the adventure when you have been particularly lucky. Details are given whenever this occurs. Remember that, as with SKILL and STAMINA, your LUCK score may never exceed its *Initial* value unless specifically instructed.

SKILL, STAMINA and LUCK scores can be restored to their *Initial* values by calling on your goddess (see later).

ALTERNATIVE DICE

If you do not have a pair of dice handy, dice rolls are printed throughout the book at the bottom of the pages. Flicking rapidly through the book and stopping on a page will give you a random dice roll. If you need to 'roll' only one die, read only the first printed die; if two, total the two dice symbols.

WIZARDS:
HOW TO USE MAGIC

If you have chosen to become a wizard you will have the option, throughout the adventure, of using magic spells. All the spells known to the sorcerers of Analand are listed in *The Sorcery! Spell Book*, which has been reprinted at the end of this book, and you will need to study this before you set off on your adventure.

All spells are coded with a three-letter code and you must learn and practise your spells until you are able to identify a reasonable number of them from their codes. Casting a spell drains your STAMINA and each has a cost, in STAMINA points, for its use. Recommended basic spells will get you started quickly, but are very uneconomical; an experienced wizard will use these only if faced with choices of unknown spells or if he/she has not found the artefact required for a less costly spell.

Full rules for using spells are given in the Spell Book.

DON'T FORGET! You may not refer to the Spell Book once you have started your adventure.

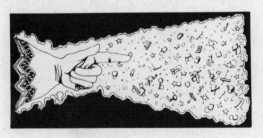

LIBRA –
THE GODDESS OF JUSTICE

During your adventure you will be watched over by your own goddess, Libra. If the going gets tough, you may call on her for aid. *But she will only help you once in each adventure.* Once you have called on her help, she will not listen to you again.

There are three ways in which she may help you:

Revitalization: You may call on her at any time to restore your SKILL, STAMINA and LUCK scores to their *Initial* values. This is not given as an option in the text; you may do this if and when you wish, but only once in each adventure.

Escape: Occasionally, when you are in danger, the text will offer you the option of calling on Libra to help you.

Removal of Curses and Diseases: She will remove any curses or diseases you may pick up on your adventure. This is not given as an option in the text; you may do this if and when you wish, but only once in each adventure.

EQUIPMENT
AND PROVISIONS

You start your adventure with the bare necessities of life. You have a sword as your weapon, and a backpack to hold your equipment, treasures, artefacts and Provisions. You cannot take your Spell Book with you, as the sorcerers of Analand cannot risk its falling into the wrong hands in Kakhabad – so you may not refer to this book at all once you have started your journey.

If you have not played any of the previous adventures, you have a pouch around your waist containing 20 Gold Pieces, the universal currency of all the known lands. If this is the second, third or final stage of your journey, your quota of Gold Pieces will already have been decided. You will need money for food, shelter, purchases and bribery throughout your adventure, and 20 Gold Pieces will not go far. You will find it necessary to collect more gold as you progress on your way.

You are also carrying Provisions (food and drink). As you will find, food is an important commodity and you will have to be careful how you use it. Make sure you do not waste food: you cannot afford to run out of Provisions.

SORCERY! ADVENTURE SHEE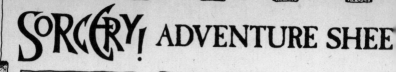

SKILL *Initial* *Skill=*	STAMINA *Initial* *Stamina=*	LUCK *Initial* *Luck=*

GOLD AND TREASURE	PROVISIONS

EQUIPMENT AND ARTEFACTS

BONUSES, PENALTIES, CURSES ETC.

CLUES AND NOTES

MONSTER ENCOUNTER BOXES

ill=
amina=

Skill=
Stamina=

Skill=
Stamina=

ill=
amina=

Skill=
Stamina=

Skill=
Stamina=

ill=
amina=

Skill=
Stamina=

Skill=
Stamina=

kill=
amina=

Skill=
Stamina=

Skill=
Stamina=

THE LEGEND
OF THE CROWN OF KINGS

Centuries ago, in the time we now call the Dark Ages, whole regions of the world were undiscovered. There were pockets of civilization, each with their own races and cultures. One such region was Kakhabad, a dark land at the end of the earth.

Although several warlords had tried, Kakhabad had never been ruled. All manner of evil creatures, forced from the more civilized lands beyond the Zanzunu Peaks, had gradually crawled into Kakhabad, which became known as the Verminpit at Earth End.

Civilization and order had spread throughout the rest of the known world ever since the discovery of the Crown of Kings by Chalanna the Reformer, of Femphrey. With its help, Chalanna became Emperor of the largest empire in the eastern world. This magical Crown had mysterious powers, bestowing supernormal qualities of leadership and justice on its owner. But Chalanna's own ambitions were not of conquest. He wished instead to establish peaceful nation-states, aligned to Femphrey. Thus in his wisdom he passed the fabled Crown from ruler to ruler in the neighbouring kingdoms, and, with the help of its magical powers, one by one these lands became peaceful and prosperous.

The path was set. Each ruler would own the Crown of Kings for a four-year period in which to establish order within his kingdom and fall in with the growing Femphrey Alliance. So far the kingdoms of Ruddlestone, Lendleland, Gallantaria and Brice had taken their turns under the rule of the Crown. The benefits were immediate. War and strife were virtually unknown.

The King of Analand duly received the Crown of Kings amid great ceremony, and, from that day onwards, the development of Analand was ensured. No one quite knew how the Crown of Kings could have such an enormous uplifting effect on a whole nation. Some said it was divinely inspired; some that its power was merely in the mind. But one thing was certain – its effects were unquestionable. All was well in Analand, until the night of the Black Moon.

The King was the first to discover that the Crown was missing. Carried off on that starless night by Birdmen from Xamen, the Crown was on its way to Mampang in the outlaw territories of Kakhabad. News came from the Baklands that the Crown was being carried to the Archmage of Mampang whose ambitions were to make Kakhabad his kingdom.

Although Kakhabad was a dangerous land, it was in itself little threat to the surrounding kingdoms. The lack of rule meant it had no army and its own internal struggles kept it permanently preoccupied. But with the Crown of Kings to establish rule, Kakhabad could potentially be a deadly enemy to all members of the Femphrey Alliance.

Such was the shame that fell on Analand for the loss of the Crown that all benefits from two years under its rule soon disappeared. Law, order and morale were breaking down. The King was losing the confidence of his subjects. Neighbouring territories were looking suspiciously across their borders. There were even whisperings of invasion.

One hope remained. Someone – for a military force would never survive the journey – must travel to Mampang and rescue the Crown of Kings. Only on its safe return would the dreadful curse be lifted from Analand. You have volunteered yourself for this quest and your mission is clear. You must cross Kakhabad to the Mampang Fortress and find the Crown!

KAKHABAD

THE ZANZUNU PEAKS

ILKLAR

TINPANG R.

L.ILKLALA

VISCHLAMI R.

VISCHU

VISCHLAMI SWAMP

MAMPANG FORTRESS

HIGH XAMEN

LOW XAMEN

REST OF THE SNATTA

AVANTI WOOD

KHARABAK R.

NACOMANTI R.

ADU

ASTLINE

D SEA

1

Like a gigantic claw clutching at the sky, the Mampang Fortress is a foreboding image etched into your mind. Although it is the goal of your mission, its appearance in the distance gives you no sense of relief at the approach of your journey's end. The feeling is rather one of apprehension and danger as you pick your way towards the great castle on high, which is partly obscured by the billowing clouds which shroud the uppermost peaks of the Zanzunus.

The going becomes harder as your trail climbs through Low Xamen. The Zanzunu foothills are evidently little used by creatures on foot, and the path is indistinct. Where the way is muddy you can make out hoof-marks along the trail; they are days, if not weeks, old. *But what sort of creature has made them?*

The sun fades behind dense clouds and the sky darkens. Perhaps a storm is brewing? A deep distant rumbling from the heavens confirms your suspicion. You had better prepare yourself. It is already late in the evening, so perhaps it would be wise for you to find a suitable place to camp for the night. There is plenty of shelter under the vegetation to avoid the rain, but you would feel safer in a cave of some sort if you are going to get some sleep.

You pause to consider which way would offer you the best chance of shelter. To the east and west, leaving the trail, the undergrowth would make the going heavy, with no real cover which you would be happy to sleep under. No, the path ahead to the north is really your only way forwards. Your eyes follow it. A few hundred metres ahead it turns to the right around a rocky ridge. With a bit of luck there may be a nook of some sort in the side of the ridge in which you will be able to shelter. You press on.

When you reach the bend in the path you are able to see what lies ahead. To your right you see exactly what you were looking for. Not one, but *three* caves are set into the rock! The nearest one has the smallest entrance, which probably opens into quite a shallow cave. The central cave looks large enough for you to light a fire inside, although the cave could be quite deep and therefore dangerous. The third cave is of a similar size but, looking at the trail, you notice that the hoof-prints lead off into this cave. Which cave will you try for shelter?

The smallest cave?	Turn to **222**
The middle cave?	Turn to **136**
The far cave?	Turn to **534**

2

Your next step is painful! Your leg has brushed against a sharp blade which gashes it. Deduct 1 STAMINA point and choose your next few steps from the following: **349**, **180** or **249**.

3

You select a jar labelled Ant Meatballs and pop a couple in your mouth. In spite of their name, they taste quite palatable! You turn to ask the Hobgoblin how they are made, but she is giving orders to the Minions and pays no attention to you. You begin to feel warm inside and your muscles glow. These strange balls have a peculiar effect which is most invigorating. You may restore your SKILL and STAMINA scores to their *Initial* levels! Now turn to **375**.

The room you are in is at the top of the tower. A single window lights the room, which is bare except for a shiny plate on the floor behind the door. The remains of a meal are on the plate. Your immediate thought is worrying. *Are you alone in this room?* The answer, quite clearly, is *no*, and this is confirmed when you feel a slight tugging at your elbow.

'Are you all right? Have you been injured?' A squeaky little voice is addressing you. You whirl round. A smile spreads across your face as you recognize Jann, the Minimite you met just outside Birritanti! 'The gods be praised!' he says. 'My friend from Analand! Oh dear, I hoped this would not happen. I'm sure your capture is my fault.' Your smile drops as you remember how troublesome the little creature was. You were quite happy to rid yourself of the Minimite at the time and perhaps his reappearance will be bad, rather than good, fortune. Nevertheless, you certainly want to know how he came to be trapped in the Archmage's tower.

'Our departure was a sad occasion for me,' he starts. 'I felt I had found a good friend, and one who certainly needed my help in crossing Kakhabad. I came after you. I missed you in Kharé – for I will not venture into the cityport – and searched for you in the Baklands. Fenestra the sorceress is one of my good friends and she told me of your movements. I almost caught you at Lake Ilklala, but you crossed in the boat before me. I could not fly that far without rest and had to skirt the lake.' You notice the creature's wings – or lack of them. 'These black-faced, swill-bellied butchers!' he moans. 'They cut my wings! I was captured by the Red-Eyes and brought to this place. My wings were clipped to prevent me escaping.'

You ask Jann why the Archmage himself should want to bring you into his own tower. 'No, my friend, you have it wrong.' He shakes his head. 'This is not the Archmage's tower. This is a *prison* tower! The Archmage's most prized prisoners are kept here.' You are astonished. Will you tell him Farren Whyde's story (turn to **69**), or do you think you ought to try planning an escape (turn to **98**)?

5

You tell them a little of your journey, being very careful not to reveal its true purpose. They listen to you, enthralled, for She-Satyrs have a strong ambition to visit lands beyond their own. They talk constantly of their intended journeys far from home. But alas, their ambitions can never be fulfilled, as they may breathe only the rarefied air of the high mountains. To them, you are a source of wonder, and they quiz you endlessly about the places you have visited and the creatures you have met. They lay down their weapons and the three of you talk for some time. 'Let me put you right in one respect, traveller. You are passing through our domain, it is true. But you are no longer in Low Xamen. This is *High* Xamen.' This news is a shock to you. You must be nearer to the Fortress than you think! You look towards it, but it is hidden for the present among the clouds. If this news is true, your journey must almost be done. Lost in contemplation, you suddenly realize that the She-Satyrs are again throwing questions at you. The larger of the two stands up. 'We would like to know more – *everything* – of your journey. Please, do us the honour of coming with us to our village. Our sisters must hear of your adventures.' You consider for a moment. You do not want to waste valuable time in idle chatter, but it is possible that the She-Satyrs may be able to provide information about the Fortress. Will you accept their invitation (turn to **545**), or will you tell them that you must make the Mampang Fortress by nightfall, so you must continue your journey (turn to **260**)?

6

The heavy door is locked. Being solid metal, you do not fancy your chances at breaking it down. If you have a silver key, you may try it in the lock by turning to the reference corresponding to the number cast into the key. If the reference makes sense, the key fits; if not, it does not. Otherwise you can knock on the door by turning to **178**.

7

You both sit down on a hard wooden bench and he composes himself. 'I have no wish for all this violence and treachery,' he starts, 'for I am a man of peace. It's this god-cursed Mampang that causes all these problems. I cannot even trust visitors any more.' You assure him that you will do him no harm and he tells you his story. Turn to **79**.

8

You have three ways onwards, depending on whether or not you want to avoid the creatures within the courtyard. Ahead to your left is a group of guards whose rowdy behaviour leads you to suspect that they are off duty: if you want to head towards them, turn to **532**. Ahead to your right is another group of creatures which look vaguely familiar: to find out more, turn to **325**. If you wish to avoid both these groups, continue straight ahead by turning to **135**.

9

You think quickly. Will you tell them you have come to see whether they would like any food while they wait (turn to **275**), will you make out that you have travelled a great distance and ask them for news of the Fortress affairs (turn to **166**), or will you try to be polite and ask them how they and their families are (turn to **200**)?

10

Did you spend last night in the cave with the hoof-prints outside? If so, turn to **247**. If not, turn to **113**.

11

The flask is slimy to the touch. You pick it up, keeping one eye on the creature. You shake it: there is a small quantity of liquid inside. But before you can uncork it and find out what is inside, the creature shambles forwards. Will you prepare to fight it (turn to **516**), or drop the flask and leave the room (turn to **96**)?

12

You have angered the Red-Eyes and given them the excuse they need for a fight. They draw out weapons and attack. You may attack either with your weapon (turn to **159**) or with a spell:

YAZ	KIN	RES	TEL	DOZ
664	748	708	639	720

13

Which candle will you use to light your way – the blood candle (turn to 38) or an ordinary candle (turn to 72)?

14

With your weapon at the ready, you grope around deeper into the cave, following the line of the wall. You find no hidden tunnels, nor any more Jib-Jibs in the back of the cave. The whole cave is perhaps three or four metres deep and is, thankfully, empty. But as you feel about, your hand touches something cold. You grasp hold of the object and bring into the light to get a closer look. You have found a dirty old bottle with a stopper firmly jammed into its neck. The glass is a dark brown colour and it is difficult for you to make out whether there is anything inside. The weight of the bottle indicates that it is empty, but there is a faint sound as you tip it up and down. Do you want to risk opening the bottle? If so, turn to 318. If not, turn to 99.

15

You stand up in the room, with your weapon at the ready. The shuffling sound is moving around towards the door and your skin chills as a dark, bulky shape is silhouetted in the doorway. Whatever it is has blocked the door! The next sound is a *pinging* noise like the twang of a bowstring. And the next sound is a scream – your own! For something has pierced your arm. You grasp hold of a shaft and draw it from your flesh. The shaft is not an arrow, as you first suspected, but a spine, like the spine of a giant porcupine. Another *ping* is followed by another scream as another spine pierces your leg. The last *ping* comes from a more accurate shot; its aim was true. This spine has passed through your throat. Your scream is more of a gurgle. Your mission has ended.

16

You can find nothing which will be particularly useful, but there is one idea which occurs to you. If you have a strong weapon, such as a sword or spear, you may try to wedge it between the floor and the ceiling, to try to hold the floor down. But the floor seems to be powered by some mechanism that is a good deal stronger than a mere weapon. Nevertheless, you may try this if you wish. And you had better hurry up! The floor's rise is already causing you to kneel down. If you wish to try wedging a sword, turn to **55**. If you wish to use a spear, turn to **134**. If you don't want to risk breaking either, turn to **269**.

17

Your magic and your weapon will do you no good against such numbers so, as a last resort, you decide to try the hardwood spear. As you thrust it out, the guards gasp. You touch one of them with its tip. The guard slumps to the ground! This enrages one group, and five of them charge towards you. Using the spear as a bat, you fight all five guards. Eventually, all five fall to the ground, dead. But not before they have inflicted 4 STAMINA points of wounds on you. The others, watching this holy magic, are now decidedly nervous. Flushed with your new-found confidence, you advance to attack them. Minutes later, they all lie dead at your feet. The only one left is the little Gnome, whimpering in the corner. You pause to think: should you spare his life or not? The poor little thing looks so wretched . . . But no. He offered you no mercy; why should you spare him? You drive your spear through his throat. You may now leave the room and head for the double doors. Turn to **392**.

18

'Off you go then,' he says, stepping aside to allow you into the room. You walk over to the left and open the door. There is a short passageway which ends at another door, and you open this one next. The room inside is a disgusting scene. Broken wood, weapons, bones and glass are scattered around the floor, and thick slime lies everywhere. Slumped in one corner is a bulky creature with blubbery skin. Its head is hideous, with a short trunk-like snout in the middle of its face. Your arrival has startled it and it climbs slowly to its feet. Two doors lead from the room; one directly opposite and the other in the wall to your left. The creature is now standing on its feet; it is the size of a bear and it is holding one hand up to its ear as if trying to hear what you are saying. But so far you have said nothing. Will you ignore it and rush towards one of the other doors (turn to **515**) or will you pause and talk to it (turn to **480**)?

19

The Ogre chuckles behind his hand. 'My question to you is: What is the name of my wife?' You get angry, claiming that there is no way you could possibly know that. But he is adamant. A deal is a deal. Will you comply with his wishes and let him have his way with you (turn to **285**)? Or will you put up a fight (turn to **270**)?

20

You give him the gold as you promised and he fingers it greedily. 'Very well. Since you have kept your side of the bargain, I will now keep mine. Step up to the large double Throben Doors leading to the inner keep and whisper "Alaralamalatana". The handle will turn. Make any mistake with this password and your mind will be lost.' You thank him for his advice and leave the room. Turn to **141**.

21

Before you can find your choice in your pack, the creature is upon you. Turn to **296**.

22

The Red-Eye who ran off will warn the Fortress of your presence. You have lost the advantage of secrecy which you had and must now stop using your special advantage of turning to alternative references whenever the person you meet is aware that an Analander is expected. Continue by turning to **171**.

· ·

23

The Birdmen are angry. You are refusing their help. But you are adamant in your wish not to follow their companion into the room. The creatures draw their weapons and advance towards you. Will you face them with your weapon (turn to **462**), or cast a spell?

GOD	NAP	DUM	YAZ	MUD
707	**647**	**790**	**758**	**605**

24

You tell Colletus about your discovery of the dead creature in the cave. 'Ah, the She-Satyrs!' he nods. 'Finding a cave in which to die in peace is one of their strange customs. The trembling disease is spreading through their race like the plague. Only yesterday I was speaking to Sh'houri herself about this disease. I am able to cure it, you see, for I am blessed with healing powers. They have promised me their protection if I will act as their medic. Of course I have agreed; for anyone so blessed must not keep his power selfishly. It must be made available to the poor and the sick everywhere.' You ask him if he will share this power with you, by healing the disease you may have contracted inside the cave, and he agrees. For a few moments, he lays his hands on your forehead. 'Indeed you did have the trembling disease,' he tells you. 'But I now have it here in my hands. You are cured!' You thank him for his help; your meeting with him has been a fortunate event. Do you now wish to continue the conversation by asking him about the Fortress (turn to **103**) or would you like his help as a holy man (turn to **283**)?

25

You try your best to reach the double doors before the statue can attack again, but it is no use. In your half-crippled state, you are no match for your opponent's tremendous speed. It slams into you again and knocks you – as luck would have it – over towards the doors ahead. But the blow has caused you quite some damage. Deduct 4 STAMINA points and turn to **224**.

26

'I have not seen you around these parts before,' she says, 'but you must be one of the Archmage's officers. You are welcome to eat from my special store. I have just pickled some juicy dung-beetles. How does that sound to you?' The thought is not too appetizing. But you have taken the Hobgoblin in; she thinks you are someone else. Maybe she would be willing just to let you continue without eating any of her nauseating 'delicacies'. Turn to **137**.

27

'Ah, would that you could, stranger,' she sighs. 'For my life would once again be worth living if my tormentors were dispatched to the gods. But why should you do this for me? I *can* make it worth your while, though I cannot tell you what I can offer, as no one must know they are in my possession. But, as far as an old, impoverished woman is able, I will reward you if you will do this for me.' If you wish to take up the old woman's offer, you must find the creatures she refers to as 'her tormentors' and kill all three. When they are all dead, deduct 100 from the reference you are on when you are searching the bodies and turn to this new reference to return to the beggar woman. Now leave her by turning to **8**.

28

You feel around the walls for any signs of secret passageways, but find none. You do, however, find the answer to your puzzlement over the purpose of this room. Turn to **182**.

29

'Why have I been disturbed?' demands the She-Satyr. 'Who is this? Ah, you have brought me a human for my amusement!' The other two creatures protest, but she will not listen to them. Guards are called and you are taken deeper into the cave to a large pit. The pit is wide but not deep and in the bottom is a large, hungry WOLF. 'Let's see what amusement our human can provide for us!' she laughs. And with a snap of her fingers, you are pushed into the pit. You must fight the Wolf:

WOLF   SKILL 7   STAMINA 7

If you defeat the Wolf, turn to **209**.

30

The confusion eventually clears as the spell wears off. Your feet once more touch the ground and you may take in your surroundings. You are outside the Fortress, high up in the mountains, standing on a narrow path through the rocks. Turn to **539**.

31

You hold your chosen object against the centre of the double doors, just above the lock, and wait for something to happen. Moments later, something does. Small pin-holes appear in the wood around your hand. And instantly, before you can react, sharp needles spring out of the door! You howl in pain as the needles pierce the flesh of your hand. Deduct 2 STAMINA points *plus* the number you roll on one die. If you are still alive, turn to **63**.

32

You speak your password. With bated breath you wait for something to happen. A tiny *click* sounds hopeful. You gather your courage and reach for the large handle. You turn it. The door opens! You have now managed to pass through two Throben Doors and you may enter the inner keep. Turn to **538**.

33

You breathe a sigh of relief as you step out of the darkness and into a brightly lit room. Your eyes smart in the light and you are forced to close them momentarily to adjust. Hurried by relief, you step through the doorway, perhaps a little too quickly. Caution should have been your watchword.

As you step into the bright room, hands grab your wrists! Guards! You have been captured! The two sentries march you proudly over towards two doors in the left-hand wall. Their gruff voices cannot conceal their excitement as they bundle you in through one of the doors to present you to their captain.

Cartoum, Captain of the Guards, sits behind a wooden desk, which is covered in papers. You are surprised to find that he is no Beastman, as are the other guards. He is tall, slim and his long hair falls down to his shoulders. Although he is a human, he is not from Analand. Most probably he is a renegade from the lands to the east of Kakhabad. Will you face the captain to see what he has to say (turn to **508**) or would you rather try to make a break for it before the door is closed behind you (turn to **154**)?

34

The Red-Eyes have the power of heat vision. They do not use it often as it can be dangerous even to their own kind, so they keep it sealed behind their closed eyes. However, to defend themselves (and sometimes to cause a little mischief) they will not hesitate to use it. Every time you inflict a wound against a Red-Eye, you must roll one die to see whether its heat vision burns you. The more often they use this power, the more accurate they get. Thus, the first time they use it, a roll of *less than 6* will mean they have missed you. The second time they use it, you will need to roll less than 5 to avoid it. The third time you must roll less than 4 and so on. If a Red-Eye's heat vision burns you, you must roll one die to see how many STAMINA points you lose. If a Red-Eye's heat vision hits you twice, you will die. Now return to **225** to finish the battle.

35

The captain believes your story. He will escort you himself to the Archmage so that you may relate your message in person. The guards release your arms and you walk with the captain out of the room and across the light chamber towards a large door on the far side. Turn to **301**.

36

You continue along the path, which winds along the side of the mountain past two more similar giant nests. Thankfully, there are still no signs of whatever lives in them. But your relief is short-lived, for a flickering shadow appears around you. You look up towards the sun and can make out a large shape hovering in the air. Two great wings are beating to keep the creature aloft. You shield your eyes from the sun and are able to see more clearly what is watching you.

A human shape is held in the air by the huge feathery wings. Its mouth is a sharp, hooked beak and wild black hair blows in the wind. Its arms and legs all end in sharp talons, and the creature is watching you intently. Of course! This is the land of the BIRDMEN! These creatures are among the most hated and feared in all the Zanzunus! The Xamen Birdmen were responsible for your mission in the first place, as it was they who stole the Crown of Kings from the court in Analand! Do you want to seek shelter behind a bushy shrub on the side of the path (turn to 513), or will you instead hail the creature and try to talk to it (turn to 338)?

37

The door is not locked. It opens to reveal an odd-shaped room, forming a rough crescent. It is dark and lit only from a lancet window in the left-hand wall. The floor is rough stone and scattered with straw. A doorway is set towards the far end of the right-hand wall. But what really catches your attention is a festering smell of decay which hangs in the room. Will you enter and look around (turn to 114), or leave this room and try the other door (turn to 465)?

38

You take the candle from your pack and concentrate. Suddenly a flame flickers and appears at the wick – just in time, as the door behind you slams shut of its own accord! You are alone in the room, but your candle lights up some of the way. You gasp as you look at the floor! Sharp blades protrude through the wooden floorboards at irregular intervals! Your balance will have to be perfect as you pick your way through this deadly maze. Will you be able to keep your footing? Choose your next few steps by turning either to reference 288 or to 367.

39

In your weak state, your resistance is less than usual. Eating dirty food such as this is not the wisest of moves. You begin to feel ill and your stomach heaves. You excuse yourself from your host and move away quickly. Deduct 2 STAMINA points for being sick, and then turn to **8**.

40

In the narrow confines of the doorway, the guards will attack you two at a time. The first pair moves in to fight:

First GUARD	SKILL 7	STAMINA 7
Second GUARD	SKILL 6	STAMINA 7

You may choose which guard to attack each Attack Round. Fight your chosen opponent as normal, but roll also for the Attack Strength of the other guard. If his Attack Strength is higher than yours, he will inflict a normal wound on you. If his Attack Strength is lower, he has missed – but you will not wound him, as you have chosen to attack his companion. As soon as one of the guards dies, a guard from the other pair will move up to take his place:

Third GUARD	SKILL 7	STAMINA 8
Fourth GUARD	SKILL 8	STAMINA 7

If you defeat the guards, turn to **129**.

41

You are naturally suspicious of such an important-looking door being open. It *looks* safe enough, but are you walking into a trap? You pick up a piece of branch lying in the hallway. It is a length of Oak Sapling, which you may keep with you if you wish. You touch the door with the branch. Nothing happens. You shove the door open a little further and then you realize the trap. A roaring flame and blast of heat flare up from behind the door, causing you to shield your face! The door opens directly into a burning inferno! Your heart sinks. There seems to be no way through here. Do you want to let the door close and try the ornate door, perhaps to return here later (turn to **54**), or will you risk an all-or-nothing run through the inferno (turn to **541**)?

42

'My name is Valignya,' he starts, 'First Assistant to the Lord Treasurer of Mampang. I collect taxes, and I collect gold. May I now have my Gold Piece?' He is becoming impatient. The Jaguar growls under his table. Will you give him the Gold Piece he is asking for (turn to **542**), or continue to refuse (turn to **132**)?

43

'A message for the Archmage?' he asks. 'I am Cartoum, Captain of the Archmage's Guards. Do not try to hoax *me* with your puny story. You have come to seek out our leader. Is this not true?' Will you admit that you have come to destroy Mampang (turn to **122**), or will you continue with your lie (turn to **243**)?

44

The room is undecorated and dirty. The only furniture is a table and two chairs, and there is nothing particularly unusual about them. The table does, however, have a drawer in it. You open the drawer and inside you find a single large key on a ring. You may take this with you and leave the room. The double doors at the end of the archway have a strong lock and your hope is that this key will open the lock. Making sure that there are no close sounds on the far side of the doors, you try the key. It fits! The lock turns and you are able to open the doors wide enough to get through. Turn to **467**.

45

Their eyes light up as they see how wealthy you are. You hand one of them the 3 Gold Pieces. 'Very well,' he says. 'You are wise to ask for advice about the dangers within Mampang. For there are many who would attack and rob you of a wealth such as you carry. Many . . . *including us!*' And with those words, the Sightmasters draw their swords. Turn to **90**.

46

You start to pick your way across the bridge. Several yards along, your foot slips! Your leg drops through the rope and you hang on desperately, to prevent yourself plummeting to your death. You do manage to hang on, but you must decide whether or not you wish to continue across the bridge. If you want to turn round, you can climb back and try the other path up the mountainside instead (turn to **339**). If you will not be put off, you must roll two dice and compare the total with your SKILL score. If the number rolled is less than or equal to your SKILL, turn to **117**. If the number exceeds your SKILL, turn to **151**.

47

There is no other way onwards. Turn to **256**.

48

Your answer stops them dead. Their mouths drop open. '*An Analander?* In Mampang? Surely not!' One of them turns to another and whispers something quickly. Too late you realize your blunder, as one of the Red-Eyes turns and runs quickly to the far side of the courtyard. He has most probably been told to warn the guards that an Analander is in the Fortress. Your advantage of surprise has been lost. If you defeated all seven Serpents in the Baklands, turn to **22**. Otherwise turn to **171**.

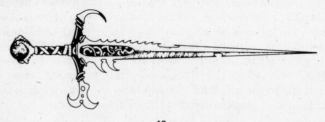

49

One by one, the heads of the other Mampang gods form on the Hydra's necks. A black face with large yellow eyes turns towards you and lowers its eyelids. When its eyes close completely, the dim light in the room is snuffed totally. Lunara, goddess of the moon, has cast her spell of darkness! In pitch blackness you can hear the great creature advancing towards you. Will you turn and run for the door (turn to **250**), or allow it to advance and prepare yourself for battle (turn to **324**)?

50

The effort of holding on to your perch is beginning to tell. Your fingers and arms are trembling with the strain. Roll two dice and compare the total with your SKILL score. If you roll a number *greater* than your SKILL, turn to **133**. Otherwise turn to **273**.

51

You search round the floor and find nothing particularly interesting. The flask that rolled to your foot contains a small quantity of a type of cooking oil – probably what the creature was drinking and what makes the floor of the room greasy and sticky. You may take this flask and the oil it contains with you if you wish, but if so, you must leave behind one item of equipment if you are carrying more than ten. Leave the room by turning to **96**.

52

At last! Your hand touches the wall ahead of you and feels the outline of a door! You grasp the handle and turn it. Turn to **33**.

53

Roll two dice. If the total rolled is less than or equal to your SKILL score, the door will burst open (turn to **112**). If the roll is higher than your SKILL, the door holds firm. Each time you try the door (including a successful attempt), you must deduct 1 STAMINA point for bruises. You may either keep trying until you open the door or give up at any stage, go back to the entrance-room and try the other door, explaining that you have made a mistake (turn to **18**).

54

The carvings on the door itelf are interesting, but give you no useful information. Grasping the handle, you open the door. Inside, you find a bare room with a mechanical contraption of some sort standing alone in the centre of the floor. It is made of brass and iron, with wheels, bands and cogs linked together in a way that suggests some sort of machine designed to work metal. But it is still. If you wish to try to discover how it works, *Test your Luck*. If you are Lucky, turn to **460**. If you are Unlucky, turn to **514**. If you do not wish to waste your time with it, turn to **81**.

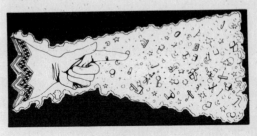

55

You wait for the floor and the ceiling to get closer together and then hold your sword between them. The sword catches and bends. It is doing nothing to halt the trap! The sweat is running down your forehead and into your eyes as you watch in desperation. Finally, the matter is decided. With a sharp snap, your sword breaks in two! You have now lost this weapon and if it is your only one, you must deduct 3 SKILL points in any battles until you find another. But probably this will be no real cause for concern. Within the next few moments, you are likely to be crushed to death! Turn to **269**.

56

You draw your weapon and march forwards. The noise dies down as you enter the room. *Test your Luck*. If you are Lucky, turn to **235**. If you are Unlucky, turn to **299**.

57

The creatures are only further excited by your attempts to avoid them. They run towards you and stop directly in your path. As you walk through, they trip you up. 'Clumsy oaf!' scorns one. 'Can you not see where you're going? How dare you kick my friend's foot here and not apologize. Apologize immediately – and *lick his boot clean*!' You pick yourself up and nod a silent apology. But sure as Libra you are not going to lick anyone's boot clean. The Red-Eye holds out his boot while the other two taunt you. Your anger rises and, in a temper, you twist the boot, bringing its wearer tumbling to the ground. This was a mistake. For this was the excuse that the Red-Eyes were looking for. Together, they open their eyes, directing their fiery stares at your arm. You howl in pain as six lines of fire burn your arm. The arm drops to the ground and with it fall your hopes. The pain is excruciating; you pass out. When you regain consciousness, you will find yourself on the ground next to your arm, alive, but unable to complete your mission . . .

58

Do you have anything you may be able to use against this creature? If so, turn to **152**. If you simply want to run for the double doors as quickly as possible, turn to **363**.

59

The trail curls behind a large boulder and continues. You are a little concerned about the fact that it is now leading you round the side of the mountain concealing the Fortress. A crevasse is preventing you from heading on towards Mampang. You must find some way across it. A short while further on, you find what may be your answer – a wooden bridge spanning the two sides of the crevasse. Will you try crossing this bridge (turn to **183**) or would you prefer to continue along the trail (turn to **257**)?

60

The Birdmen are taken aback by your offering. They have never seen such a spear before. While the three are engrossed in studying it, you are able to step quietly back through the door. Turn to **479**.

61

You press a Gold Piece into her hand. The old woman begins to tremble. 'Why, this is a *Gold* Piece!' she stammers. 'The gods be praised! Never before has anyone been so generous to poor Javinne. A harvest of thanks on you, stranger. Javinne is your friend for life. But no! I must hide my joy. For if those god-cursed mongrels who have more than their fair share of what I lack learn of my good fortune, I will surely suffer. And it is too early to seek help from my friends from Schinn. No, I must keep this news a secret. I must hide.' Several things she has said have caught your attention. Before she shuffles off to hide, you may question her. Will you ask her about 'the mongrels who have more than their fair share of what she lacks' (turn to **302**)? Would you like to know more about her friends from Schinn (turn to **372**)? Or will you ask her how she lost her sight (turn to **388**)?

62

The creature's flesh is cold! The body rocks on its seat and falls over backwards. This corpse is quite dead. And another surprise is in store. The body is not that of a man, but a female of some sort. And although its torso is human, its legs are hairy and end in hoofs. Its face is a strange blend of human and goat-like features, with two horns on its forehead.

You quickly recover from the shock and compose yourself. The rest of the cave seems to be empty and there is more than enough space to make yourself comfortable. If you wish to bed down for the night here, and perhaps eat some Provisions, turn to **293**. If you would rather try one of the other caves, turn to **419**.

63

You have survived the deadly defences of the courtyard door, but not for long. For the needles are coated with a quick-acting poison. In a few minutes, you will begin to feel groggy. Then you will pass out. The poison is effective and there is no antidote. Your journey has ended here.

64

The morning star bashes into the side of your head and knocks you reeling. Blood oozes from a nasty gash in your temple. Deduct 3 STAMINA points. When you have recovered sufficiently, you may enter the room. Turn to **251**.

65

Courageously, you advance against the Hydra. Perhaps, if you can attack it before its heads have fully materialized, it will not be at its full strength. But deep down you are not optimistic. For how can you fight against the gods themselves? Another head appears. This one is green and scaly with a pointed nose and gills in its neck. It is Hydana, god of the waters. His mouth opens and a torrent of water bursts out at you, knocking you backwards to land painfully on your ankle. Deduct 1 STAMINA point and let the battle commence:

GOD-HEADED HYDRA   SKILL 17   STAMINA 24

After the first Attack Round, turn to 458 if you wounded the Hydra, or 305 if it wounded you.

66

Valignya will accept from you anything which has some sort of ornamental value (a medallion, jewel, etc.). Choose something and offer it to him. He will accept it and you can then demand help in entering the inner keep. If you are able to offer him something, turn to 276. If you have nothing to offer, return to 160 and choose again.

67

You dash forwards through the pass before any keen-eyed observer within the Fortress can spot you. As you do so, you notice two guards slumped on the floor asleep at their posts. An empty wine flagon tells the story. They are *drunk*! Will you ignore them and run on through the pass (turn to 342), or do you think it would be wiser to run them through with your sword, just in case they should wake and spot you (turn to 289)?

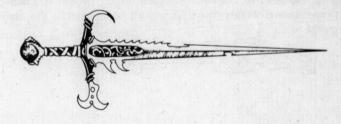

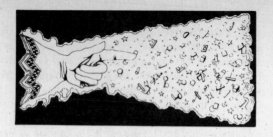

68

They look a little suspiciously at you, but talk to you nevertheless. 'Old Naggamanteh is sharpening his axe,' chirps up one of the Birdmen. 'For the Archmage has promised him new victims. But you know the old Cyclops . . . He won't be happy until he's torturing one an hour! The Archmage himself hasn't been seen for a time; locked himself away in his tower, he has. Some say he's expecting visitors. Anyway, enough.' You bid them good-day and leave the room. Turn to **479**.

69

You tell Jann of the ageing weapons specialist who revealed the tower to you. The Minimite smiles. 'Farren Whyde is no "weapons specialist" at all,' he sniggers. 'This man was the Archmage himself in disguise! And what a crafty demon he is. He has persuaded you to enter his own prison and become his prisoner – almost of your own accord!' You cannot believe your ears. You have already met the Archmage – and you have let him go! This is valuable information. Should you once again meet Farren Whyde, you will know his secret. Deduct 111 from the reference you are at if you come across him again and turn to this new reference to expose him. Now you had better plan an escape from this tower. Turn to **98**.

70

You may either investigate the door at the end of the passageway (turn to **144**) but only if you have not investigated it previously, or you may leave the hallway. If you choose the latter, you can either turn left and try the large double doors (turn to **253**), or you may walk up to the door across the archway (turn to **493**).

71

You pull out your scroll and start to unravel it. But before you can do anything, the creature is speeding towards you. Turn to **296**.

72

You take the candle from your pack and concentrate. Suddenly a flame flickers and appears at the wick – just in time, as the door behind you slams shut of its own accord! You are alone in the room, but your candle lights up some of the way. You gasp as you look at the floor! Sharp blades protrude through the wooden floorboards at irregular intervals! Your balance will have to be perfect as you pick your way through this deadly maze. Will you be able to keep your footing? Choose your next few steps by turning either to reference **87** or to **239**.

73

You open the door slowly and peer into the room. It is dark, with only a sealed window, but as your eyes become accustomed to the light, you can see what sort of room you have entered. You are standing in the guards' *latrine*! When you take your first breath, your stomach rises. The smell is horrendous! The room is filthy, with hundreds of flies buzzing round a hole in the ground. You fight down the urge to vomit, but must lose 1 STAMINA point. You can continue searching around this room if you wish by turning to **186**. Otherwise you can step back into the passage and investigate the other door (turn to **144**) but only if you have not investigated it previously.

74

This was not a wise choice. For as you open the door and rush out into the hallway, you practically bump into the three Birdmen you were originally running from! The ones you left behind in the room also come after you, and you are now surrounded by Birdmen. They grab you quickly, before you have a chance to react, and bundle you off into the Fortress. Turn to **333**.

75

Over and over you tumble in weightless space before the spell begins to wear off and your surroundings become clearer. Below you is a figure who looks more than familiar. This figure is standing outside a wooden door set into a solid rocky tower. With a look of determination, the figure sets its shoulder and charges at the door. At that very moment, your own body descends from the air and merges with it. You brace yourself for the shock. Turn to **102**.

76

'Pah!' he says. 'Three Gold Pieces? Why, that is only one each. And anyway, I will have all your gold once you are marched to the cellars! Take the miserable Half-Orc away!' The guards grab you roughly and shove you through the door. But before you go, they toss your gold pouch and backpack to the captain. You are destined to spend the rest of your life in the dungeons of Mampang. Mercifully, the rest of your life will be short . . .

77

You are standing to leave the table when a voice speaks your name. 'Do not be so hasty to leave, my friend. Allow me to speak to you!' The voice is familiar. You look all around you, but see no one. But gradually an image forms in mid-air. The ghostly image is familiar but it is not until it is fully formed that you recognize it. *Shadrack!* You ask him what he is doing here. 'Have you forgotten my powers?' he laughs. You remember the face in the tree. 'I may be where I wish *when* I wish. But this distance is greater than I have travelled before, and it is very tiring to me. My stay will be brief. You have survived many dangers and have proved yourself a worthy champion of your kingdom. I for one wish your mission to be successful, but there are further dangers you must face. The Throben Doors must be opened and their secrets are held by the most cunning of the Archmage's followers: Valignya the miser, Naggamanteh the torture-master and one other. But I am unable to discover who is the last. Your allies are few. But seek out the Samaritans of Schinn for, like you, they seek an end to the Archmage's ambitions of power.'

You thank Shadrack for his warning and advice and ask him why he has travelled so far to give you this message. 'Two nights ago, the Archmage's guards arrived at my cave. Their ways with the power of pain are persuasive. I am an old man and could not resist their tortures. I was forced to tell what I knew of your journey. For providing the information, they rewarded me well; I have been staked, on a cross, outside my own cave ever since. My body gave up its life this morning. How else could I revenge myself on these torturers of old men? My spirit can travel much faster than their horses. I have arrived before them, to aid you however I can.'

Shadrack's image begins to fade. His powers are weakening. As he disappears, you vow your revenge on the murderers of the hermit. You stand up to leave. Will you storm back out of this place into the courtyard (turn to **141**), or will you turn left and head for the room with the message over the door (turn to **428**)?

78

Did you spend last night in the cave with the dead goat woman? If not, then turn to **153** and make another choice. If you did spend the night there, turn to **24**.

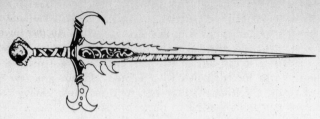

'I can assure you,' he says, 'that I am not a native of Mampang. Nor am I from anywhere in Kakhabad. My name is Farren Whyde and my kingdom is Ruddlestone, way to the west beyond the Zanzunus. My profession is the art of science and my speciality is in weaponry. In my own kingdom I was renowned for my discoveries. My most important discovery was a flash powder which would propel a missile further than any arrow could be fired. It was this cursed discovery which attracted the attentions of the Archmage. His allies, the hook-billed Birdmen, were sent after me. I was captured as I slept and brought to this hell-pit in these very clothes. Since that time his threats have kept me working on my project. But I fear that his own ambitions will see its use only for conquest, not for the defence of peace.'

You tell him a little of your own story, but only that the Archmage has similarly wronged your kingdom by stealing the Crown of Kings. The old man nods. 'I have heard of your Crown. The Archmage is said to keep it with him at all times.' You ask him where you can find the Archmage. 'Ah, now that is a secret I can help you with. Come with me!' He leads you over to a window and points out. 'The Archmage does not often visit the Mampang Fortress.' Your jaw drops. Has this journey been wasted? Farren Whyde continues: 'He considers this place unsafe from his enemies. He leads the world to believe that this is his home, but in fact it is *there*!' You follow his finger. It points out to the peaks of High Xamen – at nothing in particular.

You groan. Must you find your way safely out of the Fortress and start another journey? 'Do not despair, my friend. Let me show you another trick I have learned!' Farren Whyde cups his hands round his mouth and calls three words in a language you have never heard before. You watch dumbfounded as the enchanted words cast their spell.

Outside the tower you are in, a shimmering haze disturbs the air. As it rises slowly, the old man's story makes more sense. *Another* tower, concealed under its spell of invisibility, forms before your eyes! Farren Whyde looks at you proudly. '*There* is the Archmage's tower. That is where he stays!' You realize you must now reach this tower – and quickly, before the light fades. Will you ask the man for his advice (turn to **245**), or cast a spell?

DOC	YOB	FAR	SAP	HUF
587	626	742	774	658

80

The fat man applauds your skill. 'A worthy warrior,' he nods. The Jaguar limps off back under the table to lick its wounds. 'But warrior or not, you must still pay the price to enter this room.' This angers you and you ask him what right he has to demand gold from you. Turn to **42**.

81

You step back out into the main hallway to decide a way onwards. Will you investigate the large double doors (turn to **256**), or will you instead look for another way (turn to **47**)?

82

'Friend,' chirps the first Birdman, keeping his voice down. 'I can tell that you are concealing from us the real reason why you are here. But that is wise. Caution is wisdom in Mampang. But whether or not you came upon us by accident, you have made a lucky discovery. For we can help you more than you think with your mission. My name is Peewit Croo. We three are known as the *Samaritans of Schinn* and our goal is the overthrow of the Archmage. He is a power-crazed madman and his ambitions must be stopped! Find the Crown of Kings. If you do, we will all have our wishes. If we can help you, we will. If you need our help, blow on this. We will come to your aid if we can.' Peewit Croo hands you a small silver whistle which you place safely in your pack. You thank him and the other Samaritans and leave the room. They offer their best wishes as you do so. Add 2 LUCK points for this encounter, and turn to **479**.

83

Test your Luck. If you are Lucky, turn to **441**. If you are Unlucky, turn to **314**.

84

Your skills are worthy of the Battlemasters of the Academy at Chawberry, having fought so well against such a powerful beast. Again your weapon flashes and a head drops, but again two more heads grow to replace it. The effect is demoralizing and your concentration lapses momentarily. The creature strikes forward at you. Turn to **305**.

85

The cutlass is not enchanted; the merchant is simply a good salesman, having rid himself of this piece of junk. If you use it in a battle, you must deduct 1 SKILL point, for its rusty blade will do less damage than a normal sword. Now turn to **473**.

86

Desperately you try to fight down your nausea, but to no avail. You race from the room into the hallway and are violently ill. The thought occurs that someone may be able to hear you, but there is nothing you can do about it. Voices from the room at the end of the passage confirm that someone *has* heard you, but then the laughter that follows gives you some relief. Most probably the noise you are making is not an uncommon sound around the latrine. You compose yourself and may now choose your next action. But first you must lose 1 STAMINA point; you are feeling weakened by the experience. Turn to **70**.

87

You inch your way slowly across the room. For your next few steps, choose either **488**, **341** or **359**.

88

You drop to the ground as quietly as possible and turn to step inside the door. *Aaaaahh!* You jump with fright as you find yourself face to face with a guard in heavy armour! The guard is as surprised as you are and he bellows loudly. From outside and within, four guards come to surround you and you must now face all of them. If you attack them, turn to 40. If you would rather try a spell, you may choose one:

FOG	WOK	TEL	DUM	DIM
766	636	599	718	656

89

'Of course we will escort you,' chirps the Birdman. Two of them advance and open the door behind you. 'You will be safe with us,' he claims proudly. Looking outside, they find the way clear. You stand awkwardly between them as they walk down the hallway in a series of half-jumps. You are pressed tightly between their feathered bodies. Half-way down the hall, you realize that you are not merely sandwiched between them, you are tightly gripped! You struggle to free yourself, but to no avail. Turn to 333.

90

With swords drawn, the three Sightmasters are ready for battle. Will you draw your own weapon (turn to 110) or cast a spell?

FOG	SIX	MAG	TEL	NIP
739	657	699	588	627

If you have a hardwood spear which has been blessed by a holy man, you may try using it by turning to 313.

91

The door to the room is already open and you step inside. As you would expect, the walls are ribbed with shelves, on which hundreds of trinkets, artefacts, knick-knacks and treasures are displayed. A plump, yellow-skinned merchant sits behind a table in one corner and eyes you suspiciously. He seems to be undefended and you cannot see how he prevents his customers from stealing his wares. Do you have any money? If so, you may purchase some of his merchandise (turn to **494**). Otherwise, you may attempt to steal something. If you want to do this, you must *Test your Luck*. If you are Lucky, turn to **116**. If you are Unlucky, turn to **267**. If you don't want to steal and you haven't any gold, leave the room and try the door at the end of the passageway (turn to **310**).

92

How did you come by this vial? Were you given it by a woman (turn to **241**), by a man (turn to **278**), or did you find it on your own (turn to **491**)?

93

The door opens to reveal dirty living-quarters. An unmade bed is in the corner and a table and chair are set against one wall. A jug is standing on the table, along with a metal bowl. A wooden box protrudes a few inches from underneath the bed. This could be the torture-master's home. But then again, perhaps it is not. There are virtually no possessions in the room. This could of course mean nothing, as an Ogre's possessions are limited anyway. Do you want to step inside and investigate further (turn to **272**), or will you leave this room and try the other door leading from the torture-chamber (turn to **236**)?

94

'You could be right,' he says, eyeing you slyly. 'Are you offering your services?' You nod. 'But how do I know whether or not you are the fighter you claim to be? If I am to hire you, first you must prove your worth. *Hashi, attack!*' At the sound of his voice, the Jaguar leaps up at you from under the table. You must resolve your combat with the cat:

JAGUAR   SKILL 8   STAMINA 7

If you kill the beast, turn to **146**. If you reduce it to 2 STAMINA points and decide to spare its life, turn to **80**.

95

The creaking noise gets louder as you open the door wider. When it is half open, you can see that it leads into a short corridor. Two doors are set into the passage; one on the right and one at the end. But suddenly your ears prick up at the sound of voices! The creaking door is attracting someone's attention! You decide to close the door quickly and try another way. Will you try the large double doors (turn to **253**) or the other door across the archway (turn to **493**)?

96

Taking care on the floor you reach the door and try the handle. It opens into a hallway that widens at the far end. You follow it. Turn to **124**.

97

You thank them for the ale and drink it down. To your relief, it seems to be ordinary ale and it is a welcome drink. You may add 2 STAMINA points as you drink it. Again, you thank them for the gift. 'Gift?' laughs the Red-Eye. 'We do not hand out gifts! We charge 2 Gold Pieces for our ale!' The others join in the laughter and press you for the payment. If you have 2 Gold Pieces, you may pay for your drink and turn to **425**. If you do not have 2 Gold Pieces, or you refuse to pay, turn to **12**.

98

Your situation looks hopeless. The door is sturdy and you have already seen the size of the lock on the door. The window is one possibility, but it is a long way up. A jump would certainly kill you. Perhaps you could plan to ambush one of the guards when you are brought your food? Will you:

Try to break the door?	Turn to **120**
Ask Jann his opinion?	Turn to **414**
Use something from your pack?	Turn to **259**

Or will you cast a spell?

NIP	WAL	ZEN	FAL	ZIP
673	767	696	604	725

99

If you have any food with you, you may now eat. If you have not yet eaten today, you will gain 2 STAMINA points for this meal. If you have already eaten you will gain only 1 STAMINA point. If you do not have any food with you, you gain no STAMINA points. Make the necessary adjustments on your Adventure Sheet and prepare to settle down to sleep for the night. Turn to 384.

100

You inch your way slowly across the room. For your next few steps, choose either 52, 227 or 2.

101

You pass along the hallway and through the Mucalytic's room. At the end of the next passageway, you open the door to the entrance-chamber. The short, stocky creature that let you in is no longer there. You open the door to the courtyard and step outside. The way is clear to the large double doors and you follow the wall towards them. Turn to 392.

102

The door bursts open and you fall headlong into the chamber inside. You roll over on the straw-covered floor and take in your surroundings. The room is not at all elegant, as you would have expected. It is simply a bare room. Two doors lead from it and you must now choose which to take. You may try either the one on the left (turn to 37) or the one on the right (turn to 465).

'The Fortress?' he asks. 'Why? You are not intending to visit it, are you? For if you are, you will be cursed with eternal damnation! The evil in Mampang is like a living thing, which devours all those who cross its threshold. You have no business in there. Repent your sins now, and join with me in offering our worship to Throff – the one on high! The one true mistress of all beings! The Goddess of the Earth! Fight the dark demons of Mampang and live in eternal truth! Now! Repent now!'

The old man is getting quite excited and you really do not want to get into an argument with such a fanatic. You explain that you *are* intending to fight the evil within Mampang, that is the purpose of your mission, and that you will succeed or die in the attempt. Colletus listens and shakes his head. 'None but the gods can succeed in destroying the dark forces within Mampang,' he says. 'When I was younger, like you, that was my own mission in life. But the cursed gods within Mampang dealt with me thus!' He touches his eyes. 'But I can sense that your will is strong. Nothing I can say will dissuade you from your mission, so I will help you by revealing a sample of what you will face within the Fortress. Here, watch me.' He turns to face the Groaning Bridge and holds up his hands. *Another* bridge, looking much stronger than the first, appears next to it. 'The Groaning Bridge is naught but an illusion,' he explains. 'Had you crossed the illusory bridge, its spell would have been broken half-way across and death would have been the reward for your courage. If your cause is as you say, then I can offer you three treasures to help you on your mission. I have two potions which may aid you. The first will restore your strength, and the other has been blessed in the name of the gods. My last gift is a cloth skullcap, which may also aid you. Now go. And may the luck of Cheelah go with you.'

You thank the holy man for his help. You would certainly have died had you tried the bridge without realizing its secret. He hands you his gifts: a medicinal potion, a brass vial of holy water and the skullcap. And his last words were no idle blessing. You may increase your *Initial* LUCK score by 1 point and restore your current LUCK to 8 (if it is currently higher than 8 anyway, ignore this bonus). Now you may cross the *real* bridge to the other side of the crevasse. Turn to **411**.

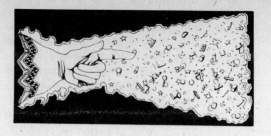

104

One of the Sightmasters takes your backpack, while another helps you off with your own tunic and on with his. The tunic is warm and comfortable but, as the Sightmaster does up the ties, its tight fit is a little discomforting. Will you protest, asking them not to draw it so tight (turn to **282**), or will you make some quip about having to lose some weight (turn to **231**)?

105

The mutation you are waiting for slowly takes effect. Your right leg begins to ache and, before your eyes, it gradually changes shape! The foot shrinks and a pointed stump appears at the end. It is turning into a tail! This now leaves you with only one leg on which to walk, although your new tail will help as a crutch. You must reduce your *Initial* SKILL by 3 points and reduce your current SKILL to this level if it is higher. When you are ready to leave, you may hop out of a back door leading further into the keep. Turn to **448**.

106

They are deeply insulted by your harmless remark, and your attempts to smooth over the tension are not too successful. The tallest Black Elf steps towards you, a sneer spreading across his lips. 'Let's teach this ugly pus-ridden human some manners, eh?', he snarls. The other two rise to their feet. You are about to have a fight on your hands. Will you use your weapon (turn to **510**) or cast a spell?

MAG	HOW	POP	NAP	NIF
793	614	775	727	671

107

The Archmage's transformation is nearly complete. If you can attack the creature quickly, before it is fully formed, then you will stand a chance. If you are not quick, you will have little hope against a Netherworld deity such as this.

NETHERWORLD DEMON   SKILL 7   STAMINA 7

If you defeat the creature within five Attack Rounds, turn to **351**. If you do not defeat it, turn to **172**.

108

The nest and golden egg are a mystery. Could they be useful if you come across Birdmen? Does the egg have any value? Or are they both simply luxurious ornaments? Will you find out? Turn now to **473**.

109

As you approach the group, you can make out three creatures talking among themselves. Their shapes are familiar. They are thin, spindly types, dressed in ragged clothes. When you are even closer, you can see that they have large eyes, but they are keeping their eyes *closed*! Immediately, you are on your guard. RED-EYES! A warning bell rings in your mind as you remember your previous encounters with the Red-Eyes. You try to avoid the group by a detour away from them. But one of them has noticed you and is calling you. Obviously he is aware that you are trying to avoid them and he is mocking you. The other two look towards you and call you over. Will you approach as they wish (turn to **242**), or will you ignore them and continue regardless of their taunts (turn to **216**)?

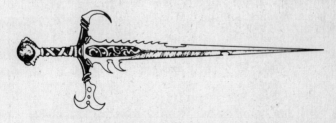

110

The Sightmasters surround you and attack together. Each Attack Round, you must choose which of the three you will fight and conduct your battle against this one as normal. Roll for the others' Attack Strengths in the normal way. If either Attack Strength is higher than your own, you will take a wound. Otherwise you will avoid their blows.

First SIGHTMASTER	SKILL 7	STAMINA 4
Second SIGHTMASTER	SKILL 6	STAMINA 4
Third SIGHTMASTER	SKILL 6	STAMINA 5

If you defeat the Sightmasters, turn to **340**.

111

The door opens. You push it slowly – and a good thing too, as it has been booby-trapped. A heavy morning star hangs above the door in such a way that its deadly spiked ball would swing into the face of anyone who entered quickly. You avoid this trap, and step into a rather sinister-looking room. Turn to **251** to find out what sort of room you have entered.

112

You fly forwards headlong into blackness. You land on a hard floor lined with straw and look around. It is pitch-black and you can see nothing. But an ominous sound puts you on your guard. From one of the corners of the room, you can hear shuffling and scraping, as though someone were dragging a bundle of twigs across the floor. Will you arm yourself (if you can) and turn to **15**? Or will you cast a spell?

DOZ	SIX	ROK	LAW	KID
682	594	672	783	644

113

The dawn has not quite broken when you rise to continue your journey. You have not yet formulated your plans for entering the Fortress, but you are sure it will not be easy. You may add 2 STAMINA points for last night's rest. But if you ate nothing yesterday, you must deduct 3 STAMINA points. You pack your things and set off for the gate.

The huge wooden gate towers above you as you approach. You are apprehensive about being spotted, but until the sun rises, this would be highly unlikely. The silhouetted outline of the Fortress against the early-morning sky is a haunting image and you cannot help but feel puny and helpless in comparison with its size.

You step up to a small door set into the gate. Will you knock on the door, knowing this will attract the guards? If so, turn to **304**. Alternatively you may cast a spell:

MUD	DOP	ZEN	YAP	YAZ
791	643	736	749	667

114

Trying to be as quiet as possible, you step into the room. You glance around at the floor for any signs either of creatures or of objects, but find none. You quicken your steps, heading towards the door. Half-way there, you stop. A shape at the far end of the room has caught your attention. It is a large, bulky shape and it is making no movements. Will you step over to investigate (turn to **369**), or ignore it and continue towards the door (turn to **470**)?

115

You chat pleasantly during your meal and eventually you decide you must continue. You may add 2 STAMINA points if you have not yet eaten today but only 1 STAMINA point if you have eaten. Now turn to **8**.

116

You smile pleasantly at the merchant, who nods back and watches you intently. You will have no opportunity to steal anything secretly, so there is only one alternative – a snatch. You choose your moment. You grab a handful of trinkets from the shelf in front of you and race for the door. The merchant does not move. But when you reach the doorway he makes a sharp clicking sound with his teeth. Immediately, sharp iron spikes shoot across to bar the exit. But you are lucky: you just manage to beat the spikes. At least, you *almost* manage to beat the spikes. For as you jump through, the sharp points nick the hand which is clutching the merchandise. You howl with pain (deduct 1 SKILL and 2 STAMINA points) and draw your hand in quickly. You have still held on to one item. To find out what you have stolen, roll one die. If the number rolled is odd, turn to **382**. If the number rolled is even, turn to **417**.

117

You manage to hold on as the bridge sways under your weight. When you reach the other side you breathe a sigh of relief and continue along the trail. Turn to 380.

118

The Birdmen are taken aback by your offering. They have never come across such a talisman before. While they are engrossed in studying it, you are able to step quietly back through the door. Turn to 479.

119

You manage to control your revulsion and work your way around the room, overturning stones and shifting bits of wood with your feet. If anything is in there, you will find it. Unless, that is, it is in the hole. For *no one* would search around in that disgusting hole. But your search is fruitless. There is nothing hidden in the latrine. At least, nothing you can *see*. For if you did but know it, you have found more than you bargained for in this room. The swarm of flies that has followed you round the room carries an unpleasant illness, which you have now contracted. For the time being, its effects are only slight. You must lose 1 STAMINA point and you must also lose 1 SKILL point *in battles only*. By the time you reach the Archmage – if you survive that long – its effects will be more noticeable. You must lose another STAMINA and another SKILL point when you first encounter him. After that, its effects will depend on whether or not you are able to find a doctor before the disease becomes fatal. You may complete your mission, but you may not survive long afterwards. Leave the room now by turning to 70.

The Minimite warns you that your efforts will be futile. Nevertheless, you are determined to try. You charge at the door as hard as you can. The little creature was right. This was a waste of time, and a painful one at that. Your shoulder gives a loud *crack* as you hit the door, and your worst fears are realized. You have done some serious damage to your shoulder. You try to move it but pain shoots across your chest. You must lose 4 STAMINA and 3 SKILL points until you can find some way of healing your injury. Turn to 476.

They are insulted that their hospitality has been refused. Will you reconsider and take their ale (turn to 97), back off and try to move away from them (turn to 57), or wait to see what happens next (turn to 12)?

122

Your bold announcement does credit to your bravery, but not to your intelligence. For you are hardly in a position to issue threats! The captain and his guards laugh loudly. 'Take the miserable Half-Orc to the dungeons,' commands the captain. His guards obey. You will now spend the rest of your life in captivity. Mercifully, this will not be for long . . .

123

The beast inside must be taught a lesson. Its howling will not prevent *you* from resting in its cave! Do you wish to enter with weapon drawn (turn to **286**), or will you cast a spell?

DOC	FAR	HOW	YAP	KIN
635	607	782	697	669

124

The passageway widens until you reach an open hallway which is evidently a main thoroughfare. Several passages open out into this area and the way onwards is a choice of two doors. Ahead are two heavy wooden double doors, standing some three metres high. Your caution is aroused by the fact that one of these doors is slightly ajar. The other door is a more ornate affair, a few yards to the left of the double doors. Carvings are set in its wooden timbers. Do you wish to investigate the large double doors (turn to **41**), or will you instead try the smaller door (turn to **54**)?

125

'From Kristatanti, eh?' laughs the Red-Eye. 'And you expect us to believe that? You are no more from Kristatanti than we are. If you were from Kristatanti, you would not wear your hair as you do. Their tradition is to wear their hair high up on their heads, held in place by pins and bones!' Will you admit that you are not from Kristatanti and that your home is Analand (turn to **48**), or will you insist that you *are* from Kristatanti (turn to **291**)?

126

You take out your Provisions and eat. If you have not yet eaten today, you may add 2 STAMINA points for the meal. If you have already eaten, you may add only 1 point. When you have finished, turn to **358**.

127

You touch the door lightly and it swings back, allowing you into a rather dirty room. A table and chair are set in a corner of the room. Asleep in the chair, slumped across the table, is a strange, smooth-skinned creature in leather armour. It has a bald head – in fact there is not a trace of hair anywhere on its body – and its shoulders look wide and powerful. As you step inside, the creature snorts and wakes up. Seeing you, it leaps to its feet, reaches for an axe and in a roaring voice demands to know why you have disturbed its nap. Will you draw out your weapon and strike the creature to get in the first blow (turn to 360), apologize for disturbing it and try to calm it down (turn to 466), or raise your voice and yell back at the creature that you didn't know he was asleep (turn to 506)?

128

The Goblin champion roars loudly, and this noise serves as a war-cry to the others. As one, they join in the fight, surrounding you and battering you with kicks, bites and blows. You fight valiantly, but you are no match for such numbers. One heavy blow knocks you to the ground. A dozen sets of spiky teeth bite into your body. The pain is unbearable and you cry your last. Your mission has ended. You will provide the best meal these foul creatures have had in their miserable lives.

129

You quickly close the door in the gate behind you and step forwards. You are in a wide archway inside the main gate. The way ahead is blocked by another gate, almost as large as the main entrance. It is a large double door with a heavy brass handle and lock. To your left and right are two smaller doorways which may open into rooms in the main wall surrounding the Fortress, which is several metres thick. Which way will you proceed? Will you try the door to your left (turn to 206), the door to your right (turn to 493), or the double doors ahead (turn to 253)?

130

You describe the boots to the captain and promise them to him if he will release you. He appears to be interested, but then snaps his fingers. The guards bustle you through the doors, throwing your backpack – and your gold pouch – back to the captain as you leave. After all, why should he release you for these boots when he can steal them? They will be no use to you in the dungeon beneath Mampang, where you are destined to spend the rest of your days.

131

They try once more to persuade you to accept their advice and put on the tunic, but you will not be persuaded. One of them snaps angrily, 'We are wasting our time. Let us persuade this miserable human in our own way!' The others nod and draw their swords. Turn to **90**.

132

You may have a bargain in mind, that if he helps you into the inner keep, you would be willing to give him his Gold Piece. If you wish to do this, you will find that he is a bargaining man and you will have to strike a deal. You may offer him 1, 2 or 3 Gold Pieces. Choose your 'final offer' and roll one die. If you offer him 1 Gold Piece, you must roll a 5 or 6 for him to accept. If you offer 2 Gold Pieces, a roll of 3–6 means he accepts. If you offer 3 Gold Pieces, a roll of 2–6 means that he will accept your price. If he accepts, turn to **20**. If he does not accept, or if you have no gold to offer, or if you do not wish to offer him any gold anyway, turn to **160**.

133

Try as you might to hold on, you cannot force your muscles to keep their grip and you drop to the ground with a thump. The noise immediately attracts the attention of the guards, who wheel round to face you. Roaring loudly, they leap towards you, swords drawn. You step back into the doorway, hoping that this will give you some protection and hoping also that no more guards appear! You must resolve your combat with the guards. Since you are standing in the doorway, you may fight them one at a time:

First GUARD	SKILL 7	STAMINA 7
Second GUARD	SKILL 6	STAMINA 7
Third GUARD	SKILL 7	STAMINA 8
Fourth GUARD	SKILL 8	STAMINA 7

If you defeat the guards, turn to **129**.

134

Anxiously, you wedge the spear between the rising floor and the ceiling. You are both shivering and sweating at the same time as your weapon takes the strain and bows a little. You whisper an unheard prayer to your god as the wood creaks. Will the spear hold? Your question is answered a moment later. *Crack!* The weapon breaks in two from the pressure. Your heart sinks. Your hopes are dashed. You have now lost this spear. If this was your only weapon, you must deduct 2 SKILL points in any future battles until you find a replacement weapon. But this is hardly of any concern to you at the moment. You are about to be crushed to death! Turn to **269**.

135

You are approaching the far side of the courtyard. Two large wooden doors loom upwards and, to progress into the keep, you will have to pass through them. A few yards in front of the doors a peculiar-shaped metal post, as tall as two men, has been driven into a mound of earth. To the left is nothing. To the right, a smaller wooden door is set into the wall. Will you step up to the double doors and see whether you may be able to get through (turn to 397)? Do you want to investigate the metal pole (turn to 502)? Or will you walk over to the door in the corner of the wall (turn to 519)?

136

You step up to the cave entrance and peer inside. It doesn't smell particularly pleasant in there, but it seems to be safe enough. The thing that is a little worrying, though, is the depth of the cave. You cannot see the back: the cave just disappears into the blackness. If you feel you would be safer in one of the other caves, you may approach either the smallest cave (turn to 222) or the other cave (turn to 534). If you will venture inside this cave, turn to 507.

137

She shuffles over to you and leads you into a foodstore. 'Help yourself!' she offers. 'All this is good for stamina. All the troops are given some of my special recipes for added strength.' You try to explain that she has mistaken you; you merely wish to take a short cut into the keep. But she will have none of it and becomes angry; she finds your refusal offensive. Will you try some of her food to keep her happy (turn to 3) or will you reassert your wish to leave (turn to 297)?

138

The strange creature holds out his hand and mumbles a few words. A shape forms in the air and rests on his hand. As it becomes more distinct, your eyes widen. *The Crown of Kings!* You reach out for it, but he pulls it away. 'Not so fast there, human!' he laughs. 'We made a bargain. If I give the Crown to you, you must be gone and leave this place. And to ensure that you cause no harm on the way, you must leave behind your weapon.' Will you agree as he says (turn to **234**)? If not, you may either draw your weapon and attack him (turn to **162**), or cast a spell:

WOK	FIX	MAG	KID	GOB
650	786	687	706	730

139

You watch both sides of the pass as you approach, keeping your eyes peeled for signs of life. You stop when you hear a rasping noise ahead. Slumped on the floor, on the right-hand side of the passage, are two heavily armoured guards. They are not moving and appear to be asleep. One of them is gripping an upturned wine flagon in his hand and the contents are seeping out. They are *drunk*! You may try creeping past them. *Test your Luck*. If you are Lucky, turn to **342**. If you are Unlucky, turn to **264**.

140

The door is unlocked and you open it. It leads into a dark passageway. You are considering whether or not to enter, when a noise from the courtyard behind you forces your decision. The sounds of marching become louder and louder. It is not well-disciplined marching, but one thing is for certain: a fair number of guards are approaching! You step through the doorway and close the door behind you. It is dark inside, but within a few moments, you are able to follow the passage. It leads more or less straight on, first winding to the left, then the right. Eventually you can see a door ahead of you. Turn to **357**.

141

You pass along the hallway and through the Mucalytic's room. At the end of the next passageway, you can hear voices in the room beyond. You open the door. 'There you are! I told you! The Analander! And when you capture the dog, remember to tell our master that it was I, Ridd the Gnome, who gave you this information.' You curse: the little Gnome has summoned guards to capture you. In his room are at least a dozen armed guards, and they rush towards you. Do you have a blessed hardwood spear with you? If so turn to **17**. If not, turn to **266**.

142

You start your battle with the guard. You have the advantage of surprise, but the guard has the advantage of *reinforcements*. As the struggle commences, the guard bellows loudly. Six more guards race into the room and, before you can react, they have pulled the two of you apart and are holding your arms pinned behind your back. A sergeant walks in and looks at the scene. His own guard is nursing a sore arm. The sergeant roars angrily at the guard for his incompetence, then looks at you. He nods to the two holding you captive and turns to leave the room. The sergeant's back is the last sight you see in the world as an unseen sword slides through your chest from behind. Your journey has ended . . .

143

The Ogre reflects for a moment. 'Uhhh, when I was new to this job I did have a particularly *nice* torture,' he starts. 'A Klattaman was caught thieving and wouldn't reveal where he'd hidden his ill-gotten gains. We put fat needles in his arms and scraped his bones first of all, then we put ground glass under his eyelids, then we cut the sinews at the back of his ankles. The killjoy told us where he'd hidden his thievings as soon as we started putting the needles in, but we ignored him. After all, we had to have our little fun, didn't we? What else did you say? The Archmage? He's in his tower, where he always is.' Now he has a question to ask you. Turn to **19**.

There are voices coming from within the room. You step up to the door and press your ear close, to hear what is going on and to discover how many are inside the room. There are probably only a couple of creatures inside, as you can only hear two voices. But suddenly, the door swings open! Before you can react, you are grabbed by the wrist and yanked into the room. 'I thought I heard something,' says a tall BLACK ELF to two others sitting round a table. 'An ugly, human creature. But look at the colour of its skin! Horrible! Ugh. Imagine having skin like that!' The other two laugh and all three of them look at you. Will you:

Laugh with them and try to befriend them?	Turn to **295**
Challenge them for daring to insult you?	Turn to **536**
Try to run from the room?	Turn to **335**

145

The two guards immediately spring on you. Fight these two together. In each Attack Round, choose whichever you will direct your attention towards and conduct this fight as normal. The remaining guard will inflict a normal wound only if his Attack Strength is higher than yours (but you cannot wound him):

First GUARD	SKILL 8	STAMINA 7
Second GUARD	SKILL 7	STAMINA 7

If you kill the guards, you may turn your attentions to the captain:

CAPTAIN OF THE GUARDS	SKILL 8	STAMINA 9

If you wish to spare the captain's life, you may turn to **347** when you reduce him to 6 STAMINA points. If you wish to continue the fight, turn to **391** when you have reduced him to 6 STAMINA points.

146

A tear appears in the corner of the fat man's eye as you deliver the final blow to his pet. 'That was unnecessary!' he sobs. 'My Hashi! What have you done?' You turn your attention to the man. You step over and grab his throat. You are a hired sword and you do not spare your victims' lives. You demand to know how to get inside the keep. You claim to have some business to attend to inside, and promise to come back if he wants to hire you. 'Very well, then,' he sighs. 'To enter the keep, step up to the doors and whisper this password to the lock: "Alaralaramalana". The handle will then turn to open the doors. Now release me!' You let him go and leave the room. Turn to **141**.

147

Libra continues: 'I must tell you also some bad news, which may affect the success of your mission. Last night you spent the entire night in the same cave as a carrier of the *trembling disease*.' She then goes on to describe the effects of the disease. Turn to **247**.

148

Do you have a silver whistle or holy water from the Tinpang River with you? If so, you may use either of these. If you wish to use the silver whistle, turn to **800**. If you wish to use the holy water, turn to **537**. If you have neither of these, turn to **351** and choose again.

149

They all exclaim in unison, 'From Kharé!' One of them smiles and grabs your wrist. '*We* are from Kharé, my friend, though we left the cityport two seasons ago. Ah, how we would love you to tell us what is happening there now. Tell me, is the holy man of Slangg still performing his miracles?' You tell him of your own experience in the chapel of Slangg and they praise your wisdom. 'If you really went through the test of Slangg, you will know the holy man's name,' says one of the Red-Eyes. 'I am trying, but I cannot remember the great man's name myself. What is it?' The other two look at their companion strangely, but then it dawns on them what he is trying to do. This is a test for you. What will your answer be:

Courga?	Turn to **195**
Salen?	Turn to **570**
Vangorn?	Turn to **549**
Tristan?	Turn to **327**
You do not know.	Turn to **457**

150

A sign over the door catches your attention. It reads 'Chamber of Night'. You pause for a moment before you try the door. What can the *Chamber of Night* hold in store? Night creatures? Sleeping gas? There is only one way you will find out. You turn the handle.

The door opens to a room as black as coal. Not a beam of light comes from the room. Even the dull light from the area where you now stand cannot penetrate its blackness. Do you have a candle which you can use to light your way through this room? If so, turn to **13**. If not, turn to **308**.

151

You are almost on the far side of the gully when your foot slips again. Desperately you try once more to clutch the rope bridge to prevent your falling. But this time you are not so lucky. The bridge quivers like a bowstring and your hand misses its grip! Down and down you plunge to your death in the river-bed below. You have come to the end of your journey – and so close to your goal . . .

You may try:

A Yellowfruit Skin	Turn to **21**
A Parchment Scroll	Turn to **71**
An Enchanted Compass	Turn to **252**
A Glass Vial of Liquid	Turn to **92**
None of these	Turn to **363**

153

You remember the message and call out for Colletus. What will this mysterious person be like? Will he be there at all? Is he even still alive? You call his name again and, a few moments later, you hear footsteps on the rock. From over the edge of the chasm, a short distance further on, a shape appears. An old, bald-headed man in a long, dirty, brown robe walks towards you. 'Who is calling my name?' he asks. At first you remain quiet – it is fairly obvious who has been calling his name! But as he approaches, you notice that he is not heading towards you, but rather slightly to your left. The old man is *blind*! His eyes have been painted black and you remember the tradition in Kristatanti. You call him over towards you and he shifts direction quickly. 'Well?' he snaps. 'Who are you? And in which direction are you heading? And what do you want of a priest with the black-eye curse?' Will you ask him for information about the Mampang Fortress (turn to **103**), would you like to call on his professional skills as a holy man (turn to **283**), or will you ask him whether, as a holy man, he has powers of healing (turn to **78**)?

154

Test your Luck. If you are Lucky, turn to **412**. If you are Unlucky, turn to **529**.

155

You tell them you were raised in Kharé by a holy man from Dhumpus when your mother abandoned you. She took the faith of Slangg, the god of malice, and was ordered to leave you to your death as proof of her commitment. Thus your accent is a cross between the broad dialect of the cityport and the slower, more pronounced speech of the southlands. You tell them you are on your way to the Fortress at Mampang, for you have been summoned by the Archmage. At the mention of his name, your two inquisitors look at each other shiftily. There seems to be a look of fear in their eyes. 'Be on your way then, stranger,' says one of the creatures. 'We will not hinder your journey. Continue.' Evidently they fear the power of Mampang and you have intimated that you are connected with the evil that rests within. They allow you to pass. Turn to **441**.

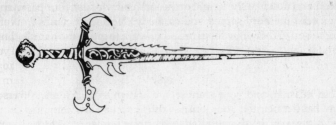

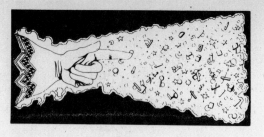

156

Trying desperately not to panic, you stand motionless while the floor rises. As you wait in hope, you are suddenly aware that your teeth are chewing hard and painfully on your lower lip! But the floor shows no signs of halting and your head is now only a foot or so from the ceiling. You had better try something more positive. Will you search the floor for something useful (turn to **168**), or look through your own belongings for something you can use (turn to **16**).

157

You bend down to the height of the lock and whisper your password. Has your memory served you correctly? No sound comes from the door. You gather your courage and prepare to grasp the handle. Turn to **344**.

158

Your mission, and your identity, are known to your host. Although you have concealed your journey thus far, it is now common knowledge that you have penetrated the Fortress's defences. Return to **198**.

159

Resolve your battle with the three Red-Eyes. They will all attack together. Choose which you will direct your own attack against and conduct this battle as normal. Roll Attack Strengths for the other two in the normal way: a higher Attack Strength than yours will inflict an automatic hit, but a lower result does not mean that you wound one of them, since you are not attacking them.

First RED-EYE	SKILL 6	STAMINA 3
Second RED-EYE	SKILL 5	STAMINA 2
Third RED-EYE	SKILL 5	STAMINA 3

When you have inflicted your first wound on the Red-Eyes, turn to **316**. If you defeat them, turn to **425**.

160

'I see we have a visitor who does not like to part with gold! Or perhaps our friend has something else to offer?' Will you offer him something else from your backpack (turn to **66**), draw your weapon and leap across the table at the fat man and his Jaguar (turn to **205**), or cast a spell?

DUD	SAP	NAP	NIF	FAR
652	693	621	763	735

161

You step into the room just in time, as three Birdmen turn round a corner and head towards you. You breathe a sigh of relief and turn round to lean back on the door. But as you do so, your heart stops! Out of necessity, you did not check the room before you entered. Now you can see where you are. There is an old Baklands expression which is appropriate here: 'Hiding from Snattacats in a Stranglebush' . . .

Rising to their feet, and glaring at you over pointed beaks, are three *more* Birdmen! What will your reaction be? Will you try to talk to them (turn to **9**), will you think desperately of a good excuse and leave as soon as possible (turn to **258**), or will you just race out into the passage (turn to **74**)?

162

You pull out your weapon and advance towards him. He simply smiles. 'Do you think you could harm me with that oversized butter-knife?' he taunts. 'Put it down. For I can make it *my* ally if I so wish.' You ignore his threats. 'Very well, then. Have it whichever way you will . . .' He gestures in the air with his hands and your weapon feels heavy in your hand. You try to lift it and find that it is tugging itself free from you. It pulls hard and breaks your grip, flailing in the air, as if with a mind of its own! And then, to your horror, it turns to face you, cutting in the air to force you back against a corner. 'And now, to complete my little show,' the sorcerer continues, 'a rope trick!' Again he gestures with his hands. This time, a rope flies up into the air. Serpent-like, it hangs, awaiting his instructions. At his command, the rope flies towards you and wraps itself around your wrists. You have been captured! '*Guards!*' he calls. From a hidden doorway in one of the walls, three guards rush into the room and grab you. The guards bundle you off back through their door and up a narrow staircase into the top of the tower. A heavy lock is set in the door at the top. This is evidently a prison room of some sort. They unlock the door and fling you inside. Turn to **4**. But remember that you have now lost your weapon. If you do not have another one with you, you must deduct 3 SKILL points in any future combats.

163

You may now either leave the room (turn to **96**) or search for anything that may be useful to you (turn to **51**).

164

The guards are disappointed. They offer to lend you 2 Gold Pieces if you are short although, if you win, you will have to pay back 4 Gold Pieces from your winnings. If you agree to this, turn to **481**. If you are not interested, turn to **397**.

165

Securing your possessions, you grab the rope firmly and once more check that it is well fastened to the rock above. You take a few steps backwards to get a good run at the crevasse. Swinging across the gully should be an easy matter. You run forwards and leap from the ledge. Then it's all over in an instant.

Even though you tested the rope thoroughly, it was not as safe as it appeared. This short cut to the Mampang Fortress was a trap designed to catch unwanted intruders such as yourself. In mid-air, the rope began to stretch quickly so that, when you arrived at the other side, you were not at a height to land on the ledge. Instead you slammed into the rocky mountainside with such force that you immediately knocked yourself out. Your fall deep into the crevasse has killed you, but at least you were not conscious when your death came . . .

166

Will they believe your story or not? *Test your Luck.* If you are Lucky, turn to **68**. If you are Unlucky, turn to **370**.

167

You sit down at the table and rest. If you have any Provisions with you, you may eat a meal. If you do so, you can add 2 STAMINA points if this is your first meal of the day or only 1 if you have already eaten. Have you visited anyone called Shadrack on your travels? If so, turn to **77**. If not, turn to **306**.

168

Quickly you drop to your knees and rummage through the straw and dust on the floor. You find plenty of small stones and broken bits of wood, but nothing which will really help you. And time is running out! The floor is rising steadily and would now be forcing you to stoop if you were standing up. A cold sweat breaks out across your forehead. You had better search your own backpack for something to use. Turn to **16**.

169

Have you already tried either of the other two caves? If you have not already tried the smallest cave, you may do so by turning to **222**. If you have not already tried the middle cave, you may do so by turning to **136**. If you have already tried both of them, then you had better settle for the one you have just looked inside – return to **534** and make another choice.

170

The Birdmen listen intently as you tell your story. They are fascinated by your adventures. 'Of course we'll help you,' one of them declares. 'In fact I have just the "seeker" you will need to locate the Crown. Come with me.' He walks into the back room. Will you follow him in as he motions (turn to 203), or remain where you are and ask him to bring it out (turn to 23)?

171

You try to reach the running Red-Eye, but his companions step in front of you. They draw their weapons and attack. You may attack either with your weapon (turn to 225) or with a spell:

SUN	ZIP	ZAP	FOF	POP
745	584	695	660	590

172

Your effort has been valiant, but in vain. The Demon now stands fully formed before you. You rush up to strike a blow with your weapon. A blast of fiery breath from the creature's great nostrils hits you full in the face. In agony, you hold your hands up to your face to stop the pain. Your hair is on fire; your face is scorched beyond recovery. You drop to the ground, defeated, as death takes you. Your journey has ended – so close, so very close, to your goal . . .

173

At the mention of the Crown, the Elves look at each other shiftily. 'Why? Who wants to know?' asks the tallest Elf. From the way they are looking at each other, you decide that you had better not pursue this line of questioning. You apologize for bringing up the subject and explain that you had only heard that it was on show within the Fortress and you had hoped to get a look at it. 'You are wasting our time, human,' the Elf continues. 'No one is allowed near the Crown save the Archmage himself. As long as those cursed Samaritans of Schinn are about, he would not dare put the Crown of Power on show.' You change the subject quickly. Turn to 377.

'If you have spent some time in contact with the trembling disease, then you will no doubt begin to feel its effects soon,' continues Sh'houri gravely. 'But all is not lost. Word has just reached us that Colletus the holy man is able to heal the disease. This is the tragedy of the situation. Had we known this two days earlier, then we could have saved the life of poor Sh'himbli. Nevertheless, stranger, he is not an easy man to find, although he has been seen on the way to that black Fortress. If you discover Colletus's whereabouts, you may summon him thus.' She cups her hands to her mouth and makes a whistling sound. If at some time in the future you think you know where the holy man is, repeat this sound by deducting 30 from the number of the reference you are at and turning to this new reference. If Colletus is there, he will appear to you. Sh'houri continues: 'And we thank you for the news of our sister.' The She-Satyrs want to give you some gift for the news you have brought. Sh'houri tells you first about the Mampang Fortress, the end of your journey. 'You must beware of the Fortress,' she starts, 'for it is a chaotic place. Keep your eyes open in front and behind if you wish to survive in there. The way through the Fortress takes you through the four *Throben Doors*; they are large sets of double doors, yet much more to those who try to pass through. Do not mistakenly believe that they are not protected, for they are deadly to all who try to open them unawares. They appear as heavy double doors, but nothing about their appearance gives any clue as to their real purpose.' She has noticed that you are listening intently, and is glad to have been able to give you some information of interest. As you stand to leave, she motions to one of the other creatures, who rushes off, to return later with a leather bag. Within the bag are several items which may be of use. She will allow you to take with you any of the items in the bag, but for each you must exchange one item of your equipment (but not food or gold). If you are playing as a warrior, turn to **564**. If you are playing as a wizard, turn to **435**.

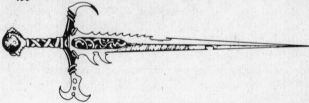

175

You inch your way slowly across the room. For your next few steps, choose either **349**, **554** or **2**.

176

As you approach the double doors, you keep your eyes peeled for any signs of activity. Through the doors, you can hear the early-morning sounds of the inhabitants preparing for the day ahead. But there is no sound coming from the short passageway in which you stand. You grasp the great brass handle and turn it. The doors are locked. Looking down the narrow slit between the doors, you can see that a heavy bolt holds them fastened. It looks as though you will need a key to open them, unless you can think of another way. Do you want to turn back and try the door on the right (turn to **206**), or will you try another plan (turn to **193**)?

177

The meal is fairly basic and not at all appetizing. Cornbread and grits do not exactly make a banquet. Nevertheless, you may add 2 STAMINA points for the food if this is your first meal today, or 1 STAMINA point if you have already eaten. Then you sit down and wait. Turn to **214**.

178

Your knock is heard by someone inside the room. A voice bids you 'Come in!' and the tumblers in the lock turn. You open the door and step inside. As you do so, you fling yourself backwards instinctively! For above the door hangs a morning star, a vicious weapon consisting of a solid metal spiked ball hanging from a handle by a length of chain. As you opened the door, it took the ball outwards to swing back at your face! *Test your Luck*. If you are Lucky, turn to **190**. If you are Unlucky, turn to **64**.

179

You open the door. As you rightly deduced, you have entered the kitchen. Servant MINIONS, small, nervous creatures with squeaky voices, are fussing around preparing food for the guards. The smell is not too pleasant. Today's menu is swine offal and lizard entrails. A larger creature, a HOBGOBLIN of some sort, stands in the middle of the kitchen, barking orders. As her Minions rush past, she whacks them on the head with a sapling branch. No one has noticed you. Will you announce yourself (turn to **422**), or will you instead try to creep through the kitchen unnoticed (turn to **437**)?

180

Your next step is painful! Your leg has brushed against a sharp blade which gashes it. Deduct 1 STAMINA point and choose your next few steps from the following: **249, 227** or **349**.

181

'So, this arrogant worm refuses our help, eh?' snaps the Sightmaster angrily. 'Then let us show the wretch what dangers are to be faced in Mampang!' You have offended the Sightmasters. They draw their swords and grab at you. Turn to **90**.

182

A noise from the doorway makes you spin round quickly. What you see makes you leap frantically towards the door. But you are too late. The heavy portcullis has already dropped in the doorway, barring your escape. *Of course*, you think. The answer is now obvious. This room is no one's living-quarters. It is a prison cell! And the heavy bars will not be budged either by your strength or your magic. You are a prisoner of Mampang and your journey is now over.

183

The wooden bridge seems to be quite strong. But you are not one to trust appearances and will not risk this bridge without first testing it carefully. You put a foot on to it, then your whole weight, holding tightly on to the rope handrail. As your weight is taken by the wooden links of the bridge, a strange sound seems to come from it: *Ooooohhhh!* The soft moan makes you jump back on to the ground! *What was that?* As soon as you step off the bridge, the noise ceases. Again you try stepping on to it, and again the groaning sound comes. Trying a few steps towards the middle of the bridge, the sound is quite disturbing: *Oooohhh! Aaaaahhh! Ooooohh!* Although the moaning is somewhat unnerving, the bridge itself seems strong enough to take your weight. If you want to try crossing it, turn to **424**. If you want to try another way across the crevasse, you may either return to the swing-rope and try that (turn to **323**) or follow the trail along a bit further to see whether there is another way across (turn to **257**).

184

A sudden pain shoots through your forehead. You feel around for signs of anything and notice a bump in the centre, growing larger and larger! Shortly, you have a sharp horn growing in the centre of your forehead. The meatballs have had their effect. Although this horn is a little unsightly, it will be useful in battle if you do not have a weapon to use. If you are disarmed and must fight without a weapon, you need only deduct 1 SKILL point as a penalty and ignore whatever SKILL penalty you previously incurred. Leave the kitchen by turning to **448**.

185

You try the key in the lock. It turns awkwardly, as if the tumblers have not quite caught. Turn to **344**.

186

You hold your breath and step further into the room. You move towards the hole in the ground and peer into it. Your presence disturbs the flies and they swarm into the air around you. Indescribable filth is down the hole and the sight makes your stomach heave. *Test your Luck*. If you are Lucky, turn to **119**. If you are Unlucky, turn to **86**.

187

The Hobgoblin throws off her apron and stands before you ready for battle. She grabs a meat-cleaver and threatens you. Will you fight her with your weapon (turn to **281**) or cast a spell?

DOC	DUD	KIN	MAG	KID
602	726	755	690	668

188

You stand defiantly, weapon at the ready, and accuse them of a number of shameful misdemeanours involving members of their families. The two become angry; their tempers rise. But the tension is finally broken by one of the creatures who laughs out loud. 'Well, Sh'haarzha, we have certainly found a spirited one here! Do you think the sisters would like to meet this character? I think so, don't you?' The other She-Satyr nods and they both order you to follow them to their village. Will you go along with them (turn to **545**), or set off with them, but take advantage of the first opportunity to run away and continue your journey (turn to **456**)?

189

You must be quick to climb the stairs and reach the Archmage before the guards are alerted. Panting heavily, you arrive at the secret door at the top of the stairs. But how can you open the door? You try your password again and the door opens. But you are expected! Rough hands grab you as you open the door. Shouts go up and you find yourself in the grip of a tall, grimy guard. Around the doorway are other guards. You were not expecting to be discovered this quickly! Turn to **430** to face the guards.

190

Just in time you managed to avoid the full impact of the morning star. It swings past your ear and catches you across the temple. Deduct 1 STAMINA point for the graze and enter the room. Turn to **251**.

191

You apologize for your blunder and explain that it was 'just a little human joke'. You will have to remember to be careful with Black Elves, as their sense of humour does not include being able to laugh at themselves. They calm down and you are able to speak to them. Do you want to ask them how to get further into the Fortress (turn to **377**), or whether they know anything which will help you find the Crown of Kings (turn to **213**)?

192

The man is terrified at your threats. He agrees to tell you anything you want to know. He is not at all like the other creatures of Mampang. You allow him to tell his story. Turn to **79**.

193

You may wish to cast a spell here:

DOC	HOW	ZIP	FAR	RAP
776	649	741	640	761

Alternatively, you may want to hold something you found on your travels against the door to try to open it (turn to **31**).

194

The door opens slowly and you step into a dimly lit room. A tiled stone floor is slightly greasy underfoot and there does not appear to be much in the way of furniture inside. An oily smell hangs in the room. On the far side of the room, a faint crack of light outlines a doorway. Do you want to head straight across for this door (turn to 96), or will you investigate the room (turn to 523)?

195

'Ha!' exclaims the Red-Eye. 'Just as I suspected. This thick-skulled impostor is not from Kharé at all! Imagine thinking that was the holy man's name!' Your attempts at trickery have been found out. Turn to 12.

196

Throwing caution to the wind, you grab the handle and turn it. Although the handle turns in your grip, the door does not open! It is locked! You curse and turn to face the creature, which is now almost on top of you. Turn to 296. If you have a key to use in the lock, return to 224 to try it. If you key is correct, you will know what to do.

197

They immediately snap to attention and pretend to be busy, polishing their weapons and armour. One of them thanks you for the advice and you turn to leave the room. Turn to 479.

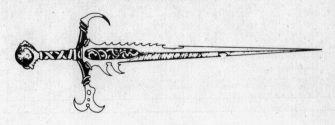

198

The door opens into an office of some kind. Straw again lines the floor, but charts and maps are pinned to the walls. Some of these are charts of the heavens, and there is a strange contraption pointing out of the window at the sky. Sitting behind the table across the room is a scrawny-looking fellow with spiky black hair. He looks up at you over half-moon glasses and smiles a sinister smile. Could this be the Archmage himself?

'And who do we have here, then?' he asks. 'As if I did not know. *The Analander!* I wondered whether you would make it this far. My congratulations on your skill and your courage. You are indeed a worthy enemy. But here is where your luck runs to an end. For now you face no cowardly Black Elf, no brainless Klattaman.' You state defiantly that your journey will not end until the Crown of Kings has been returned to its rightful guardians in Analand. 'Ah yes,' he says. 'The Crown of Kings. What say I give it to you now and you be gone? I for one am anxious to remove the cursed thing from here.' This is a strange offer. Will you accept and ask him for the Crown (turn to **138**)? Would you prefer to draw your weapon and fight him (turn to **162**) or cast a spell?

MAG	KID	GOB	FIX	WOK
687	706	730	786	650

199

'My favourite weapon?' He stares dully into the air. 'Ummm, I suppose I like my whip. Yes, my whip! I'm very good with this. I can take out a blackfly's back teeth from four metres with my whip. Do you want to see?' You don't, and you press on with the next part of your question, about the Crown. But you are out of luck. 'Never heard of it,' he shrugs. Now it is his turn to ask you a question. Turn to **19**.

200

They look at each other strangely. The situation is puzzling. A human comes bursting into their room as if being chased by a Spectre, then starts asking about their families! They cannot make sense of it. Confused, one of them steps forwards and, in a twittering voice, says, 'Our blessed mothers are well. But what business is this of yours?' Will you take advantage of their confusion, apologize for the intrusion and ask permission to leave (turn to **527**), or apologize for offending them and continue the conversation (turn to **429**)?

201

The captain listens with interest to your story. He is undecided whether or not you are telling the truth. How good are your powers of persuasion? Roll two dice and compare the total with your SKILL score. If the total is equal to or less than your SKILL, turn to **35**. If the total is higher than your SKILL, turn to **423**.

202

With your weapon poised to strike, you rush at the creature, screaming a loud war-cry. *It does not react!* Your weapon smashes into the side of its skull and its head splits open. Still the creature has not reacted! Now feeling quite safe from any danger, you reach out to touch the body. Turn to **62**.

203

You walk across the room and follow him into the dark room beyond. 'It's in here somewhere,' he is twittering. But as you step into the darkness, you feel a blow on the head. You lose consciousness. Turn to **333**.

204

You show him the hardwood spear and explain how you came across it. 'Ah, Sh'houri and her band,' he smiles. 'An unruly lot, and prone to outbursts of violence, of that you can be sure. But it is not evil which rules their hearts – though at times it is not far away! Pass me the spear. I will bless it as you wish.' Colletus places the spear on the ground and lays on his hands to bless it. From now on, this blessed spear will aid you in your battles against some of the creatures of Mampang. You thank Colletus and then bring the conversation round to the Fortress at Mampang. Turn to **103**.

205

You leap across the table and grab the man by the throat. His pet snarls at you, but you threaten Valignya with his life if he does not call off the Jaguar. Nervously, he does so. You demand to know how you may get through into the inner keep. Turn to **276**.

206

The door is not locked, but its hinges are rusty and, as you inch it open, it makes a creaking sound. Will you burst through it, weapon at the ready, to surprise whatever is inside (turn to **416**)? Or would you prefer a more cautious approach and continue inching the door open, trying to keep the noise to a minimum (turn to **311**)?

207

Your heart is thumping as you open the door and you slam it shut behind you to keep the Marbled Ram out.

You pause to collect your thoughts. You are about to come face to face with the Archmage. Your mission is almost done! If only you can take the dark lord of Mampang and rescue the Crown . . . The door opens on to the foot of a spiral staircase. You climb the stairs way up into the tower until you reach a door at the top. The door is unlocked. You open it. You are expecting an elegant study, well decorated and lined with books. What you see is exactly the opposite. Turn to **321**.

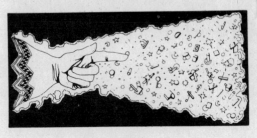

208

The silver pieces are worth more than the gold you paid for them. But they will prove to be more trouble than they are worth. The pouch that the merchant would not sell you is capable of magically generating more of these coins, so he has lost nothing. Outside of their pouch, the coins will burn through anything you put them in. You will not notice this until afterwards, when you have lost them. A short while after you have placed them in your backpack, they will have burnt a hole in your pack and and dropped out. You will also have lost one item from your backpack. Cross off the *Third* item on the Equipment List – and the coins – and turn to **473**.

209

'A fine battle!' declares Sh'houri, Queen of the She-Satyrs, as you are raised from the pit. 'Now, what was it you wanted this human to tell me?' Will you tell her about your journey across Kakhabad (turn to **371**), or will you tell her about your encounter with Sh'himbli – but only if you know who Sh'himbli is (turn to **354**)?

You confront the snivelling creature before you. You have learned the Archmage's secret and you tell him so. Farren Whyde steps back, aghast. His whimperings cease. His expression changes as his eyes narrow. 'So!' he exclaims. 'The Analander knows our secret. Our foe is more competent than any of us had imagined. I offer my admiration for your skill. Such skill should be well rewarded. You have come for the Crown of Kings. No doubt you would like to set eyes on it.' The old man moves towards the desk and opens a drawer. From within, he pulls a shining golden crown and lays it on the desk. *The Crown of Kings!* You recognize instantly the treasured Crown and your eyes widen in awe of its beauty. At last it is within your grasp!

But while your concentration is focused on the Crown, you have taken your eyes off Farren Whyde, and a transformation is taking place. You wheel round towards the old man. Farren Whyde, dressed in his long undergarments, lies on the ground, still as death. Standing over the old man, a fearsome creature is forming before your very eyes. Your thoughts of the Crown disappear and you must quickly decide what to do. For the creature forming before you is a NETHER-WORLD DEMON of some sort, with a huge, bullish face, hoofed feet, and a black, hairy body. Smoke curls from its nostrils. You must attack, quickly, before it forms fully. Will you draw your weapon and attack (turn to **107**) or will you cast a spell?

ZEN	RES	ZAP	GAK	HOT
798	628	683	717	582

211

'A visitor!' exclaims the torture-master as you enter the room. 'And, I feel, one with a sense of fun! No one comes into this room unless they wish something from Naggamanteh. I will offer you a bargain. Ask of me what you require. If I can help I may. Then I will ask you a question. If you cannot answer, then you shall be my amusement for the rest of the day. What say you?' If you will accept his offer, turn to 361. If you refuse, turn to 557.

212

The Birdmen are taken aback by your offering. They have never seen such a beautiful collar before. While the three are engrossed in studying it, you are able to step quietly back through the door. Turn to 479.

213

At the mention of the Crown, the Black Elves' faces drop and they glance at one another quickly. 'So *you* are the Analander who has come to steal our master's Crown!' their leader says. 'We had expected a much more fearsome enemy! The Archmage will reward us handsomely for your head. Cannu! Blindi! Let us claim our reward! Attack the human!' Quick as a flash, the three Elves attack. Will you draw your weapon (turn to 510) or cast a spell?

HOW	NIF	NAP	POP	MAG
614	671	727	775	793

214

At last, a commotion outside gives you hope. The lock rattles and four guards enter the room. You rise to your feet. A sergeant steps forwards and addresses you. 'Analander,' he starts, 'I have special instructions from the Archmage himself.' Already your mind is planning how to break free from your escort as you enter the Archmage's chambers and leap on him. But the Archmage's instructions are not as you expect. The sergeant continues: 'The Archmage considers that you are too dangerous an enemy to Mampang to be allowed to live. You are to be executed immediately!' You are crestfallen. In a state of shock, the blood drains from your face and the room spins. You slump to the floor in an unconscious state. The guards are merciful. They carry out their order immediately without waiting for you to regain consciousness. Your journey ends here.

215

He falls silent as you pay your respects. You have appealed to his sense of professional pride. 'No one has ever complimented me before like that,' he sighs. 'What your business is here, I do not know. But those kind words deserve thanks. You wish to know about the Throben Doors? Well, I will tell you this. If you leave this room through the door on the left you will eventually arrive at a Throben Door. This door is open. But when you open the door, you will seemingly step into a pit of hell-fire. Ignore this, for it is naught but an illusion, and will burn only those who believe in its existence. But you must plunge in at your first opportunity. Any hesitation or dawdling will destroy your belief in the flame as an illusion – let nothing sidetrack you. That is all I will tell you. And tell not a soul that Naggamanteh revealed its secret to you.' You thank him for his advice and leave the room. He seems to have forgotten all about asking you a question in return. If you follow his advice and find a large double door, then when you step through it into the fire beyond, turn to **399** instead of the reference mentioned, because you know its secret. Continue now by turning to **230**.

216

As you would expect from thugs such as these, they walk towards you to intercept your course. Sensing that you are trying to avoid them, you have now become a victim and they are determined to cause trouble. One of the Red-Eyes opens his eyes, and a flash of fire sears through the air into the ground ahead of you. Will you change direction to approach them (turn to 242), or continue regardless (turn to 57)?

217

You sit down with her and the two of you start your meal. She breaks hard crusts from the loaf and hands them to you. You crunch the stale bread and wash it down with the water from her flask. Is your STAMINA score greater than 8? If so, turn to 115. If it is less than 8, turn to 320.

218

'Save your lies for those simple-minded enough to believe them!' scowls the Red-Eye. The three are angry at you for trying to deceive them. Will you try to walk away from the group (turn to 57), or will you wait to see what happens next (turn to 12)?

219

The creatures are ugly, black-skinned chaotics of some kind. You search through their belongings and find nothing particularly interesting. On the wall behind them is a long horn, which is presumably for them to sound the alarm. It is really too long for you to carry, but if you wish to take it, you may do so if you leave behind three items from your Equipment List. Apart from that, you find only 2 Gold Pieces in their pockets and a meal's worth of Provisions. You may either take the Provisions with you or pause to eat them now. If you choose to eat them now, you may add 2 STAMINA points if this is your first meal of the day, or 1 STAMINA point if you have already eaten. Continue when you are ready by turning to 342.

220

Gingerly you reach forwards and grasp the handle. Expecting the worst, you are relieved to find that the handle, at least, is not trapped. You turn it. The click from within sounds normal. The door is not locked. With a nervous gulp, you swing the door open, releasing the handle. No spikes or explosions or shocks! The door is perfectly normal. Beyond the door is a spiral staircase leading upwards. You step through the doorway and peer up the stairs. At the top is a wide door which is heavy-set and edged with brass. This seems to be your only way through, so you set off up the stairs. The upper door is a grand affair, and is presumably the entrance to some sort of important room. Could this lead to the confrontation you have been waiting for? Turn to **198**.

221

The little creature stands aside, and you open the door. It leads down a short passageway to a door at the far end. This door is locked. If you wish to break down the door, turn to **53**. If you want to try a spell, choose one:

RAZ	YAP	DOP	ZAP	RAP
630	795	702	662	750

If you would rather not go this way, you may turn back, tell the little creature you have taken the wrong door, and go through the other one (turn to **18**).

222

You step up to the small cave mouth and kneel down to look inside. Although you will be able to crawl into the cave, the entrance will be a tight squeeze. But as your eyes become accustomed to the darkness, you can see that there will be enough room for you to fit comfortably. The back of the cave is black, so you are unable to tell whether or not the cave is completely empty. You get down on all fours and poke your head into the cave.

Oooowwouou! A shrill howling comes from inside the cave and all but deafens you! Instinctively you jerk your head out again, away from the danger. The noise sounded as though it came from a hound of some sort. You spring to your feet and draw out your weapon, ready to face whatever is inside. But nothing emerges from the cave. When your courage has returned, you must make a decision. Will you enter the cave and face whatever is inside (turn to **123**), or instead try the middle cave (turn to **136**) or the far one (turn to **534**)?

223

As the shadows flit backwards and forwards across the room, your balance sways. Your calf comes down alongside one of the blades, cutting your leg. Deduct 1 STAMINA point and choose to turn to either **367** or **484**.

224

The tall double doors are closed. You scramble up to them and must decide quickly what to do. Time is short. The ramming statue is picking up speed towards you already. Will you turn the handle and step through the doors (turn to **196**), or will you try to avoid the creature speeding towards you (turn to **415**)?

225

Resolve your battle with the two Red-Eyes. They will both attack together. Choose which you will direct your own attack against and conduct this battle as normal. Roll for the second's Attack Strength in the normal way. A higher Attack Strength than yours will inflict an automatic hit, but a lower Attack Strength does not mean that you wound it, since you are not attacking it.

First RED-EYE	SKILL 6	STAMINA 3
Second RED-EYE	SKILL 5	STAMINA 2

When you have inflicted your first wound on the Red-Eyes, turn to **34**. If you defeat the Red-Eyes, turn to **425**.

226

He has on his shelves some of the artefacts that you may need for the spells listed in your Spell Book. Furthermore, he will let you have two artefacts for 8 Gold Pieces, three for 10 and any others you may wish to buy will cost you only 1 Gold Piece each. He can offer you: A Jewel of Gold, Yellow Powder, A Gold-Backed Mirror, an Orb of Crystal and a Jewel-Studded Medallion. Decide which and how many you will buy, then turn to **473**.

227

Your next step is painful! Your leg has brushed against a sharp blade which gashes it. Deduct 1 STAMINA point and choose your next few steps from the following: **410, 349** or **249**.

228

You scramble up the rock-pile to view what lies ahead. On your way up your foot slips. You twist your ankle and must lose 1 STAMINA point. But on the other side of the rock fall is an even more welcome sight than you had hoped for. The landslip has occurred at a point where the crevasse had become narrower and the fallen rocks now form a sturdy bridge towards Mampang. You scramble across to the other side of the crevasse without incident. You are now in Mampang itself and are very close to your goal. Turn to **551**.

229

Eventually your visions cease and the world once more takes form around you. As the spell wears off, you are aware of your surroundings. The prison tower has vanished. You are in an underground cavern which seems strangely familiar. Your memory returns when you recognize a sound you had hoped never to hear again. Turn to reference **195** of Book 1 of the *Sorcery!* series.

230

You have a choice of two doors leading from the torture-room. They are both in the wall ahead of you, leading further into the inner chambers. Will you take the door in the corner on the left (turn to **236**) or the other door to its right (turn to **93**)?

231

Your quip causes them to laugh loudly. You tell them that no one could possibly recognize you wearing this tunic as it is squeezing you into a totally different shape. You must now look like an Ogre's thigh-bone! Again, this causes laughter. But the tunic is beginning to feel painful. Turn to **282**.

232

What can you offer the captain? Do you have 3 Gold Pieces to tempt him with? If so, turn to **76**. If you have a locket, found along your journey, turn to **290**. If you have any Borrinskin Boots, turn to **130**. If you have none of these, turn to **385**.

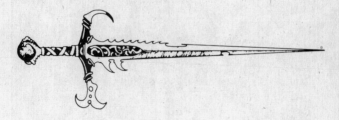

233

You walk towards what you take to be a bundle of rags lying on the ground. But to your surprise, your approaching footsteps bring the shape to life. You have woken up a creature of some sort, sleeping underneath the rags. A head raises itself, squinting in your direction, but without opening its eyes. A dirty, misshapen body stands up and scratches itself, trying to sort some order out of the rags it is dressed in. Its toothless mouth grins a gummy smile as you approach and its squeaky voice addresses you: 'Spare an old woman a Copper Piece, enough to buy a crust of bread. Bless you for helping a blind woman whose days are coming to an end.' A *beggar*, you think, and a blind one at that. Sometimes the blind can see more than a hawk-eyed Sightmaster. You consider whether or not you will talk to this woman. Do you wish to toss her a Gold Piece and stop for a chat (turn to **61**), will you chat to her anyway, but not part with any gold (turn to **287**), or will you ignore the beggar and continue across the courtyard (turn to **8**)?

234

You place your weapon on the ground and kick it over to him as he asks. 'You poor fool!' he exclaims. 'How can you have survived so long in Kakhabad with such trust of strangers? *Guards!*' From a hidden door along one of the walls, three burly guards enter the room behind you and grasp your wrists. 'Our friend here has given up his weapon without a struggle. Very wise. Show the Analander how grateful we are!' The guards bundle you off back through their door and up a narrow staircase into the top of the tower. A heavy lock is set in the door at the top. This is evidently a prison room of some sort. They unlock the door and fling you inside. Turn to **4**. But remember that you have now lost your weapon. If you do not have another one with you, you must deduct 3 SKILL points in any future combats.

235

The Goblins stare at you as you walk across the centre of the room. Some of them look at one another to see whether any of them is willing to make the first move. But none of them is. You reach the door on the other side without incident. Turn to **426**.

236

You open the door and step out into an arched cloister. The cloister runs round a sort of yard. You follow it round, turning the first corner and looking for a suitable way onwards. At the mid-point of the second wall, a passageway leads out from this courtyard back into the main building. Doors lead off on both sides of this passageway and, at the far end, there is another door. Towards the end of the passage, on the right-hand side, a sign swings in the gentle breeze. It reads: 'NYLOCK – Merchant – Open'. Before that, another door reads: 'Inner Sanctum'. If you wish to try the earlier right-hand door, turn to **140**. If you wish to see what the merchant has for sale, turn to **91**. If you wish to continue down this passage and leave through the door at the end, turn to **310**.

237

The seven Serpents had been carrying a message of your arrival back to the Archmage at Mampang. Since you have defeated all seven of the Archmage's messengers, no news of your mission has reached the Fortress. If, during your adventure, you come across a creature or group of creatures who recognize you as 'The Analander', you may ignore the particular reference you are on at the time and turn to a new reference in which you will find that you are *not* recognized. To get to the new reference, deduct 40 from the reference you are on. If you did not kill all the Serpents in Book 3, you should not be reading this message! Now turn to **1** to begin your adventure.

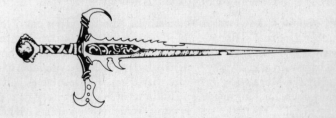

238

The fat man snaps his fingers and, from behind a curtain in the corner of the room, emerges a slim, dark-skinned girl with flowing black hair. Her face is half-covered with a silky veil and she carries a tray. On the tray are a silver tea-pot and two silver cups. The serving-girl pours two cups and leaves the room. The fat man offers you one. You accept and the two of you drink your tea. A little caution would have been wise here; perhaps the clue was that this tea was ready for your arrival. For the tea you have just finished was drugged. The greedy miser wants your gold at any cost. After you have lost consciousness, you will be robbed, killed and dumped outside the Fortress. Your mission has ended.

239

You step carefully between the blades. The flickering candlelight makes it difficult for you to see the room clearly, but your next few steps are safe. To take a few more steps, choose to turn to either **262**, **359** or **488**.

Remembering your promise to Javinne, you look around for the beggar woman. She has moved across the courtyard towards the large double gate at the far side. You gather up some evidence from the bodies to substantiate your claim and run over to her. She is overjoyed at your news; small tears force themselves through her closed eyelids. 'You do not know what it will mean to me to have been freed from these tormentors,' she sobs. 'You have made an old woman very happy. And for this you must be rewarded. Take this pendant. Although it has done little for me, it is blessed with luck.' When you first put the pendant on, you can increase your *Initial* LUCK score by 1 and restore your LUCK to this new level.

She continues: 'And I will also offer advice. Ahead of you is one of the Throben Doors. Do not attempt to open it without discovering the password. Would that I knew it and could tell you, but alas I do not. The password is known by Valignya, but to reach him you must first pass by the Mucalytics. Take care with them.' She also gives you a small pouch. Looking inside, you find a small stoppered flask made of shiny metal. 'This flask,' says Javinne, 'contains a few drops of Holy Water from the Tinpang River. Its healing properties are well known. I have no use for it – it can do nothing for my curse – but you may find it useful.' You thank Javinne and continue towards the doors. Turn to 135.

You draw out your vial and grab the stopper. It is stuck! The creature is now heading towards you and accelerating fast. In desperation, you fling the vial at the statue and, as luck would have it, you score a direct hit! The vial shatters on its head! Immediately, the creature stops dead in its tracks and totters on its legs. It seems to be struggling with something. The liquid within the vial has a pungent, acidic smell, which fills the air and seems to be having some effect on the statue. Steam rises from the creature's neck and it loses its footing. One leg slips, causing it to fall to the side. This is enough for you. You race for the doors at the far end of the room while the creature is incapacitated. You reach the doors safely but, when you look back at the creature, your blood chills. The Marbled Ram is rising to its feet! The effects of the liquid are wearing off! Turn to 224.

242

'What have we here?' asks one of the Red-Eyes. 'Courga take my eyes if this overfed oaf is a native of Mampang. Where are you from, fathead, and what is your purpose here?' What will your reply be? Will you claim to be:

From Analand?	Turn to 48
From Kristatanti?	Turn to 125
From Kharé?	Turn to 149

If you don't wish to get caught up in a conversation with them, you can ignore them and continue (turn to 57).

243

The captain becomes angry. He motions to the two guards holding you and they shove you forwards into the desk. But you are nimble-footed. As you are flung over the desk, you kick backwards with your feet, catching the shins of both guards! They howl in pain and release their grip. Your arms are free! Will you now draw your weapon and prepare to fight your captors (turn to 145), or cast a spell?

GOD	FAR	DIM	ZIP	JIG
747	722	679	593	642

244

Slowly, you rise from behind your rock, watching them carefully. You apologize for trespassing on their territory and tell them that you did not realize that they claimed this area of Low Xamen as theirs. As you speak, their expressions change, and they look at one another in amazement. 'Your tongue is strange, human. Are you not of Kakha-bad? For never have we heard the language spoken in such a way.' What will your answer be? Will you tell them that you are from Analand, away to the south (turn to 5), or do you think it best not to let them know (turn to 155)?

245

'I can offer you a little help,' he says, 'but whether or not you will be able to make use of it I do not know. Outside of this door, to the left, is a solid wall. A secret doorway is hidden in the wall. It is released by a password, but it is well protected against all unauthorized people. The passageway behind the door runs down stairs to the outside of the Fortress. When the Archmage *did* live here, this was his private escape-route. I know what you are thinking. *Does he know the password?* Alas I do not. For if I did, I would certainly have escaped long ago. Your only other alternative is to work your way back through the Fortress and find your own way outside.' You thank him for his information and hurry outside. Will you turn left and investigate the stone wall (turn to **546**), or head downstairs to make your way back through the Fortress (turn to **486**)?

246

You hand 3 Gold Pieces to one of the Sightmasters. 'You are wise to ask for our advice,' starts the Sightmaster. 'For there are many dangerous races living within the Fortress.' You wait for further advice, but you get none. You protest that this information was hardly worth 3 Gold Pieces. The Sightmasters laugh. Will you challenge them and demand your money back (turn to **90**), or would you rather not cause a fuss and leave them alone, even though you have just been robbed of 3 Gold Pieces (turn to **322**)?

247

The dead creature that you encountered in the cave was a She-Satyr. It had died from an extremely contagious disease which, through spending the night in the cave, you picked up. It is an unpleasant malady called the *trembling disease*. The ailment takes a full day to take effect but, so long as you remain uncured, it will affect you in two ways. Firstly, from now on you may not *regain* any STAMINA points; the disease prevents the body from recovering strength. Secondly, it befuddles the brain under pressure, making concentration difficult. From now on, if you wish to choose a spell from the options given in the text, you must throw one die. Imagine that the options are numbered 1–5 from left to right: you can only choose the spell corresponding to the number you roll. You are calling for more concentration than your mind can cope with under the effects of the trembling disease, and the results are unpredictable. If the number rolled is a 6, then you may ignore these instructions and choose whichever spell you wish for that particular encounter. You would be well advised to seek a cure for the trembling disease! Now turn to **113**.

248

The box is heavy and you strain to tug it out from under the bed. The lid has rusty hinges and is difficult to open. To your dismay, you find it empty. However, while you are struggling with the box, your previous doubts about the purpose of the room are answered. Turn to **182**.

249

Your next step is painful! Your leg has brushed against a sharp blade which gashes it. Deduct 1 STAMINA point and choose your next few steps from the following: **175, 227** or **410**.

250

You race for the entrance. In the blackness you catch your foot on a rock and trip over. You land hard and bang your knees on the rocky floor. Deduct 2 STAMINA points. But you scramble back to your feet and reach the door, slamming it firmly shut behind you. You must now try the other door across the hallway. It opens.

As your eyes adjust to the light, you can see that the room is circular and, thankfully, empty. There is no furniture inside, nor are there any windows. The walls are smooth and stony, with long scratches stretching from floor to ceiling at several points round the edge of the door. On the far side, you see what you are looking for – the foot of a staircase. Will you enter the room and look around (turn to **355**), or head across the room for the staircase (turn to **381**)?

251

The large room inside is a fearful sight. The walls are black and festooned with chains; what it lacks in furniture it makes up for in traps, cages, racks and innumerable other amusements designed for the torture of hapless victims. In one corner of the room stands a brutally ugly OGRE, with a patch over one eye and a whip in his hand. As you step into the room, a smile curls across his face. 'So!' his voice booms at you. 'The Analander! The master's Serpents did not lie. We have been expecting you. You have saved us a great deal of trouble by coming here of your own accord. You would have wound up in this room anyway. But no doubt not of your own choosing . . .' He laughs hard and deep and cracks his whip as if to emphasize his joke. What will your reaction be? Will you draw a weapon to fight him (turn to **270**), will you offer him a rich reward if he will help you (turn to **373**) or will you cast a spell?

TEL	ZIP	POP	SUN	NIF
592	619	794	752	709

252

The compass gives you a reading. North is directly ahead, in the direction of the large double doors. Meanwhile, the creature is charging. Turn to **296**.

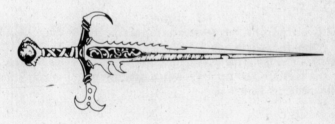

253

As you approach the double doors, you keep your eyes peeled for any signs of activity. Through the doors, you can hear the early-morning sounds of the inhabitants preparing for the day ahead. But there is no sound coming from the short passageway in which you stand. You grasp the great brass handle and turn it. The doors are locked. Looking down the narrow slit between the doors, you can see that a heavy bolt holds them fastened. It looks as though you will need a key to open them, unless you can think of another way. Do you want to go back to the door on the right (turn to **206**) or the door on the left (turn to **493**) in search of the key? Or do you have another plan (turn to **193**)?

254

Their gruff voices plead with you to join in but you continue on your way regardless. One of them comes running over to try his best to persuade you, but to no avail. Eventually, he gives up and allows you to continue. Turn to **397**.

255

Before you can react, the statue is on top of you. Its head butts you in the rump and sends you flying into the wall behind. Deduct 2 STAMINA points for the blow and collect yourself together quickly. For the creature has turned towards you again and is ready for another charge. Turn to **58**.

256

You are naturally suspicious of such an important-looking door being open. It *looks* safe enough, but are you walking into a trap? You pick up a length of wood lying in the hallway and touch the door. Nothing happens. You shove the door open a little further and then you realize the trap. A roaring flame and blast of heat flare up from behind the door, causing you to shield your face! The door opens directly into a burning inferno! Your heart sinks. There seems to be no way through here. Do you want to let the door close and try the ornate door, perhaps to return here later (turn to 336), or will you risk an all-or-nothing run through the inferno (turn to 541)?

257

Continuing around the side of the mountain, you walk for another ten minutes or so. Your hopes sink as you see that a rock fall has covered the trail between two great boulders. The way ahead is blocked. But you may be able to climb over the rock fall, and if you do so, turn to 228. If, on the other hand, you would prefer to turn back and try one of the other ways across the crevasse, you can either return to the swing-rope (turn to 323) or the wooden bridge (turn to 59).

258

What will your excuse be? Will you ask them whether they would like any food while they wait (turn to 275)? Or will you try to bluff them by telling them to look lively as the Captain of the Guards is doing a tour of inspection (turn to 197)?

259

Do you have a silver whistle? If so, this may be of help to you and you may blow it by turning to **274**. If you do not have a silver whistle, you will find none of your possessions much use and you will have to try something else. You may either ask the Minimite for his advice (turn to **414**), try breaking down the door (turn to **120**), or you may plan an ambush on the guard when he comes to bring your food (turn to **476**).

260

They are shocked, and somewhat offended, that you refuse their hospitality. You try to explain that time is of the essence in your journey, but they seem not to hear you and look at one another angrily. Will you bid them farewell and set off on your way (turn to **314**), or will you instead *Test Your Luck* and leave your fate to fortune (turn to **83**)?

261

Within moments, your face starts to change. Your skin turns jet black and hair sprouts all over your face and hands. When the change is complete, you could easily be mistaken for one of the guards. In view of this, you will not be recognized in future. Whenever you come across an encounter in which you are recognized and described as 'The Analander', ignore the reference, deduct 40 from its number, and turn to this new reference. You will find a reference which is similar, but in which you are not recognized. Leave the kitchen now by turning to **448**.

262

You inch your way slowly across the room. For your next few steps, choose either **87**, **488** or **52**.

263

You leave the room and step out into the passageway behind the door. You wonder whether the commotion will have alerted the stocky little creature who let you in. But then you remember his words about 'tormenting' the Mucalytics. Perhaps this sort of thing is quite commonplace. From where you are, you can see two options. To your left is an empty room with no door – empty, that is, except for a table and chair. It looks like a suitable place to rest and perhaps eat some Provisions. But the raised portcullis above the doorway is a little worrying. Ahead is another door, above which is a sign: 'Enter Only Those Who Will Pay the Price'. Where will you go next? Into the empty room to rest (turn to **167**), or ahead to try the door (turn to **428**)?

264

Your footsteps crunch on the ground, and one of the guards snorts and sits up. His eyes flick open! As he sees you, he panics into action, bellowing loudly and waking up his companion. The two leap to their feet and stagger about. They are still feeling the effects of the wine! One of them picks up his sword and steps towards you, while the other grabs for a long horn hanging on the wall. You must quickly attack the first guard and prevent the other from reaching the horn. The element of surprise, plus the drunken state of your opponent, gives you a great advantage here; one blow will be enough to cut him down:

GUARD   SKILL 7   STAMINA 2

If you kill him within two Attack Rounds, turn to **387**. If you do not kill him within two Attack Rounds, turn to **487**.

265

You step back to gather your thoughts. Should you ignore the warning? Or should you look for another way onwards? Perhaps the other door outside? Suddenly a noise startles you. It seemed to come from outside. You had better find a place to hide just in case this is one of the Archmage's guards. The gloomy corner at the end of the room is your best bet and you creep further into the darkness. The bulky shape that you noticed earlier may provide cover. But you are still not sure what it is. The shape remains a mystery as you walk up to it. As you get nearer you can notice certain things about it. It appears to be inanimate, since it remains motionless. Perhaps it is a bundle of rubbish in a huge sack? The sack is slightly shiny, resembling a hide of some kind, perhaps like a *reptile's skin*? You stop in your tracks as the realization dawns on you. At the same time, the shape rises . . . Turn to **499**.

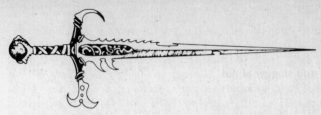

266

You fumble with your weapon to defend yourself but it is too late. The guards surround you and pin your arms behind your back. You swear at the miserable little Gnome, now beaming proudly, as you are frogmarched out of the room. You have been captured and you will not now succeed in your mission.

267

You smile pleasantly at the merchant, who nods back and watches you intently. You will have no opportunity to steal anything secretly, so there is only one alternative – a snatch. You choose your moment. You grab a handful of trinkets from the shelf in front of you and race for the door. The merchant does not move. But when you reach the doorway he makes a sharp clicking sound with his teeth. Immediately, sharp iron spikes shoot across to bar the exit. You leap through the doorway and, as you jump, the sharp points nick the hand which is clutching the merchandise. You howl with pain (deduct 1 SKILL and 2 STAMINA points) and draw your hand in quickly. He has foiled your snatch and you are now locked outside his room with an injured hand. You decide to open the door ahead at the end of the corridor. Turn to **310**.

268

The cave extends deep into the rock and becomes gradually gloomier, with only the dim light from the entrance to help you. Your hand is following the left-hand wall. Your foot kicks something soft. Instinctively, you spring backwards! That was not a rock – that was something *animal*! Your fears are confirmed when a shuffling and a growling noise arise from the spot. Suddenly a blow catches you square across the chest and knocks you sprawling backwards! You curse. You were standing between this creature and the entrance! Although you could not see it, it could see you clearly! You must deduct 2 STAMINA points for the blow, which has partially winded you.

As you run back to the entrance, the roaring beast pursues you, and in the light you can see what it is. The distinctive black and white fur and long, bushy tail are unmistakable. You have stumbled across the lair of a great SKUNKBEAR! Will you run from the cave and escape the creature (turn to **469**), will you draw your weapon and attack it (turn to **490**), or will you instead cast a spell?

DOZ	KIN	ZEN	DUD	YAP
638	611	686	788	757

269

Slowly the floor continues to rise, causing you further agonies in your hopeless situation. You must now lie outstretched on the ground and you close your eyes to the sight of the rocky ceiling inching closer and closer . . . In a last desperate attempt, you raise your arms to press against the ceiling as if your own strength could halt the floor's progress. But it is no use.

You are not destined to die like a fly swatted against the ceiling in the Floortrap Chamber. The purpose of the trap is more cunning than that. For the Archmage can gain no useful information from *dead* enemies. Much better to frighten them witless and *then* interrogate them. With the ceiling inches from your chest, and the heat of your own panting breath reflecting back into your nostrils, another noise sounds from above. This one is again mechanical and similar to the floor's motor, but is one which you are truly relieved to hear. A crack appears along the centre of the ceiling and the light floods in! Turn to **561**.

270

The Ogre advances, cracking his whip. This is his idea of sport! With his other hand, he grabs an axe. Resolve your battle with him:

OGRE   SKILL 9   STAMINA 11

He will constantly try to catch you with his whip during the fight. Roll one die for him before you start each Attack Round. A roll of 1 means that he has snared you with his whip and you must deduct 3 SKILL points for the next three Attack Rounds while you fight to free yourself. If you defeat the torture-master, turn to **230**.

271

They seem to accept your explanation, although they are not certain whether or not you are telling the truth. 'Well, even if that is the truth,' says the Red-Eye, 'I'm sure there is one Kristatanti tradition that you will not have rebelled against. Your kind are fond of their ale. A drunken lot, you are. Perhaps you'd like a swig of this!' He pulls out a flask of ale from his pocket and offers it to you. Will you accept his offering (turn to **97**), or will you tell him that you *have* given up this Kristatanti tradition (turn to **121**)?

272

Do you wish to check the walls for secret passages (turn to **28**), or will you pull the box from under the bed and open it (turn to **248**)?

273

You manage to keep your grip, but the strain is considerable. No more guards come through the door, and you are having second thoughts about whether or not to drop to the ground and try for the entrance. You look back at the guards. And then your hopes fade . . .

Having decided that the disturbance at the pass was of no concern to them, they have turned back towards the door. And there you are, perched above the door like a hunter's trophy! The guards roar with rage and draw their swords. There is nothing you can do. They stand beneath you, waiting for you to drop. You cannot either draw your weapon or cast any spells, for releasing either hand would make your fall certain. The guards jab you with their swords. Your cause is hopeless. You will be captured and imprisoned forever within the dungeons at Mampang. Your mission is over.

274

You walk to the window and blow the whistle. A shrill, warbling sound comes out. You blow again. Searching the skies, you await the help of Peewit Croo and the other Samaritans. Sure enough, your call is answered! In the sky, circling round from the Fortress, three Birdmen are flapping towards you. A sudden thought chills you. *Can they see the tower?* But your fears are eased when they respond to your waving and hover by your window. Peewit Croo smiles. 'You have the Crown? You have thwarted the Archmage's plans?' You shake your head sadly. The Birdmen are outraged. 'Do you know what risks we are taking by even coming here?' he screams. 'If we are spied, our cause is lost – and all for a miserable Analander with high hopes but no real skills at all!' He is furious, but calms down a little when you tell him of the information you have gained. 'All right, Analander,' he agrees. 'We will take you from this tower even though it may cost us our lives. I hope for your sake as well as ours that we are not being watched. But I am not taking that Pixie, whether or not he is a friend of yours. Those mischievous creatures are naught but trouble.' You turn to look at Jann, who waves you on your way. Without wings, he considers his life to be ended anyway – and your cause must not be lost. You say your goodbyes and grasp Peewit Croo's talons.

The Birdmen carry you down to the base of the tower and drop you by the secret exit from the Fortress. Wishing you well, they fly off quickly to avoid capture. Will you enter the tower again (turn to **358**) or will you rest to take Provisions (turn to **126**)?

275

The three look at you suspiciously. They have just had their midday meal! One of them pulls a sword from under the table and nods at his companions. Prepare yourself for battle. Will you use your weapon (turn to **462**), or will you cast a spell?

NAP	GOD	MUD	DUM	YAZ
647	707	605	790	758

276

'All right!' he agrees. 'I will tell you the password you will need to pass through the Throben Doors.' You stop him and demand that you must have *proof* that it is the right one. A quick flash of disappointment flickers over his face, and you smile. You have guessed right. He would have tried to trick you. 'You are a shrewd one, and no doubt,' he says. 'But I will do as you say.' He opens a drawer in the table and pulls out a book. Handwritten on its pages are diagrams of the courtyard and sketches of the lands of High Xamen. It is the drawings of the courtyard that take your attention. He points to a representation of the double doors. Written in ink next to the doors is a meaningless word: 'Alaralatanalara'. 'And that,' he says, 'is the password. Whisper it to the lock on the gates and the handle will turn. Now be gone, and leave me in peace.' You leave the miser's room. But after such an encounter you are not feeling at your most honest. You cannot resist pocketing a small pouch lying on his desk. Outside of the room you open the pouch. Your guess was right. Inside are 10 Gold Pieces. Add 2 LUCK points for the snatch and turn to **141**.

'You were very wise to leave the cave,' continues Sh'houri, 'or even now you might have been feeling the effects of the trembling disease.' The She-Satyrs want to give you some gift for the news you have brought. Sh'houri tells you first about the Mampang Fortress, the end of your journey. 'You must beware of the Fortress,' she starts. 'For it is a chaotic place. Keep your eyes open in front and behind if you wish to survive in there. The way through the Fortress takes you through the four *Throben Doors*; they are large sets of double doors, yet much more to those who try to pass through. Do not mistakenly believe that they are not protected, for they are deadly to those who try to open them unawares. They appear as heavy double doors, but nothing about their appearance gives any clue as to their real purpose.' She has noticed that you are listening intently, and is glad to have been able to give you some information of interest. As you stand to leave, she motions to one of the other creatures, who rushes off and returns with a leather bag. Within the bag are several items which may be of use. She will allow you to take with you any of the items in the bag, but for each you must exchange one item from your Equipment List (but not food or gold). If you are playing as a warrior, turn to **564**. If you are playing as a wizard, turn to **435**.

You quickly hurl the vial at the speeding creature before it can reach you. The glass shatters, spraying liquid all over the statue. But to your dismay, it has no effect at all! Now the statue is almost upon you. Turn to **296**.

279

Do you have any of the following with you? If so, you may offer one to the Birdmen:

A wooden spear	Turn to **60**
A studded dog-collar	Turn to **212**
A lucky talisman	Turn to **118**

If you have none of these items, return to **511** and choose again.

280

The door continues to creak as it opens, but you manage to keep the noise minimal. Through it, you can see a short passage. There is a door on the right of the passage, which you may investigate by turning to **307**. At the end of the passage is another door, which you may investigate by turning to **144**, but only if you have not investigated it previously.

281

You must fight the Hobgoblin cook until you reduce her to a STAMINA of 3 or less, when she will run off into the kitchen and hide:

HOBGOBLIN COOK   SKILL 7   STAMINA 7

If you manage to beat her off, you may leave the kitchen (turn to **448**).

282

'It is indeed a tight fit!' laughs the Sightmaster. 'For that is its design. What is the use of a Holding Jacket if it does not fit snugly?' The three of them laugh, while you try to flex your arms. Their words have alarmed you – a *Holding Jacket*! These are used to march prisoners between cells! Too late you have discovered their trap. The treacherous Sightmasters have captured you. Your journey and your mission end here.

'You have come all this way to look for a holy man?' he asks. 'Then you have found one. Indeed I am the only lawful priest in these parts for many days' journey. What can I do for you?' He seems genuinely flattered that you have made such a journey to see him. Do you have a hardwood spear with you? If so, turn to **204**. If not, you may ask him for any information he may be able to give you about the Mampang Fortress (turn to **103**).

284

The rumbling continues. You lose your footing and stumble forwards and it is only then that you realize what is happening. For that stumble was no clumsiness on your part. *The floor is moving!* Quickly you glance towards the archway. The dark staircase has disappeared. You can see only a solid wall within the arch! You wheel round to consider your other way of escape but, as if in answer to your question, the door slams firmly shut. Only now can you understand the scratchings on the walls. The floor is rising up towards the ceiling. You are about to be crushed to death! Will you search through the straw on the floor in the hope of finding something that may help you (turn to **168**), will you wait to see what happens in case the floor does not rise all the way (turn to **156**), or will you search your own equipment for something to use (turn to **16**)?

285

Your fate is assured. The torturer will have no mercy. Your death will be slow and painful.

As you enter the cave, the howling starts again. It is horrendously loud. You give several thrusts into the blackness to warn whatever is inside that you are armed. You touch nothing. Pushing yourself right inside, you slash about with your weapon. It hits the side of the cave walls, but nothing else. Suddenly, the howling stops and you feel something brush against your ankle! A scurrying noise catches your attention and you watch as a small ball of fur, no bigger than a cabbage, races out of the cave on two short, stumpy legs.

You breathe a sigh of relief and chuckle. This must have been a JIB-JIB. Although this has been your first sighting of such a creature, you have heard about them from the scholars of Analand. Possessing neither teeth nor claws, Jib-Jibs defend themselves with their tremendous voices, which deceive would-be attackers into thinking they are facing dangerous beasts! You watch the harmless little creature scurrying into the undergrowth.

But what of your intended home for the night? The cave itself seems to be ideal. Its narrow entrance will easily be defended and, although you are not able to stand up inside, there is room for you to be comfortable. You have not yet discovered how deep the cave is, but there is no sound coming from the back. Do you now wish to eat a meal (turn to **99**), do you want to reassure yourself that there is nothing else in the back of the cave (turn to **14**), or will you just settle down to sleep for the night (turn to **384**)?

You apologize to the woman but explain that you do not have a Copper Piece. 'Then you and I are as wretched as each other,' she says. 'Is my profession yours also?' Thinking quickly, you tell her it is. A smile comes to her lips and she reaches into her rags. 'A fellow beggar! Then we must have a beggar's banquet.' She pulls out a loaf of bread and a flask of water and bids you sit down to eat with her. You are a little unsure whether or not to do as she wishes, as this is neither the most appetizing nor the cleanest food you have seen. If you want to refuse her offer, turn to **8**. If you are hungry, you may sit down with her and eat (turn to **217**).

288

You step carefully between the blades. The flickering candlelight makes it difficult for you to see the room clearly, but your next few steps are safe. To take a few more steps, choose to turn to either **440** or **352**.

289

Test your Luck. If you are Lucky, you manage to kill both guards without either waking up (turn to **219**). If you are Unlucky, turn to **264**.

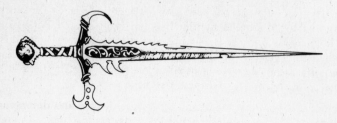

290

You mention the locket to him and describe the portrait painted within. The captain's jaw drops. 'Let me see it!' he demands. You get him to agree to release your hands and you fish for the locket in your bag. Realizing its significance, you concoct a story, telling him how it was given to you in Kharé by a beautiful woman who gave you instructions to pass it to a Captain Cartoum, with her love. A tear appears in the corner of the captain's eye and he waves the guards away so that he may talk to you in private. You continue your story and he listens earnestly, believing every word. In return for bringing this locket, he agrees to help you. He pulls a key from his pocket and hands it to you. The key has the number 17 cast into it. This key will open the next Throben Doors you come to, at the foot of the Archmage's tower. When you arrive at the next set of Throben Doors, you may use this key by deducting its number from the reference you are on and turning to this new reference. Now you may leave the captain, pining for his lost sweetheart. Turn to **463**.

291

You tell them that it was against Kristatanti traditions such as this that you rebelled when you decided to leave the village. *Test your Luck*. If you are Lucky, turn to **271**. If you are Unlucky, turn to **218**.

292

'Not thirsty? Then perhaps you would prefer a little nourishment?' He claps his hands and the curtains in the corner of the room rustle. A dark-skinned serving-girl with long, flowing, black hair steps into the room carrying a silver tray. On the tray is a bowl of hot soup and she brings it over to you. The aroma of the soup reaches your nostrils and your mouth waters. Its spicy smell is delicious! The soup tastes as it smells and you slurp it down quickly. 'That is more like it,' smiles the fat man. 'Now we shall have our little talk.' You sit down to talk to him, but something is not quite right. Your head begins to spin. The soup has been drugged! Your host smiles again. For the miser wants only one thing from you – your gold! In a moment or two you will lose consciousness, and then he will rob you, kill you and dump your body outside the Fortress. Your journey is over.

293

You find a comfortable area to bed down for the night. If you have any Provisions, you may now eat a meal and, if you do so, you may add 2 STAMINA points if this is your first meal of the day, or 1 STAMINA point if you have already eaten. Soon darkness comes, and with it the rumble of thunder in the distance. You settle down for the night. Turn to **384**.

Their gruff voices plead with you to join in but you continue on your way regardless. One of them comes running over to try his best to persuade you. As he gets close, he stops dead in his tracks. 'The Analander!' he growls as he recognizes your features. 'Here! Guards! Help me capture the slippery worm!' The other guards spring to attention and come over to see what the commotion is. You have been expected in the Fortress ever since the arrival of the first Serpent. The guards have been alerted and your description has been given. These three guards mean to capture you. You will have to battle them either with your weapon (turn to 449) or with a spell:

TEL	POP	HOW	FOG	RAZ
670	784	711	613	732

295

You quip something like, 'At least you don't lose yourself in the dark.' There is a pregnant silence as you speak, and then one of the Black Elves bursts out laughing. The other two join in. You breathe a sigh of relief. Following up your success, you ask how the black-skinned creatures keep from bumping into each other at night. The creatures fall silent. Evidently they don't find your little joke too amusing. You can either back off towards the door and try to exit from the room (turn to 335) or you can try to keep a conversation going with them. If you wish to do this, *Test your Luck*. If you are Lucky, turn to 191. If you are Unlucky, turn to 106.

296

You try your best to avoid the creature's blow, but it is no use. Its head slams into your side and hurls you against the wall. Your skull cracks against the marble and you slump lifelessly to the floor. So near your goal, you have been stopped by perhaps the Archmage's most dangerous servant, the Sleepless Ram.

297

'Officer or not,' she grunts indignantly, 'your manners are bettered by a Red-Eye. How dare you refuse my offer? Your men would give their weapons for a chance to eat from my special larder. Do not insult me thus. Or face the consequences!' Will you change your mind and choose something to eat to keep her happy (turn to **3**), or will you face whatever consequences she has in store for you (turn to **187**)?

298

You follow the path along to the rope bridge. Examining it, you find it looks strong enough to hold you, but it sways about dangerously as you step on to it. The gully that it spans is deep and a fall from the bridge would certainly kill you. *Test your Luck*. If you are Lucky, turn to **117**. If you are Unlucky, turn to **46**.

299

As you reach the centre of the room, a bellowing noise comes from a midget Goblin slumped against a wall. This seems to spur the others into action and one of them rises to its feet and hobbles towards you. This one has two arms of different sizes; its right arm is huge and muscular. This imbalance is mirrored by its legs; its left leg is twice the girth of its right. It stands directly in your path and bares it teeth. Turn to **332**.

300

You whisper your password to the lock on the door. Nothing unusual happens, but you are confident that you have remembered the password correctly and your hand reaches for the handle. Turn to **344**.

301

As he is about to open the door, a guard hails him. The two of them meet in the centre of the room and exchange frantic whispers. There is evidently an emergency of some kind. The captain returns to you. 'It is the mutants,' he says. 'They are a rowdy lot and things have got a little out of hand. I must go straight away. But here is a key which will open the Throben Doors at the foot of the Archmage's tower. Give it to him before you leave.' The captain bustles off. The key he has given you has the number 17 cast into it. When you reach the Throben Doors and wish to use the key, deduct this number from the reference you are on at the time and turn to this new reference. You may now enter the room ahead of you by turning to **580**.

302

She talks about her foes with disgust in her voice. 'Those hell-spawned *Sight-monsters*!' she spits. 'Or whatever they are called. They are as thin as saplings, with eyes the size of Bomba fruits. From the lands to the south they come. Why they should choose Mampang as their home is anyone's guess. I expect they have been exiled from their own lands, for they are a mean bunch, and that's for sure. And unquestionably loyal to the Archmage. He is said to have offered them expanses of Analand, to the south of the Shamutantis, in exchange for their loyalty and their help. I, for one, would shed no tears if they all dropped from the fly-plague for, ever since my accident, they have delighted in tormenting me.' Would you like to offer to rid her of her tormentors (turn to **27**), will you ask her about the accident she has talked about (turn to **388**), or will you ask her how you can best enter the keep (turn to **535**)?

303

As he has told you, the two candles are self-lighting. The blood candle will last longer than the normal one. Now turn to **473**.

304

You consider how you may be able to gain entrance to the Fortress. There are a number of bushes scattered around which you could hide behind if the guards could be enticed out. There is also another possible plan. Above the small door is a thick metal band on the gate. You decide quickly. You will rap on the door and perch up on the metal band. When the guard comes out, you will drop down and nip through the door. It could work . . .

You try out the perch. Hmmm. It will take some strength to support yourself while waiting for the guard, but you may be able to do it. You position yourself and then thump on the door with your foot. Seconds later, the door opens. A spiked helmet pokes out below you and a dark, hairy face grunts. The guard is surprised at finding no one about. He opens the door wider and steps outside. Should you drop on him and attack? No, this is probably not a good idea, as the guard looks to be a powerful creature. The wind rustles one of the bushes and the guard goes over to investigate. He growls something loudly and looks around, but he hasn't seen you yet. Will you drop from your perch and nip inside the door (turn to **88**), or will you wait to see what the guard does (turn to **496**)?

305

The Hydra's great tail flashes round like a whip and catches you across the chest. You prepare for the impact, expecting to be sent flying across the room, but the blow never touches you. Instead, the tail passes right through you! But how can this be? That blow would have been enough to fell a mighty champion; but you felt nothing. Then the implications dawn on you. *This Hydra is no living creature – it is merely an illusion!* The pieces fit. The smell of decay as you entered. No sign of life from the creature as you approached. You close your eyes and look again. Sure enough, the scene in the room is as it was when you entered. The dead Hydra's carcass lies harmlessly in the corner of the room.

Its spell broken, the creature will do you no harm. You are free to try the door in the wall. But if this is a room of magic, will the door also be protected? Turn to **220**.

306

You stand to leave the room and you must choose whether you will turn right and head back out towards the courtyard (turn to **141**), or left and head towards the door with the sign (turn to **428**).

307

The door is ajar, and you listen at it closely. There is no one inside. But your nose has picked up a most unsavoury smell coming from inside the door. Do you wish to open the door and investigate the smell (turn to **73**), or will you try the door at the end of the hallway instead (turn to **144**) but only if you have not investigated it previously.

308

You step into the blackness. Your foot rests safely on the floor. A creaking noise comes from behind and you are startled by the bang of the door slamming shut. You can see nothing! You must now grope your way across the room, looking for a door. To take your next few steps, choose one of the following references, either **175**, **227** or **410**.

309

You call out to hail whoever it is that is sitting in the cave. There is no reaction. Again you try and the response is the same. Either this person is totally deaf, or there is something strange going on here. You decide to investigate, keeping your hand on your weapon. Your hand reaches out to touch his shoulder and, as it does so, you jump! Turn to **62**.

310

The door opens into a passageway. To the right, the way leads onwards and the passage widens. To the left, it reaches a dead end. You decide to turn right and follow the passage. Turn to **124**.

311

Test your Luck. If you are Lucky, turn to **280**. If you are Unlucky, turn to **95**.

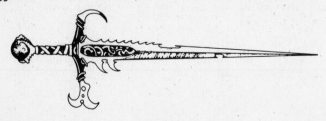

312

You whisper your password to the lock in the door. Nothing particularly unusual happens. Now you must grasp the handle and try to swing the door open. Turn to 344.

313

You hold your spear with both hands and jab it at them to keep them at bay. You are not well practised at spear techniques, but somehow you feel strangely confident. One of the Sightmasters rushes at you and, as if it had a will of its own, your spear switches round to defend you against the charge. The Sightmaster screams in agony as the point pierces its eye! It drops to the ground clutching its face. The second Sightmaster is enraged at seeing its companion so wounded and leaps forwards with its sword. Again your spear catches the Sightmaster in mid-flight, this time running it through the chest. The third creature turns to run. You fling your spear. It shifts direction in the air and catches the Sightmaster in the back. You step forwards to check the first Sightmaster, but its screamings have now ceased. The three of them lie dead. Now turn to 340.

314

'Halt!' cries one of the She-Satyrs. 'You may not leave unless we wish it.' Your stride breaks into a run and you continue along the trail. Both creatures fling their wooden spears at you as you flee. Roll two dice once for each creature. If you roll 6 or less for either of them, the spear hits you for 3 STAMINA points of damage. If you roll a *double* for either, the spear hits you in the back and its point drives through your chest and kills you. However, the She-Satyrs do not follow you and you may continue your journey if you have survived this encounter. Turn to 441.

315

You await the effects of the meatballs anxiously. Suddenly, pain rocks your head. It rises in intensity until it causes you to cry out loud! Your head is splitting! You tear at your hair. But there is no escape. Perhaps if your skull had been larger you could have made good use of the oversized brain growing within your head. But, being constrained by your skull, the effect is deadly, cutting off the blood supply to your brain. The pain causes you to black out. You never recover . . .

316

The Red-Eyes have the power of heat vision. They do not use it often as it can be dangerous even to their own kind, so they keep it sealed behind their closed eyes. However, to defend themselves (and sometimes to cause a little mischief) they will not hesitate to use it. Every time you inflict a wound against a Red-Eye, you must roll one die to see whether its heat vision burns you. The more often they use this power, the more accurate they get. Thus, the first time they use it, a roll of *less* than 6 will mean they have missed you. The second time they use it, you will need to roll less than 5 to avoid it. The third time you must roll less than 4, and so on. If a Red-Eye's heat vision burns you, you must roll one die to see how many STAMINA points you lose. If a Red-Eye's heat vision hits you twice, you will die. Now return to **159** to finish the battle.

317

You speak the word softly to the wall and wait for it to move. Nothing happens. You wait and consider what to do next. Suddenly you hear a sound! But to your dismay, it is not the sound of the doorway opening; it is the sound of a troop of foot-soldiers. As the old man warned, the secret door is protected. An alarm has sounded in the guardroom! Turn to **430** to face the guards.

318

Holding the bottle well away from you, you pull at the stopper. It is fixed firmly in place and will not budge. Again you try and, this time, it slips a little in the neck of the bottle. Giving it another twist, you manage to remove it with a soft pop.

Looking inside, you can see a small piece of parchment. It is an awkward job to pull the parchment from the bottle but, using a twig, you manage to draw it out. You unroll it and try to read it. The writing is in a language that you do not understand and you puzzle over it fruitlessly for a few minutes before giving up. You may take this with you on your journey if you wish, to try to find someone who can interpret it for you. When you *first* meet someone whom you would like to ask about this parchment, deduct 20 from the reference number you are on at the time and turn to this new reference. If that person knows how to translate the parchment, the text will make sense. If that person does not know how to translate it, the text will be meaningless to your situation. Now turn to **99**.

319

Do you want to step through the door (turn to **127**) or will you instead tug on the bell-pull (turn to **560**)?

320

Your caution was well founded. Who knows what germs the dirty food is carrying? *Test your Luck.* If you are Lucky, turn to **115**. If you are Unlucky, turn to **39**.

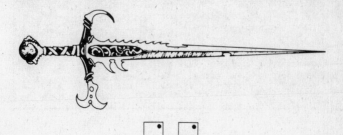

321

The room inside is sparsely decorated. It is a bed-chamber of some sort. Narrow window-slits in the bare stone walls provide a little light, although the sun has nearly left the sky. There *is* a desk in the room, but it is cheaply made. The room seems empty; no one is about. You step into the room. A sound comes from behind the door, followed by sobbing. You wheel round quickly. Standing behind the door, with a large brass pot in one hand, is a balding, plump man, dressed in long undergarments. 'It's no use,' he whimpers. 'I just cannot bring myself to do it!' Presumably he is talking about using his pot to knock you senseless as you entered. What will you do now? Will you calm the man down and try to talk to him (turn to **7**) or will you threaten him for daring to contemplate ambushing you (turn to **192**)?

322

Ahead of you, on the far side of the courtyard, are two great wooden doors which you surmise must lead the way into the keep. You head towards them. Turn to **135**.

323

You pull down on the rope. It seems to be strong enough to take your weight. You may either swing across the crevasse on the rope (turn to **165**), or cast a spell:

PEP	HOW	DOC	KIN	HUF
612	785	704	797	724

324

The sliding sound as the Hydra drags itself across the floor becomes louder as it advances. Briefly, the light returns to the room and you see a sight which astounds you. The moon goddess has opened her eyes, lifting her spell. The Hydra itself is *on top of you*! For a brief moment you panic, expecting sudden death, but then a realization of what is actually happening dawns on you. The Hydra surrounds you, its head flailing about in attack, but you can feel nothing. You are not harmed. There can only be one explanation: *this Hydra is no living creature – it is merely an illusion!* The pieces fit: the smell of decay as you entered; no sign of life from the creature as you approached. You close your eyes and look again. Sure enough, the scene in the room is as it was when you entered. The dead Hydra's carcass lies in the corner of the room.

Its spell broken, the creature will do you no harm. You are free to try the door in the wall. But if this is a room of magic, will the door also be protected? Turn to **220**.

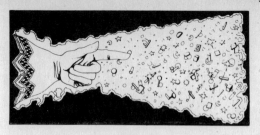

325

You walk determinedly across the courtyard. As you get closer to the group ahead, you recognize their shapes. *SIGHTMASTERS!* Their large eyes are a sure giveaway. But what are Sightmasters doing here? You remember the Sightmaster Sergeant's good wishes as you left the Outpost Settlement. These creatures, with powers of ultravision, are closely allied to the Analand Crown. You are astonished to see them in a place such as this. Could they be spies, sent to infiltrate Mampang? Or are they traitors, aligned to the powers of darkness? They seem to have recognized your origins too, and no doubt you both are thinking along the same lines. You eye them suspiciously as you approach. One of them beckons you over. Will you approach as he wishes (turn to **568**), or ignore them and continue walking (turn to **322**)?

326

'You are a native of the cityport!' caws one of the Birdmen. 'Hah! We have had some fun in that place, comrades, have we not! Come: sit down with us and share some bread and dried worms.' You agree to sit down with them and eat some of their bread, but you are not too keen on the worms. They cackle at your reluctance and pull out a loaf. You may join them in a meal and add 2 STAMINA points if this is your first food of the day (1 STAMINA point if you have already eaten). Eventually, you stand and leave. Turn to **479**.

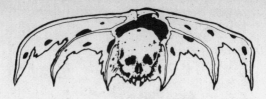

327

'What?' shrieks your inquisitor. 'What sort of a name is that for a holy man in Kharé? That is more like a name from the language of the Wild Wood Men of Avanti. A guess – a poor guess which we are expected to believe. Pah! What shall we do with the impostor, fellows?' Your choice was not a good one. Turn to **12**.

328

Taking out your food, you settle down to enjoy your meal. But before you take your first bite, a noise coming from deeper inside the cave catches your attention. *What was that?* It sounded like some*thing* inside the cave with you! You put down your food and clutch at your weapon. And then you discover exactly what you are sharing the cave with. A black furry shape, streaked with white, steps out of the darkness. A SKUNKBEAR! And a hungry one, at that. Will you face it with your weapon (turn to **490**), throw your food at it and run out of the cave (deduct 1 Provision and turn to **469**) or cast a spell?

KIN	DUD	DOZ	YAP	ZEN
611	788	638	757	686

329

You fling yourself out of the way just in the nick of time. The creature thunders past you and into the marble wall behind, with a blow hard enough to kill an armoured Troll. But this tremendous impact has not even disturbed it and it turns again to face you. Turn to **58**.

330

You stand to one side of the door and listen, hoping that whoever has just stood up is not planning to leave the room. '. . . Varack has heard about the night watch,' says a rasping voice. '. . . the Samaritans of Schinn! That's what he thinks. But me, I'm not so sure. Those damned Samaritans! This isn't their style. They don't need to worry about guards. Not unless they're armed with arrows – that's for sure. But even so, it's worrying. There are dozens of those blasted Birdmen around here. How d'you know which you can trust? I'd kill 'em all if it was up to me. Anyway, I'm away to check the gate. I thought young Hyangi was right; I heard a knock as well.'

Footsteps from the room head towards the door. Will you wait until they're close, then smash the door open into whoever is coming (turn to 446), leap into the room to surprise them (turn to 553), or try to hide quickly (turn to 396)?

331

As your hand touches the sword, you hear a faint humming in the air, and you feel an overwhelming force seize you. Turn to 451.

332

You must resolve your combat with this creature:

GOBLIN MUTANT   SKILL 8   STAMINA 8

If you defeat the Goblin within six Attack Rounds, turn to 497. If you do not, turn to 128.

333

You have been captured, and your future looks bleak. Your captors take you downstairs into a dungeon beneath the Fortress and throw you into a cell. Without weapon or equipment, and with your hands bound, your position is hopeless. You have failed in your mission.

334

The situation seems hopeless. But an idea dawns on you as you remember the genie given to you by Sh'houri. Quickly you reach into your pack and pull it out. The Minimite looks worried as you pull it out, but for the time being you are ignoring him. You grasp the stopper firmly and give it a yank. It comes out with a pop. You wait to see what happens next.

Almost immediately, a pure white smoke begins to creep its way out of the neck of the bottle. It swirls in the air and seems to hang above your hand. A disembodied voice speaks: 'I have been summoned to the material plane. Who is it that calls me?' You are unsure whether or not this genie is friendly, but you announce yourself and ask whether it is able to help your situation. 'A human!' the voice exclaims. 'It is long, very long, since I served a human. Yes, I can release you from your prison; and more than that. But I may serve you once only. Consider your request carefully.' You think over your problem. The genie is offering you wise advice. A simple escape would be helpful, but not prudent, as you might simply wind up outside the tower and then have to battle your way in once again. No, you have a better request.

You ask the genie to take you back to the Archmage! With this request you kill two birds with one stone, both escaping and confronting your enemy at the same time. The genie's voice answers you. 'Hmmm. *Back* to the Archmage? Are you sure this is what you want? Very well then. So be it!' You are a little worried about the cautionary tone in its voice. Have you said the wrong thing? What is wrong with going back to the Archmage? But there is no time to think about this. Before your eyes, the genie has grown in size! Its swirling shape now fills the room. It has cast its spell and you are tossing and turning on a weightless cloud, unable to see anything. Turn to **631**.

335

You turn and run from the room, closing the door. The Black Elves do not follow you; instead you can hear mocking laughter coming from the room behind you. You feel ashamed to have shown such cowardice, and must deduct 1 SKILL point, but only for your next battle. Now turn to **566**.

336

The room is exactly as you left it, the mechanical contraption motionless in the centre of the room. You have no other choice but to take your chances with the burning inferno. Turn to **541**.

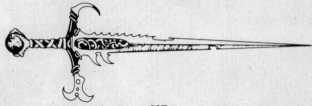

337

You start to concentrate, to prepare a spell. But Jann keeps on breaking your concentration. 'I tell you, you are wasting your time!' he says. 'No spells will work when I am around.' You tell him you are trying to find a spell which will not be affected by his defensive aura. 'There are few who know spells which Minimites have not been protected against,' he smiles, 'and I have no wish for you to waste your strength.' Do you have 'strength to waste', as he puts it? If your STAMINA is 8 or more, turn to **356**. If it is less than 8, turn to **389**.

338

The Birdman looks down at you as you try a few pleasantries. It opens its mouth to speak . . . But instead of a reply, a piercing call comes from the creature and it drops from the sky towards you, talons poised to strike. You leap aside to avoid its attack, but it catches your shoulder and tears your flesh. Lose 2 STAMINA points for the wound. It seems that the Birdman is not interested in conversation, and you will have to fight it. You may either draw your weapon (turn to **450**), or cast a spell:

YAP	HOT	FIX	ZEN	SAP
661	598	701	778	716

339

You pick your way along the rocky path, which is now rising steeply, and at times you have to *climb* rather than walk along it. The journey is extremely tiring and you must stop to rest several times along the trail. One thing is a little worrying: you seem to have picked up the hoof-marks again. But this time, they are fresh, recently trodden into the fresh mud after the storm. Mountain goats, perhaps?

The Mampang Fortress in the distance at first sight does not seem to be getting any closer, but you are definitely getting nearer. You round a narrow bend and stop dead in your tracks, as a missile whizzes past you and bounces off a rock! Instinctively, you drop down to shelter by a boulder. *What was that?* In a moment, your question is answered. Standing above you are two tall creatures holding wooden spears at the ready. Long, shaggy hair falls from their heads down to their waists. Their torsos are human, and *female*. From what you can see of their faces, they appear to be a bizarre hybrid of human and goat, with two stumpy horns protruding from their foreheads. Their lower bodies confirm this view. Their legs are goat-like and hoofed. *The hoof-prints!* Each holds a wooden spear. Have you come across any of these creatures before? If so, turn to **378**; if not, turn to **522**.

340

Your first concern is that the battle may have attracted the attention of the other creatures in the courtyard. You look around. Some interest has been aroused, but skirmishes such as this are commonplace in Mampang. The inhabitants of the courtyard resume their activities. You search through the pockets of the Sightmasters and find their ill-gotten gains: 20 Gold Pieces (plus your own 3 if you handed them over). One of them carries a backpack and in it you find two pouches, one containing sand and the other containing a vial of glue. The backpack also contains enough Provisions for 3 meals. A glint of green on one of their fingers reveals a Ring of Green Metal. Most of these possessions have no doubt come from hoodwinked travellers. Turn to **135**.

341

Beads of sweat appear on your forehead. The going is difficult as the candlelit shadows sway across the room. But so far you have not touched any of the blades. To take your next few steps, choose between turning to **262**, **239** or **52**.

342

Safely inside, you consider your best plan. Night is coming and you are feeling tired. You had better find a sheltered spot to bed down for the night and get some rest. You explore the inside rim of the mountain and find a suitable small cave which appears to be empty.

You may eat Provisions here before you get some sleep. If you do, you may add 2 STAMINA points if this is your first meal of the day, or 1 STAMINA point if you have already eaten. Then you can settle down to sleep.

Your dreams that night are vivid and frightening. Perhaps this is the influence of Mampang. Several times you awaken in a cold sweat, and you toss and turn constantly. Are you still faithful to your goddess, Libra? If so, turn to **439**. If you have chosen or have been forced to renounce your faith, turn to **10**.

343

You speak the word softly to the wall and wait for it to move. Nothing happens. You wait and consider what to do next. Suddenly you hear a sound! But to your dismay, it is not the sound of the doorway opening – it is the sound of a troop of foot-soldiers. As the old man warned, the secret door is protected. An alarm has sounded in the guardroom! Turn to **430** to face the guards.

344

You reach forwards and grasp the handle. You feel a tingle pass briefly through your body, but feel no other ill effects. You look at your hand. *What are you doing this for?* You step backwards and look around at the courtyard. *Where are you? What are you doing here? WHO are you?* You puzzle over these strange thoughts, trying desperately to find the answers. But you will never solve these mysteries. For the Throben Door you have just tried to enter has its own defence against intruders. Any unauthorized person trying to enter is subject to the same treatment. *Your mind has been wiped blank!* All knowledge of your self and your mission has been erased for good. Your quest has ended . . .

345

Keeping its head bowed, the creature shuffles off down the corridor. You wait impatiently, but soon it returns with a bowl of broth. You may take this soup and, if this is your first meal of the day, add 2 STAMINA points. If you have already eaten, you may add only 1 STAMINA point. Then choose which way you will continue. Another door is adjacent to, and just inside, the entrance to its room. If you wish to go through this door, turn to **573**. Alternatively you may walk a few paces back down the corridor and enter the door in the right-hand wall that you saw earlier (turn to **517**).

346

The creature roars loudly as your blow strikes. It steps backwards away from you and its tail rises in the air. Turning its backside towards you, the Skunkbear releases its special weapon: a horrendous stench fills the enclosed cave. You gag and fight to hold down the feeling of nausea which grips you. Meanwhile the Skunkbear moves in to attack. Continue the fight, but you must deduct 2 SKILL points during the rest of the battle. If you score a successful attack on the creature, you may escape from the cave by turning to **469**. If you continue the fight, turn to **558** if you win.

347

The captain thanks you for your mercy and promises that you will be rewarded for sparing his life. He steps behind his desk and opens the drawer. You wait to see how you will be rewarded. Your gift is not what you had expected. From inside the drawer, the captain pulls out a small hand crossbow, already loaded with a deadly dart. The bowstring sings as the dart shoots towards you and embeds itself in your chest. Its tip is treated with fast-acting poison. Your journey has ended here.

348

You unhook the lock and lift up the top of the pillory. The broad-nosed man steps back, rubbing his neck and wrists. He thanks you but is concerned not to let his escape attract attention. He points to a group of guards playing a game of some sort against the wall. Your eyes follow his finger across the courtyard. Suddenly, you feel a heavy blow on the back of your head and you slump to the ground. Turn to **418**.

349

Your next step is painful! Your leg has brushed against a sharp blade which gashes your leg. Deduct 1 STAMINA point and choose your next few steps from the following: **249**, **410** and **227**.

350

You squat down in the alcove to eat your food. It is perched up on the side of the rock and you can see part of the way ahead. The trail leads down across a rocky plateau and then finally climbs another bare crag towards the Fortress. Although you cannot see the gates of Mampang, you can see the tips of its spires hidden behind the crag. You are almost there.

You look around your resting-place. The remains of a fire in one area suggests that someone has been there before. And on the wall of the alcove is a message written in dye. You move over to see what it says. The language is your own and the message appears to be a warning of some kind. A mystic symbol – a religious diamond with a cross in its centre – heads the writing, which reads:

> *Heed this warning! Proceed no further towards the curse that is Mampang. Every step you take in its direction takes you one step nearer eternal damnation. For I, Colletus, have been there and back and know the truth of its ways. If you do not turn back, you may find me at the Groaning Bridge. You must save your own soul before it is too late.*
>
> *Colletus*

How recent the message is you cannot be sure, but its warning is certainly a little worrying. Nevertheless, you could not possibly give up your journey at this stage. You gather your things together and set off. You may add 2 STAMINA points for the meal you have just eaten. Leave your resting-place now by turning to **539**.

351

The hideous Demon drops to the ground. Its shape shrivels and disappears before your eyes, returning to its god-forsaken home. You are now alone in the room with the Crown of Kings and the body of Farren Whyde. You check the old man. He is dead. You walk over to the desk to touch the Crown. In spite of being made from solid metals, it is remarkably light. You wrap it carefully and place it in your pack. Now you must return it to Analand. Will you leave the room and step carefully down the stairs (turn to **434**)? Will you open your pack and look for something to use (turn to **148**) or will you cast a spell?

ROK	RES	NAP	LAW	SIX
637	743	591	781	703

352

Your nervousness shows as you tiptoe carefully across the room. At one point the candle flickers and your foot comes down alongside one of the blades! The sharp edge slits your calf and you fight desperately to regain your balance. Deduct 1 STAMINA point for the wound and take your next few steps by turning either to **223** or **484**.

353

She places one hand on your brow and another on the back of your neck and fixes her concentration on you. 'This is good, very good,' she smiles. 'One such as you does not belong in this place. I can tell you have a mission, though I know not what it is. But I feel reassured that my mentioning the Samaritans of Schinn has not endangered their cause.' Do you have any illnesses or diseases at the moment? If so, turn to **489**. If not, turn to **436**.

354

You tell Sh'houri of your encounter with Sh'himbli the previous day in the cave. She nods her head. 'I think we all suspected as much,' says Sh'houri grimly. 'Sh'himbli was cursed with the dire trembling disease when she was last seen at the village. Knowing how contagious it was, she did the honourable thing by leaving the village to die in a private place. Such is the way of our race. We thank you for this news. But I fear we have some bad news for you. The trembling disease is *very* contagious. If you spent the night in her cave, I am sure you will have caught it.' Did you spend the night in the cave? If so, turn to **174**. If not, turn to **277**.

355

The floor of the room is covered in dust and straw. You kick through this and occasionally your foot touches something solid. Mostly these are stones, but one particular object feels light. You bend down and pick up a facemask! It is black in colour and is carved to resemble a grotesque face. Placing it in your pack, you continue to disturb the straw to see whether you can find anything else of value. But suddenly, you stop in your tracks. Your foot has kicked a much heavier stone and immediately a deep rumbling noise comes from under the floor. Turn to **284**.

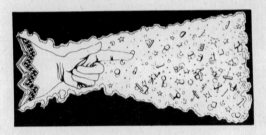

356

'Tell me of your strongest spells,' says the Minimite, 'and I will tell you whether or not they will penetrate my defences.' You run through your most tiring spells and the little creature shakes his head at every one until you reach the last. 'The ZED spell!' he shrieks. 'You know the ZED spell! If this is true, then I think we may have our solution. This spell is certainly too powerful for me to stop.' You are astounded. No one knows the powers of the ZED spell. How does the Minimite know so much about it? Turn to **374** to listen to his story. Otherwise turn to **427** to cast your spell.

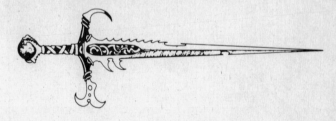

357

The door opens to reveal dirty living-quarters. An unmade bed is in the corner and a table and chair are set against one wall. A plate and a metal mug stand on the table, along with a bowl. A wooden chest is under the table. This could be the home of one of the Archmage's servants. But then again, perhaps it is not. There are virtually no possessions in the room. Perhaps this means nothing, as most of the inhabitants of Mampang seem to own little anyway. Do you want to check the walls for secret passages (turn to **28**), or will you pull the box from under the table and open it (turn to **248**)?

358

You feel around the wall of the Fortress, looking for the hidden doorway which will allow you back into the tower. A noise behind you makes you whirl round, startled. You can see nothing, but cries of battle are definitely coming from somewhere. There is a great crashing sound in the grass further along the wall. Something has dropped from the sky. You look up and can see a battle taking place high up in the air. Birdmen are attacking Birdmen. Another Birdman falls near by and your worst fears are realized. The Samaritans have been discovered! Birdmen archers high up on the Fortress walls are firing at your allies, who do not stand a chance against the arrows. Your rescue call has exposed them! There is nothing you can do to help your comrades and you fear now for your own safety, as the Birdmen will no doubt be scouting the area when they have killed off all the Samaritans. You find the doorway and step inside. Turn to **189**.

359

The room seems to shift in the candlelight, but this is a natural trick of the flickering light. You manage to keep your balance and step safely across the room. To take your next few steps, choose to turn to either **52**, **488** or **262**.

360

You take out your weapon and quickly strike the creature with it. It roars in agony and collapses to the floor. You cannot believe your eyes! Your blow was powerful, but not enough to fell such a strong-looking adversary. When it does not move, you bend down to investigate. As far as you can tell, the creature is *dead*! Your attack has finished it off! You look through its clothing, but find only 4 Gold Pieces. You must now decide your best way onwards. You can either return to the door along the corridor and try that (turn to **517**), or you can try another door just inside the creature's room, set in the left-hand wall (turn to **573**).

361

You agree to his terms. What will your first question to him be? Will you ask him casually about some of the tortures he has enjoyed in the past and then ask where you may find the Archmage (turn to **143**)? Will you ask him his favourite weapon and then ask whether he knows anything of the Crown of Kings (turn to **199**)? Or will you compliment him on such a fine torture-chamber and then ask whether he knows anything of the Throben Doors (turn to **215**)?

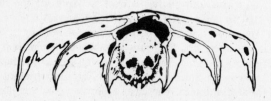

362

You examine the lock holding the pillory shut. It looks quite strong – but nothing that a hefty blow wouldn't sort out. You may either smash the lock with your weapon (turn to **505**), or cast a spell:

FAR	PEP	KID	DOC	ZAP
645	700	729	768	674

363

You panic and run for the doors as quickly as possible. *Test your Luck.* If you are Lucky, turn to **512**. If you are Unlucky, turn to **296**.

364

Your decision was wise. A third guard appears moments later and calls out gruffly to the other two. The first guard makes a noise like a knocking sound on a door and points into the distance. Perhaps they are wondering why there seems to be no activity from the area of the pass. One of them staggers about comically, imitating a drunkard, and the other two laugh. While their attention is away from you, you consider whether this would be an opportune time to drop down and nip inside. Your muscles are tiring rapidly. Will you sneak through the doorway now (turn to **474**) or wait (turn to **432**)?

365

Looking around the room, you find little of interest. The Birdmen carry swords as weapons. If you need a weapon, you may take one of these. Each carries 2 Gold Pieces – a week's pay – so you may collect all six coins. One of them also carries some bread and a pouch containing something that looks like *dried worms*! You may take the bread with you (there is enough for two meals), but you decide to leave the worms. If you are hungry, you may eat a meal now, and add 2 STAMINA points if this is today's first meal (1 STAMINA point if you have already eaten). Then turn to **479**.

366

You sit down on a rock just inside the cave where you cannot be spotted from outside. If you are carrying any food with you you may prepare a meal (turn to **328**). If you have no Provisions, you may as well settle down and prepare your bed (turn to **574**).

367

The room seems to shift in the candlelight, but this is a natural trick of the flickering light. You manage to keep your balance and step safely across the room. To take your next few steps, turn to either **440** or **223**.

368

You run as fast as you are able. Ahead is a large boulder which should afford at least some shelter from the landslide. You race forwards and squat down behind it, panting hard. Above you, the landslide is picking up momentum. Rocks are crashing around you, and several smaller ones bounce painfully off your head and back. A creaking noise raises the alarm, but you are too late to react to prevent fate from taking your life. The creaking you heard was the boulder, rolling back towards the crevasse as the landslide beats it into motion. You manage to avoid being crushed to death as it rolls away from you, but this only leaves you exposed to the landslide. Your journey has ended here.

369

The shape remains a mystery as you walk up to it. As you get nearer you notice certain things about it. It appears to be inanimate – at least, it remains motionless. Perhaps it is a bundle of rubbish in a huge sack? The sack is slightly shiny, resembling a hide of some kind, perhaps like a *reptile's skin*? You stop in your tracks as the realization dawns on you. At the same time, the shape rises . . . Turn to **499**.

370

One of the Birdmen immediately sees through your story. 'You've not travelled any distance!' he squawks. 'This fellow is an impostor!' The other two rise to their feet and you must face the Birdmen. Will you draw your weapon (turn to **462**), or will you cast a spell?

MUD	NAP	DUM	YAZ	GOD
605	647	790	758	707

You begin your story at Kharé and tell her how the guards took you captive. Your search for the four spell lines fascinates her, and other She-Satyrs sit and listen to your tales. For two hours you keep them enthralled. They are horrified as you tell of your encounters with the seven Serpents and are sad at the death of Tek Kramin, the boatman of Lake Ilklala. As a character, he was infamous throughout Kakhabad. When you finally tire of telling your stories, the She-Satyrs are disappointed. 'We must not weary our friend,' says Sh'houri. You explain that you have enjoyed the meeting but must be on your way towards the Fortress.

'I cannot understand your wish to visit that place,' Sh'houri continues. 'It is a lawless and dangerous keep. It is a wonder that even one so powerful as the Archmage can survive in Mampang. But it is said that he is well protected from the chaotic rabble surrounding him. Four strong doorways close the way to the inner keep, the *Throben Doors*. None but his most trusted servants may pass through them. If you are planning to visit the Archmage himself, you must beware of the Throben Doors, as they are deadly to those who know not of their existence. They appear as heavy double doors but nothing of their aspect gives any clue as to their real purpose.' She has noticed that you are listening intently, and is glad to have been able to give you some information of interest. As you stand to leave, she motions to one of the other creatures, who rushes off and returns with a spear and a leather bag. Both are handed to you. 'This is a fine hardwood spear,' announces Sh'houri, 'which I believe you will find helpful on your travels. It will be doubly so if you are able to find Colletus the holy man and persuade him to bless it. If you discover Colletus's whereabouts, you may summon him thus.' She cups her hands to her mouth and makes a whistling sound. If at some time in the future you think you know where the holy man is, repeat this sound by deducting 30 from the number of the reference you are on and turning to this new reference. If Colletus is there, he will appear to you. Sh'houri continues: 'Colletus will persuade you not to try to reach the Fortress, as he curses its evil. Tell him you are planning to destroy it and he will agree to help. Also, in this bag are some things that may help you. But our possessions are few. We must ask that you exchange anything that you want for something of your own.'

Within the bag are several items which may be of use. If you are playing as a warrior, turn to **564**. If you are playing as a wizard, turn to **435**.

372

'Woe betide my soul!' she moans. 'I did not mean to mention the Samaritans to a stranger. I have betrayed them!' You calm her down by saying that they are common knowledge within the Fortress. She has given nothing away. You tell her you would like to meet these creatures, for you may find that your cause is the same. 'I cannot be sure that you are telling the truth,' she says, 'as I cannot see your face. Allow me to *sense* your honesty and I may tell you more. But do not try to deceive Javinne, for her hands can feel the truth.' The old woman wants to place her hands on your head and neck to 'sense the truth' in you. This is not a pleasant prospect, as you are not certain you can trust her, and you have no idea whether she may be carrying any contagious diseases. Will you allow her to lay her hands on you? Turn to **353** if you are prepared to undergo this test. If you would rather not, you may change the subject and ask her about how she lost her sight (turn to **388**), or how you may enter the keep (turn to **535**).

373

How much are you willing to offer him for his help – 5 Gold Pieces (turn to **452**), 10 Gold Pieces (turn to **531**) or 13 Gold Pieces (turn to **478**)? If you can offer none of these, draw your weapon and turn to **270**.

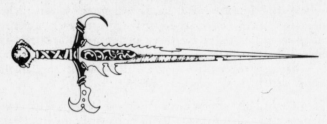

374

'If the truth be known,' Jann begins, 'we Minimites know much more about the arts of sorcery than most magic-users themselves. We have outlawed the use of magic within our own race, for our experiences were bad. Whether it is the magic itself or our own characters, we do not know. But sorcery and ambitions of power went hand in hand with our people. Eventually it split us up into a race of nomadic individuals, avoiding each other like the plague. And all because of sorcery.' The Minimite sighs for a moment, then returns to the subject at hand. 'It is thought that the ZED spell originated from Throben. This is not true. It was originally designed here in Mampang by the sorcerer-priests of Chronada, god of time. One of my own race stole the secret and brought it to the Minimites. When our people dispersed, the spell's secret was taken by its thief to Throben, then given to a Necromancer in exchange for . . . er . . . favours. It is the ultimate secret of travel – travel across distances, and travel *through time*! But it carries its own dangers. It demands perfect concentration. If you can achieve this concentration, then you may send yourself forwards and backwards through time and space. But before you cast this spell, you must concentrate hard on wherever you wish to go. You must have this image firmly in your mind, or the spell will work randomly. As with the Throben Necromancer, you may arrive at any place in any time! This is all I know about the ZED spell; how to cast it is a secret I have not learned. Nor have I any wish to do so.' Now turn to **402**.

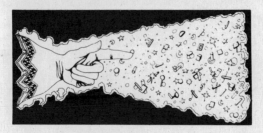

375

The Hobgoblin turns back towards you to see how you are doing. She spies the jar in your hand and shrieks! 'Oh, no!' she wails. 'Not *that* jar! Of all the choices to make!' You explain that the Ant Meatballs are delicious and compliment her on her skills as a cook. 'No, no! You do not understand!' she explains. 'Those are not *Ant Meatballs*. Look!' The label on the jar has ripped and hangs half off. When she folds the torn piece back into its proper position, the blood drains from your cheeks. You are eating from a jar of *Mutant* Meatballs!

Mutant Meatballs were concocted originally by an apothecary from Throben aligned to a rebellious Prince of Brice. On discovering their effects, they designed a plan of conquest. These potent little balls taste delicious, but are quite deadly. They wreak horrible mutations on whoever tastes them. The Prince of Brice planned to seize the throne, his troops manned by experimental mutants, bred for their bizarre powers. And you have just eaten a handful of the balls! Slowly, you will begin to mutate. What will happen to you? The effects are never predictable, usually harmful, sometimes fatal and sometimes useful. Roll two dice and consult the folowing table to see what happens to you:

Roll	Turn to	Roll	Turn to	Roll	Turn to
2	562	6	455	10	261
3	544	7	433	11	184
4	524	8	409	12	315
5	501	9	105		

376

It looks at you shiftily and shrugs its huge shoulders to indicate that there is nothing in its room. There doesn't *look* to be much in the room. Will you believe it and leave (turn to **550**), or threaten it with your weapon (turn to **482**)?

377

You explain that you are having a little trouble getting inside the Fortress proper and wonder whether they may be able to help you. 'Nah, you'll never get through,' says one. 'Not if you expect just to walk straight through the Throben Doors. You'll have to find a key for this one.' He motions outside. 'But if you're charming enough to the guards across the way . . .' The other two glare at their companion, whose tongue has been a little too loose. The three of them start to argue in their own language and you decide this would be a suitable time for you to leave. Turn to 566.

378

You remember the dead creature in the cave; these two are similar. This knowledge may be of some help, if they have lost their comrade. Or then again, maybe you should keep quiet, as your sleeping-place may have been a sacred tomb of some sort. Do you want to call to your two attackers and tell them of your find (turn to 413), or will you keep quiet and wait to see how they react to you first (turn to 522)?

379

You choose your password carefully and whisper it at the lock just below the handle. Will your choice be correct? You take a deep breath and prepare to try the handle. Turn to 344.

380

The trail winds up the mountainside and you follow it until a sight ahead makes you stop. To the left, higher up the rocky cliffs, is a strange structure made out of twigs, branches and moss. This looks like a huge bird's-nest perched on a ledge. Do you want to climb up the side of the mountain to investigate it (turn to **530**), or will you ignore it and continue along the path (turn to **36**)?

381

You step inside and walk towards the archway. As far as you can tell, the steps lead straight up into the tower. After two steps, you hear an ominous sound. A rumbling is coming from the floor beneath your feet! You quicken your pace, but already things are happening. Turn to **284**.

382

You have grabbed a small bird's-nest, inside which is a golden egg. But you have no clue as to what the egg or the nest are or do. Nevertheless, you may take them with you. You must now leave the area quickly, before the merchant can summon guards. You nip down to the door at the end of the passageway. Turn to **310**.

383

You quickly glance round to make sure no one is watching. No one is paying any attention to you. You step up to the mound and climb up to the base of the pole. Will you reach for a sword (turn to **331**) or an axe (turn to **509**)?

384

The storm breaks during the night, waking you several times. You are thankful for the shelter your cave affords. Rain pelts down, and muddy puddles form in the cave entrance. But by morning, the rain has stopped and the sun is fighting its way through the low-hanging clouds. You rise early and prepare yourself for the day. Judging the distance as best you can, you should reach the Fortress by the end of the day. If your STAMINA is below its *Initial* level, you may add 2 STAMINA points for the rest. If you did not eat at all yesterday, you must deduct 3 STAMINA points, as you are now hungry. If you wish, you may take with you some stone dust and three small pebbles which you can pick up from the cave. Now you must leave your cave and set off on your journey.

As you climb through the foothills of Low Xamen, you notice how few animals are about. Certainly animals would hide from you, but there are no *signs* of wildlife. Perhaps the terrain is too treacherous. The going is undoubtedly becoming harder and, by the late morning, you are climbing steeply. Ahead, the narrow trail splits to offer you two ways onwards. To the right, the path continues to wind up the mountainside, while to the left, a narrow rope bridge spans a gully and joins another path. Both lead upwards in the direction you are heading. Which will you choose:

To the right?   Turn to **339**
To the left?   Turn to **298**

385

The captain tries to question you, but you are tight-lipped and stubborn. Eventually he tires of you and instructs the guards to take you to the dungeons. Naggamanteh, he thinks, will have no trouble persuading you to talk. Your mission has ended. No one escapes from the Mampang dungeons.

386

The creature steps slowly forwards, holding up its hands as if to indicate that it means no harm. You stop it a few feet away and turn your ear towards it to hear what it has to say. It speaks. You can now make out the words of its message – but as it breathes, you catch a whiff of its breath. The smell is horrendous! You cough and choke. Its breath is like poison gas! In fact, the Mucalytic's breath *is* a form of poison gas, and you have just taken a lungful – a fatal dose. You crash to the ground, dead, at the creature's feet.

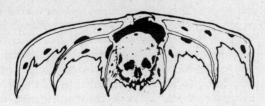

387

You must now leap over and kill the other guard, who is taking the horn off the wall. There is no time to cast a spell:

Second GUARD   SKILL 8   STAMINA 6

If you kill this guard, turn to **219**.

388

'My story is a sad one,' she starts. 'Many seasons ago, in my youth, I was skilled in the arts of healing. My master was a healer-priest from Daddu-Yadu who had been shipwrecked and washed ashore on the Earthend beaches. Being youthful and ambitious, I decided to bring my skills to Mampang, where I imagined the rewards would be greatest. But this was against the wishes of my master who wished me to travel south and use my learning to aid the lawful kingdoms. Ah, would that I had listened to the wisdom of his words! But the promise of fortune dissuaded me and I lived in prosperity at Mampang for many years. My undoing came when the Archmage recruited a new type of troop to his army. *The Mucalytics!* These creatures were a miserable lot, but totally without fear. They are almost deaf and may speak only in a whisper, and one was brought to me in the hope of a cure. But I could not undo the curse set upon these wretches by the gods themselves! Try as I would, I could not restore their voices nor improve their ears. My punishment was an "accident" which resulted in this!' And she holds her hands up to her eyes. You sympathize with her, and her head bows in sorrow. You may now either change the subject, and ask her how best to enter the keep (turn to **535**) or leave her be and continue on your way (turn to **8**). Or will you ask her about 'the mongrels who have more than their fair share of what she lacks' (turn to **302**)?

389

You describe to Jann all the spells you are capable of casting. 'I'll leave it to you if you're feeling so headstrong,' declares Jann, indignantly. 'But if you take my advice, you'll leave magic well alone!' If you'll follow his advice, you may either plan an ambush on the guard (turn to 476) or wait to see whether anyone is interested in you (turn to 214). If you *are* feeling headstrong and you want to try some magic, turn to 427.

390

With a mixture of grunts and instructions, he tells you to turn round and follow the passageway as far as you can. If you go through a metal door at the end, you will be on your way through to a Throben Door. But he has no idea how you will get through this gateway and has never himself been that far into the Fortress. If you decide to follow his instructions, turn to 6. If you do not want to take his advice, you may go through a door adjacent to the entrance to his room (turn to 573).

391

You decide wisely that the captain is still too strong to be spared. If you wish to spare his life when you have reduced him to 3 STAMINA points, turn to 445. If you have decided that this will be a fight to the death, turn to 463 when you kill him.

392

You step up to the large double doors. Will you try to open them with a key (turn to 185) or a password (turn to 498)?

393

As you approach the pillory, you can see that someone is being held captive within it. The bedraggled shape of a miserable human-like creature is slumped against the frame. As you approach, it turns its head towards you. As you get closer, you find that the creature is brawny and shaggy-haired. You would guess that it is some sort of sub-human, judging from its narrow eyes, broad nose and high forehead. 'Taunt me all you will,' it says. 'You will teach me no lesson that two days in this bane-cursed pillory has not taught already. Is my punishment not yet over? I beg of you: spare me your tongue and instead offer me some nourishment.' You pause to reflect on its words. This creature is much too articulate for a sub-human. Will you offer it some nourishment as it asks? If so, turn to 408 – but you may only do this if you have Provisions with you. Will you offer to set the creature free by smashing the lock on the pillory (turn to 362)? Will you leave the wretch alone and continue (turn to 485)? Or will you stop to taunt it (turn to 431)?

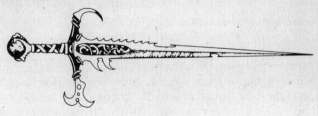

394

You must first fight the guard standing before you:

GUARD   SKILL 8   STAMINA 6

If you have a blessed hardwood spear, you may kill the guard instantly. If you defeat the guard, turn to 495.

395

You warn the creature that you will defend yourself but have no wish to harm it. Again it cups its hand to its ear, straining to hear you. You yell your warning loudly and something seems to register. The creature lifts its long snout and a faint sound comes out. Will you step closer to listen to what the creature is saying (turn to 405), or will you ignore it and leave the room (turn to 96)?

396

There is no suitable cover in the archway for you to hide. The door is beginning to move, so you quickly step behind the door as it opens. A heavy-set GUARD steps out. You wait with bated breath. The guard sniffs the air and stops. Something is not quite right! To your dismay, he grabs the door and swings it closed, leaving you exposed. He snarls at you and draws a sword. You have no time to cast a spell and must fight him:

GUARD   SKILL 8   STAMINA 6

If you defeat the guard, turn to 563.

397

You continue and reach the wall of the courtyard, stopping in front of the two large double doors. Another creature is shuffling along the wall from the right-hand corner of the courtyard. It is a slow, bulky creature with a dark, rubbery skin. As it is the size of a bear, you decide to hold back to see what it will do at the gate before approaching. You watch it press its mouth close to the handle, then grasp and turn the handle. The right-hand door opens and it steps through. Now you must decide what to do. Will you copy the creature, pressing your mouth to the door (turn to 483), will you leave the door and instead try following the right-hand wall into the corner of the courtyard (turn to 519), or will you cast a spell?

POP	HUF	ZAP	BIG	DOP
737	618	596	773	632

398

Again your weapon finds its target as you avoid the Hydra's strike. Another head drops to the ground, this time the head of Hydana, god of the water. But, as before, two new heads grow rapidly to replace it. It is now the turn of Pangara to use his powers on you. With a great puff of breath, a gale force breaks from his lips, sending you flying backwards into the wall, crashing against your shoulder. Deduct 2 STAMINA points. But you are still determined and you advance again. Resolve the next Attack Round. If you wound the creature, turn to **84**. If it wounds you, turn to **305**.

399

The flames lick your clothes and the heat begins to feel unbearable. But you have seen through its illusion. As you continue through the inferno, its effects die. The flames are cold. There is no heat. On the far side of the inferno is another door, which you walk comfortably up to. Turn to **150**.

400

You swallow hard and race for the crevasse, taking a great leap off the edge towards the far side. Your jump was strong, but no human jump could span the distance. Your fingers clutch at the sides of the rock as you plunge down, down, down to your death. You have failed in your mission.

401

The last guard does not advance. Instead the cowardly creature has decided to raise the alarm and is now running across the courtyard, roaring loudly. Within moments, a full complement of armed guards are hurrying towards you. There is no way for you to take on so many opponents. You will be captured and you will no doubt have earned the last guard a special commendation from the Archmage. You have failed in your mission.

402

The conversation has been enormously enlightening. You now know the secret of the most powerful spell in your Spell Book *and* you know how to control it. Turn to 427 to cast a spell. If you choose to cast the ZED spell, ignore the reference you are told to turn to and turn instead to 631. This is your bonus for knowing the secret of the spell.

403

You leave the smooth-skinned creature in peace and back slowly down the corridor, closing the door behind you. Will you try the door in the wall that you passed on the way to this room (turn to 517), or will you retrace your steps completely to the crossroads and take the other passageway to the metal door (turn to 6)?

404

You step up to the small cave mouth and kneel down to look inside. Although you will be able to crawl into the cave, the entrance will be a tight squeeze. But as your eyes become accustomed to the darkness inside, you can see that there will be enough room for you to fit comfortably. The back of the cave is blackness, so you are unable to tell whether or not the cave is completely empty. You get down on all fours and poke your head inside.

Oooowwouou! A shrill howling comes from inside the cave and all but deafens you! Instinctively you jerk your head out again, away from the danger. The noise sounded as though it came from a hound of some sort. You spring to your feet and draw out your weapon, ready to face whatever is inside. But nothing emerges from the cave. When your courage has returned, you must make a decision: will you enter the cave and face whatever is inside (turn to **123**), or will you instead try the far cave (turn to **534**)?

405

The creature makes no move as you step up to it and cup your hand to your ear. With an expression that looks almost sad, it reaches out its snout towards your ear and whispers to you. The sounds form into words and a message takes shape . . .

But before you can make sense of the message, the smell of its breath hits your nostrils like an acid cloud. You cough and choke, flinging your head backwards out of the way. But it is too late. The breath of a MUCALYTIC is deadly to all but its own kind. A lungful of this poison has ensured your fate. The only mercy is that your death will be quick.

406

You whisper your password to the lock on the door. Nothing unusual happens, but you are confident that you have remembered the password correctly and you reach for the handle. Turn to **344**.

407

Visions of the past flash past you as you tumble weightlessly, carried by your spell. Eventually the confusion clears and you are brought back to the ground. Still unsure what has actually happened, you look around. It is night and you are alone in a small hut, under blankets. Desperately, you want to spring out of bed and find out where you are. But you cannot. Something within is forbidding you to leave your rest and is drawing the curtain of sleep across your eyes. Your eyelids feel as heavy as lead. You cannot resist the urge to sleep. Turn to reference **1** of Book **1** of the *Sorcery!* series.

408

You open your backpack and pull out some Provisions to offer to the unfortunate creature. His eyes open wide as you hold out the food towards it. 'Aaahh, thank you, stranger,' he says. 'At this moment in time, I would gladly sell my soul for a mouthful of food. I hope your price is not that high!' You smile as you break your food up and press it into his mouth. You must deduct 1 from your Provisions. Now you may either talk to him (turn to **555**), tell him that you demand information for the food (turn to **444**) or take out more Provisions and join him in a meal (turn to **520**) – but only if you have more Provisions.

409

The front of your face starts to ache. You raise your hand to feel what is going on and withdraw it immediately. Your nose is growing! It droops down from your face like a proboscis. This is not only an eyesore, but it also makes breathing quite difficult. You must reduce your *Initial* STAMINA by 2 and deduct 2 from your current STAMINA while you are hampered by this trunk. When you are ready, you may leave the kitchen by another door. Turn to **448**.

410

You inch your way slowly across the room. For your next few steps, choose either **180**, **2** or **175**.

411

The bridge is solid and barely responds to your weight as you cross over. You pick up the path which leads south round the rim of the mountain. The Fortress itself is set on the inside of a volcano-like peak. Inside the rim is a flat plateau which forms an ideal base for the stronghold: defence is made easy by the surrounding rock. There is only one pass through to the Fortress. All you have to do is find it!

You presume that the trail leads towards the pass and follow it round. The sky is darkening now as the sun is setting. It has been a long, tiring day. Ahead, you see what you are looking for. The path widens and turns into the rock. You creep forwards cautiously; the pass is doubtless defended by guards. With each step, you can see a little further round into the inner plateau. When you stand directly in front of the pass, your jaw drops in awe. The Mampang Fortress!

Spellbound by its presence, your eyes follow its lines. Gnarled spires twist upwards towards the sky as if in agonized prayers to the heavens. Sharp angles and jagged points protrude everywhere. Demonic gargoyles line the outside walls. The sight is enough to break the courage of many a brave soldier – and its effect on you is similar. Deduct 1 SKILL point until you are inside the Fortress. You quickly snap out of your trance and plan your approach. There may be guards in the pass, but you cannot see any. But standing in the open as you are, anyone inside could certainly see you. Will you creep forwards cautiously, looking out for guards (turn to **139**), or will you run to get through the pass before you are spotted (turn to **67**)?

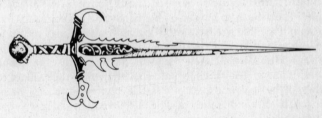

412

You break free from your captors and turn to run from the room. The captain shouts a command in a high-pitched voice, and you realize the folly of your move. Two more guards appear at the door. As you race through it, these two slam their hairy fists into your stomach. You double up and collapse on the floor. Deduct 2 STAMINA points. You are hauled back to face the captain. Turn to 508.

413

You tell the two creatures of your night in the cave and the body you found inside. At first they become excited when you tell them of the news, but later, when you explain that their comrade is dead, their expressions turn to despair. 'This is not good news for us, but it is not entirely unexpected,' says one of the creatures. 'Sh'himbli disappeared two nights ago. It is customary with our race for one who is expecting to die to venture off alone and find an unused cave in which to expire. Then she is no burden on her family and her comrades live in constant hope that she has simply lost her way and may return to the village at any time. However, Sh'himbli had been fevered for some days. I think we all knew the truth. But in any case, we thank you for this news.' They invite you to go with them to their village to tell others of the news and to eat and rest. If you wish to go with them, turn to 545. If you would rather decline their invitation and be on your way, turn to 441.

414

'If you want my opinion,' says Jann, 'even the *thought* of escape is futile. Perhaps we could ambush the guard as he enters the room. But you can bet your worth that the whole company will not be far behind him. An escape plan aided by magic is impossible. As you know, Minimites are protected from most magic with an invisible shroud of protection. Only the most powerful spells will work while I am here – and I'm sure as Courga not going to oblige you by jumping out of the window to get out of your way, if that's what you're thinking! Other than these, the only possibility is to wait to see whether anyone sends for you. Someone is bound to ask for you before long.' You consider his advice. ** Will you:

Plan to ambush the guard?	Turn to **476**
Consider a spell to cast?	Turn to **337**
Wait to see whether anyone sends for you?	Turn to **214**

415

Your heart pounds heavily in your chest as you try to decide which is your best way of avoiding the creature. It is now almost on you. Turn to **296**.

416

With your weapon in your hand, you burst through the door. Your foot catches a half-brick on the floor and you tumble headlong along a hallway, scraping your arms and knees (deduct 2 STAMINA points). You feel foolish. You have burst into a hallway, not into a room – and you have surprised nothing! However, the commotion has attracted something's attention: you can hear voices. The hallway you are in has two doors in it, one in the right-hand wall, which you may investigate by turning to 307, and another at the end of the corridor, which you may try by turning to 144. You may choose this option only if you have not investigated this door previously. Alternatively you can leave this hallway and nip back into the archway where you may either try the large double doors ahead (turn to 253) or the door opposite (turn to 493).

417

You have grabbed a bundle of two candles. One of them is a perfectly ordinary wax candle. The other is red, and is made from the dried blood of a Firefox. The two candles are self-lighting. The blood candle will last longer than the normal candle. You must now leave the area quickly, through the door at the end of the passageway, before the merchant summons the guards. Turn to 310.

418

When you regain consciousness, a feeling of despair overtakes you. You are trapped in the pillory! The broken lock has been jammed through the fastening to hold it in place and though you struggle to free yourself, there is no escape. In front of you stands your attacker. 'My friend, I am truly sorry to have to do this to you,' he says. 'But this is a matter of survival. I must have some time to escape from this place. If the pillory is found to be empty, I will surely be hunted without delay. And I will also need supplies on my journey. Your backpack will no doubt prove most useful.' You watch helplessly as he makes off with your belongings. But what he did not tell you was that he was sentenced to three days in the pillory before being executed for treason. In a day's time, his fate will be yours.

419

Have you already tried either of the other two caves? If you have not already tried the smallest cave, you may do so by turning to **222**. If you have not already tried the middle cave, you may do so by turning to **136**. If you have already tried both of them, then you had better settle for the one you have just looked inside – turn to **293**.

420

You are powerless now to prevent the spell tossing you through time. You realize the folly of using this spell, for power is awesome – and frightening – if you are unable to control it. You have no such control over it. Confused visions flash through your mind, faster and faster, until eventually your feet once more touch solid ground. You come to earth with a crash and look around. You are on a rocky plateau, surrounded by craggy peaks. The scene is familiar. Where have you come across this before? *Of course! Mampang!* You are quite right – you *are* on the rocky plateau of the Fortress, surrounded by the peaks of an extinct volcano. But where is the Fortress? Quite clearly it is not there. The answer dawns on you. *The spell!* You have travelled through time to a point either way in the past, before the Fortress was built, or far in the future, after it has been destroyed! Whichever is the case, your predicament is hopeless. You may try the spell again and again, until your STAMINA runs out, but without controlling it, you will never return to Mampang. Your mission has ended.

421

You join in with the guards and they teach you how to play their game, which they call 'Ten-up'. Each player throws one dart at a time at the board, which is marked out in black and white sections. Any dart thrown into a black number scores that many points. Any dart thrown into a white number *deducts* that number of points from the current score. Only one score is kept (not one per player) and each player's dart throw affects this score. Whoever throws the dart which brings the score exactly to either ten or minus ten wins the game. Needless to say, this is a gambling game. Each player puts 2 Gold Pieces in the kitty and the winner takes the lot. If you have 2 Gold Pieces and you would like to play, turn to 481. If you do not have 2 Gold Pieces or do not want to play, turn to 164.

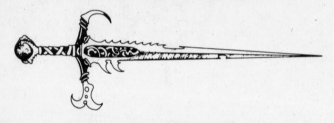

422

You address the Hobgoblin in an arrogant tone. Immediately, the commotion ceases as quickly as if a tap were turned off. The Hobgoblin turns towards you and squints. Her sight is apparently not good. 'Who told you to stop your work?' she screams at the Minions. 'You lazy ants! Get back to work this instant! The guards must be fed!' The Minions cower in fear as she speaks and work recommences. The Hobgoblin steps over and screws her eyes up to get a good look at you. 'Well?' she demands. 'You asked for the cook. What do you want?' Will you ask her for something to eat, as you are hungry (turn to 26), or will you tell her that the guards will soon need to eat, and then leave the kitchen (turn to 448)?

423

The captain does not believe your story. Instead he questions you. Turn to 385.

424

You step on to the bridge. Again, the groaning sound follows your footsteps. But, now you are used to it, the sound is quite amusing. In fact the humour of the situation is a welcome relief to the anxiety you would be feeling if you were crossing the bridge and looking down into the chasm. But in the next second, you *are* looking down into the chasm, and watching it come racing towards you! For the rope bridge of groans has disappeared completely! Not a trace of it remains, leaving you flying downwards through the air to your death. You will never know the true secret of the Groaning Bridge. Your last memory will be the sound of the groaning which has now turned to a faint mocking laughter way above you . . .

425

To your left ahead is a bundle of rags in a heap on the ground. If you wish to head towards it, turn to **233**. To your right is a group of human-like creatures – and something looks familiar about their appearance. If you wish to walk a bit closer to investigate, turn to **325**. If you want to ignore both of these and continue straight ahead, turn to **135**.

426

The door you have reached is locked in a similar way to the entrance door. You quickly grasp the handle, flick the catch, and step outside into a corridor, closing the door firmly behind you. This passage is quite short and widens at its far end. You follow it. Turn to **124**.

427

You ignore the Minimite's reservations about using magic and choose your spell to cast:

ZEN	NIP	FAL	ZED	DUM
710	666	694	753	601

If you know none of these spells, you must either plan to attack the guard as he brings you food (turn to **476**), or simply wait to see what happens (turn to **214**).

428

You step up to the door. Your hand reaches for the handle but, before you can touch it, a gruff voice calls out from inside: '*Inside!* But do not waste my time unless you carry gold!' You step inside. The room is elegantly laid out with ornaments and drapes. Sitting behind a fine table is a large brown-skinned man wearing a turban perched on top of large, bulbous ears. He is very fat. 'Ho, ho!' he laughs. 'And what have we here? Not much finery. Certainly not a merchant. Perhaps a fortune-hunter? Do you hide wealth under those tawdry rags? The price to enter this room is 1 Gold Piece. And we like our payment in advance, do we not, Hashi?' He looks down and strokes a large black Jaguar which is sitting under the table. Will you throw him 1 Gold Piece as he wishes, in exchange for information (turn to **542**)? Will you ask him his name and what he is doing here (turn to **42**)? Or will you tell him that he looks as though he could do with a hired sword to protect his possessions (turn to **94**)?

429

In a soft voice you add that you are glad to hear about their mothers and ask whether their fathers are also well. The three scowl at you, menacingly. 'Do not ask. Our mothers are well. That is all that need concern you. And what of you? Where is your home?' They are, in their own way, continuing the pleasantries. Will you tell them that you are from Analand (turn to **578**), or will you claim to be from Kharé (turn to **326**)?

430

Will you face the guards with your weapon (turn to **394**), or cast a spell?

FAL	GOB	YOB	YAZ	FIX
712	646	789	721	655

431

You laugh at the poor creature's predicament and a sadistic urge seizes you. You take great delight in calling him a 'vomit-faced pig with the brain of a lesser Goblin' and tell him he deserves a fate worse than being drowned in a bucket of Skunkbear dung. His anger rises, but there is nothing he can do. When you have tired of insulting him, turn to **485**.

432

When their laughter has died down, one of the guards steps apart from the rest and looks out at the pass. He seems to have noticed that all is not well and shades his eyes with his hand to see better. In fact, in the early-morning gloom, you doubt whether this would make any difference, but *something* has caught his attention. He barks at the other two and shouts louder to attract a fourth guard who comes out of the door and joins them. The four of them look out at the pass, pointing and snorting. Do you feel safe enough to try dropping to the ground yet (turn to **572**), or do you have another plan (turn to **50**)?

433

You wait for signs of the mutation. But you feel nothing! You are one of the rare few who are immune from the effects of the Mutant Meatballs! You may now leave the kitchen through a door leading into the keep by turning to **448**.

434

You leave the room and set off down the stairs. At the foot of the staircase, you open the Throben Doors and step through . . .

Rough hands grab you as you swing the door open. Shouts go up. You find yourself in the grip of a tall, grimy guard. Around the doorway are other guards. Although you were not expecting to be discovered this quickly, you had realized that the way back through the Fortress would not be easy. Turn to **430** to face the guards.

435

Your eyes widen as you look inside the bag. Inside are several artefacts for use with your spells! You may take as many or as few of these artefacts as you want, but for each you must leave behind 1 item from your Equipment List (not food or gold). Inside the bag you find:

A Potion of Fire Water   A Brass Pendulum
A Sun Jewel   An Orb of Crystal
A Pearl Ring   Orange Powder
A Pair of Nose Plugs

Exchange as you wish, then leave the village by turning to **441**.

436

She removes her hands and sighs deeply. 'Perhaps I should tell you all I know about the Birdmen from Schinn,' she says. 'I can sense that in many ways your missions are similar. But I must be brief. The creatures within Mampang are not all aligned to the evil ways of the Archmage. Although the Xamen Birdmen are his strongest allies, there is a faction from Schinn, to the east of the Nagomanti River, who fear his growing power. A group of Schinns have infiltrated the Fortress and are plotting his overthrow. They have become known as the 'Samaritans' and the Archmage has been mounting an inquisition to drive them from his ranks. As a result, many wrongful accusations have been made and loyal Birdmen have been tortured and executed. Thus there is growing dissent in the ranks of the Birdmen. It is impossible to tell which Birdmen are Samaritans, as they must of necessity keep their activities secret. But there is one introduction I know of which will reveal the Schinns. If you meet Birdmen, ask them about their families. Loyalist Birdmen will talk only of their fathers; Samaritans worship their mothers.' This is useful information, for which you may add 2 LUCK points. Will you continue by asking her about herself and how she became the beggar she now is (turn to 388), or would you like to know whether she can advise you how to enter the keep (turn to 535)?

437

With confident strides, you walk across the kitchen. The Minions bustle around you and bump into your legs, but no one challenges you. At least, not until you are half-way across the kitchen, when a gruff voice growls at you. 'Halt!' screams the Hobgoblin. 'What business do you have intruding on Throg's kitchen? Come to steal food, eh? The Archmage knows that his officers are welcome in here. You have no need to creep. Come with me!' Turn to 137.

438

Where will your journey take you? Past adventures flash before you in no particular order. In one instant you are watching your own birth. Then you are being congratulated by the villagers of Torrepani. Then you are battling the Serpent of Time. Roll two dice and consult the table below to find the effect of the spell:

Roll	Turn to		Roll	Turn to
2	447		7	229
3	518		8	631
4	733		9	579
5	30		10	407
6	75		11	500
			12	420

439

Thankfully, one calming dream interrupts your nightmares. The reassuring face of Libra, your goddess, appears and speaks softly:

'My loyal devotee, the end of your arduous journey is in sight. The dangers you will face within the Mampang Fortress are many, but you have so far proven a worthy choice for this mission. I have watched your progress with interest and, at times, with fear for your life. But at each stage of the journey, you have been successful. And with little help from me.

'I bring you this final message. It may be the last help I can give you, for the netherworld deities which oversee Mampang are powerful enough to keep even me out of its stronghold. If you would know the truth, I am in some danger even as I speak. *I cannot help you while you are inside the Fortress.*

'Because the netherworld gods protect Mampang, little is known of its secrets. But I will tell you this: a generation ago, another of my followers escaped from the Fortress through a secret passage. He had discovered the password which would open its hidden door. I will whisper this to you.' She speaks a word softly in your ear. If you wish to use this password at some time during your adventure, deduct 92 from the reference you are on at the time when you wish to use it, and turn to this new reference. If you are using it correctly, the new reference will make sense and take you through the secret door.

Did you spend last night in the cave with the hoof-prints outside? If so, turn to 147. If you did not, turn to 113.

440

Beads of sweat appear on your forehead. The going is difficult as the candlelit shadows sway across the room. But so far you have not touched any of the blades. To take your next few steps, choose between turning to **484** and **223**.

441

The trail continues to climb upwards into the mountains. In the distance, the dark shape of the Mampang Fortress is becoming larger by the hour. You will certainly reach its gates by nightfall. You come to a little sheltered alcove where you may rest and take Provisions if you want to (turn to **350**). If you have no Provisions or do not wish to stop, turn to **539**.

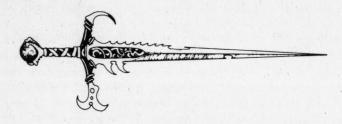

442

At the sight of the weapon, the creature lumbers towards you as if to strike the first blow. Resolve your battle with this MUCALYTIC.

MUCALYTIC   SKILL 8   STAMINA 9

If it manages to score three wounds on you during the battle, turn to **576**. If you can defeat it before taking three wounds, turn to **163**.

Before continuing, you look through the debris littering the floor of

443

Before continuing, you look through the debris littering the floor of the room. A rusty sword lies in one corner. If you have no weapon, you may take this with you, but it is not much of a weapon. When using this sword, you will fight at 1 below your SKILL score. If you have a weapon, you may only take this sword if you will leave behind one of your other possessions (not gold or Provisions). A small string of bones, fashioned into a bracelet, is hidden under a wooden plank and you may also take with you two Goblin teeth and 5 Gold Pieces which you find on the floor. Which way will you continue? Do you want to head through the door opposite the one you entered through (turn to **263**), or will you try the door in the other wall (turn to **547**)?

444

'I . . . I cannot!' he stutters. 'I cannot tell you what you want to know. For it was my loose tongue that got me into this situation in the first place. I want no more trouble.' You insist that he tells you and he relents a little. 'Perhaps I might be able to talk a little more freely if I was released from this pillory. Do you think you could help me?' he asks. Will you offer to release him from the pillory (turn to **362**), or do you think he is safer where he is now (turn to **485**)?

445

The captain is grateful for your mercy. You threaten him with the final blow unless he agrees to help you. 'My life is now worth nothing,' he sobs, 'for I have allowed you to escape, and the Archmage is a cruel master. My only hope now is that you succeed in your mission.' He pulls a key from his pocket with the number 17 cast into it. 'This is the key which will open the Throben Doors at the foot of the Archmage's tower. Without it you will get no further into his private chambers.' You take the key and tie the captain to his seat. You cannot afford to take chances with his loyalty. When you reach the next Throben Doors, you may use this key by deducting its number from the reference you arrive at and turning to this new reference. Turn to **463**.

446

You wait for the right moment. When the footsteps have stopped at the door, you heave yourself forwards, slamming your shoulder into the door. The door flies open and stops abruptly as it smashes into the GUARD who was about to open it. The guard howls in pain and falls to the ground. Inside the room are a table and two chairs, and rising quickly from one of the chairs is another guard, who grabs a weapon. You must fight the guards, but you have two advantages. Firstly, you have disabled one of the guards already. Deduct 3 points from the first guard's SKILL. Secondly, you have the element of surprise on your side. If, during the fight, your Attack Strengths are the same, you can treat this result as though you had inflicted a wound. If you are going to fight the guards, turn to 453. Otherwise you may cast a spell:

YAZ	RAP	GUM	RAZ	RES
688	738	756	765	641

447

Your life and the history of the world seem to race past you in an instant. Skimpy visions flash past, leaving you in a state of confusion. Where will this end? Eventually, the turmoil subsides. The confusion clears and the world once more settles to its normal pace. Your feet touch the ground and you take in your surroundings. All around is a barren wasteland. Are you out in the Baklands? Your questions are answered when three birds fly overhead. They have enormous wingspans and their heads are more reptilian than bird-like. You clutch at your chest. *Anteelocets! It cannot be!* This species of flying reptile has been extinct for centuries! Then the answer dawns on you. The ZED spell is the most dangerous spell in your Spell Book, not because of its powers, but because it is difficult to control. You are now lost in another time. Will you ever find your way back? Perhaps you could use the spell again – but your STAMINA will not take it for long. In any case, your mission will now never be completed . . .

448

You leave the kitchen along a passageway which no doubt leads towards the guards' mess-hall. After several paces you come to a sharp bend to the left. Around the bend you can hear gruff voices and the chink of chainmail armour approaching you! What can you do? If these are guards approaching, you would be stupid to leap round the corner and face them. You lean back against the wall into a small alcove, thinking fast.

As fate would have it, you have unwittingly discovered an escape-route in this alcove. For the wall behind you gives a little as you lean into it. There is a secret door set into the wall! You have no other choice but to nip quickly through it. In the nick of time, you close it behind you as the approaching footsteps round the corner.

The passageway behind the door is dark and damp. It descends probably to below floor-level, and continues straight onwards. Most probably, other secret passages lead into and off this corridor, but in the dark you are satisfied simply to follow it to the end. Eventually, it climbs back up to floor-level and ends at a latched door. You undo the latch and step out. Turn to **236**.

449

The guards come at you one at a time. Fight the first two first:

First GUARD	SKILL 7	STAMINA 8
Second GUARD	SKILL 7	STAMINA 7

If you defeat both guards, you may turn to face the third one. Turn to **401**.

450

There is no escaping this creature; you are in a battle to the death:

BIRDMAN   SKILL 9   STAMINA 11

If you defeat this creature, turn to **543**.

451

You fight against the force, but to no avail. You catapult forwards and slam into the metal pole. Lose 2 STAMINA points for your bruises. You quickly realize what is happening: the pole is a huge *magnet* with a lodestone core. Its effect has caught hold of all the metal objects you are carrying. You are free to move your arms and legs, but everything you have made of metal is firmly fixed in place. Perhaps this pole is used by the guards to search unknown visitors, particularly those with magic powers who may be able to disguise their weapons. There is only one way you may escape from this pole, and that is by abandoning everything you have which is made of metal. You set to work on freeing yourself. Cross all your metal objects off your Adventure Sheet and wrench yourself free from the pole. If you now have no weapon, you must deduct 3 SKILL points until you find something you can use as a weapon. Then you may step up to the wooden doors by turning to **397**.

452

'*Five* Gold Pieces? Do you call that a reward?' he laughs, and advances. 'Nooo, I think I will kill you first and *then* take your gold!' Will you draw your weapon (turn to **270**), or cast a spell?

POP	ZIP	NIF	TEL	SUN
651	619	709	592	691

453

During this battle, both guards will attack you. You must choose which of the guards you wish to attack and fight that one as normal. Roll for Attack Strength in the usual way for the remaining guard. If his Attack Strength is higher than yours, he has wounded you. If your Attack Strength is higher, you have avoided the blow but will not wound him, as you were directing your attack against the other guard.

| First GUARD | SKILL 8 | STAMINA 6 |
| Second GUARD | SKILL 7 | STAMINA 7 |

If you defeat both guards, you may search their room. Turn to 44.

454

You speak your password and wait. A creak in the rock is followed by the appearance of a crack which splits along the rock-face. A door is opening! Your heart beats quickly as it swings open to allow you through. And, judging by the commotion you can hear at the bottom of the stairs, this was not a moment too soon! You step through the door and close it behind you.

You find yourself in a narrow tunnel. Stairs lead downwards. You follow them down and down, zigzagging until you reach the bottom. At the bottom is a door. It squeaks on its hinges as you open it. This door cannot have been used for many years; the dust and debris that have built up around it make it very difficult to open. Your spirits rise again when you find the door leads, as Farren Whyde had told you, outside the Fortress! But what of the hidden tower? Has it now resumed its aura of invisibility? You look out and breathe a sigh of relief. It is still visible. Perhaps the old man's words render the invisibility spell ineffective to anyone who once sees the tower. You step across towards it.

A heavy door leads into the tower. You try it and find it firmly locked. Roll two dice and compare the total with your SKILL score. If you roll a number *less* than your SKILL, the door will open to allow you inside. If you roll a number *greater than or equal to* your SKILL (this door is particularly strong), then the door will hold fast. Deduct 1 STAMINA point for each attempt you make (including the successful ones). When you finally open the door, turn to 102.

455

Within moments, the meatballs take effect. Spines shoot out of your back, bursting through your tunic. Scales appear on your hands and face. You are turning into a reptilian! The thought horrifies you and there is another side-effect of which you are not yet aware. *You have a permanent phobia of reptiles.* If, at any time later in your adventure, you encounter a reptile of any kind (snakes, serpents, hydras, lizardmen, giant frogs, etc.), *you will drop dead on sight!* You must avoid reptiles at all costs. When you are ready, you may leave the kitchen by turning to 448.

456

The two creatures lead you up and along the rock. Following several metres behind, you wait for an opportunity to escape. *Test your Luck*. If you are Lucky, an opportunity presents itself and you manage to nip away and rejoin the trail (turn to 441). If you are Unlucky, they keep a close eye on you (turn to 545).

457

You shrug your shoulders and admit that the holy man never gave his name to you. The Red-Eyes nod their heads. 'He has never revealed his true name to anyone,' agrees your inquisitor. 'It is said that Slangg alone knows his real identity.' You breathe a sigh of relief and try to excuse yourself. You have no wish to delay things with these creatures. They can see you are impatient and they let you go with a wave. Turn to 425.

458

Your weapon strikes true. It shears one of the creature's necks! The Hydra rears up and roars, its other heads glaring angrily down at you. You watch the severed head drop to the ground. But then your heart sinks. For *two* more heads are growing where the first dropped! The legend of the Hydra was true. The sun goddess Glantanka fixes her vision on you and two fine jets of light flash from her eyes at your wrist. You scream as they find their mark and your weapon drops to the ground. Deduct 2 STAMINA points and fight the next Attack Round. If you wound the creature, turn to 398. If it wounds you, turn to 305.

459

The Sightmasters watch carefully as you open up your bag to give them their gold. How many Gold Pieces are you carrying? If you have more than 5, turn to 45. If you have less than 5, turn to 246.

460

You turn a few wheels and push a couple of levers, but nothing seems to make any difference. Suddenly it splutters! You repeat your actions and it splutters again, but this time something catches and the machine springs to life! Wheels turn, plates move up and down and steam rises from the top of the contraption. But you still cannot decide what it does. Finally, it dawns on you. This is a device for sharpening weapons and knives; it has a large grindstone rotating at the back. You may use it to sharpen your own weapons if you have any. Anything you sharpen on the machine will add a bonus of 1 point on to your Attack Strength from now on. When you have done this, you can turn the machine off and concentrate on your mission. You don't seem to be able to get through this room, so you will have to return to the main hallway. Turn to 81.

461

You turn towards the group and ask them what they're playing. The three shaggy faces invite you to join in. Suddenly one of them stops and shouts out loudly: 'Wait! The Analander! It is the one we have been warned about! The crud-faced cockroach must be captured! Quick!' The three of them quickly draw weapons and spring on you. Do you wish to face them with your own weapon (turn to **449**)? If you want to use magic, you will have to be quick, but you may just have time to cast a spell:

FOG	HOW	RAZ	TEL	POP
613	711	732	670	784

462

The Birdmen attack with their weapons and sharp talons. In the confines of the room, they may only attack one at a time. Resolve your battle with them:

First BIRDMAN	SKILL 8	STAMINA 10
Second BIRDMAN	SKILL 9	STAMINA 8
Third BIRDMAN	SKILL 8	STAMINA 9

If you kill all three, turn to **365**.

463

You leave the room and walk across the bright chamber towards a door on the far side leading onwards. You may open this door by turning to **580**.

464

A great lumbering shape about the size of a bear rises up from the corner. As it does so, it disturbs a flask which was standing in the corner. The flask rolls over towards you and stops when it bumps into your foot. As the creature rises to its feet (if indeed it has any feet at all), you can see that its bulky features are highlighted by a dull glistening. On top of a blubbery body is an indistinct head with two eyes floating about and a trunk-like snout in the middle of its face. A pudgy hand rises and cups the creature's ear as if it was listening to what you are saying. But you have said nothing. Do you wish to try to talk to it (turn to 395), will you prepare to fight it (turn to 516), or will you investigate the flask at your foot (turn to 11)?

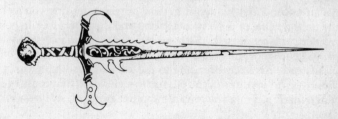

465

The handle turns and you push the door open. Expecting the worst, you peer into the room. It is dark, but there is no sound coming from inside. As your eyes adjust to the light, you can see that the room is circular and, thankfully, empty. There is no furniture inside, nor any windows. The walls are smooth and stony, with long scratches stretching from floor to ceiling at several points round the edge of the door. On the far side, you see what you are looking for. The foot of a staircase! Will you enter the room and look around (turn to 355), head across the room for the staircase (turn to 381), or ignore this room and try the other door (turn to 37)?

466

The creature listens to your apology and its anger rises once more. It screams for you to leave without delay. Will you do as it wishes and go back down the corridor (turn to 403), or defy its wishes and draw out your weapon (turn to 360)?

467

The scene inside the doors is encouraging. There is a large courtyard before you and, in the early-morning light, groups of the Fortress's inhabitants are coming to life. This is encouraging because you will probably be able to mingle with these groups and make your way inconspicuously. You close the door behind you and walk into the courtyard.

Trying your best to act naturally, you advance towards the far side of the courtyard, where it seems that the entrance to the main keep will be. You are aware that you may well be the only human in the courtyard and that this fact may arouse some suspicions, so you steer round to the right. One group, some distance ahead of you, starts to take an uncomfortable interest in your progress, making you feel a little uneasy. One of them points at you and the others look in your direction. You cannot tell whether their intentions are malevolent or not. Will you ignore this and continue towards them (turn to 325), will you instead take a route tending to the left and heading towards a pillory (turn to 393), or will you pass on the left side of the group, even though this is steering you towards another group of creatures (turn to 109)?

468

The captain looks at you curiously. The obvious similarity between your races has come as a shock to him as well. You hold his gaze, then look around the room. (The room is illustrated opposite reference 375: you may find a useful clue in this illustration.) Finally, he sits down and speaks to you. 'What have we here?' he asks. 'An intruder? Or one with legitimate business so deep within the confines of the Fortress? Well? Have you lost your tongue?' What will you tell the captain? Will you pretend you have a message for the Archmage (turn to 201)? Will you tell him you have sworn to destroy the evil within the Fortress (turn to 122)? Or will you offer him something from your backpack, perhaps as a bribe (turn to 232)?

469

You dash outside the cave and into the undergrowth. Eventually you stop to see whether your pursuer is behind you. The creature has not come out of its cave. You decide to try one of the other caves for a place to sleep for the night. Will you try the smallest cave (turn to 404) or the other cave (turn to 534)?

470

You walk across to the door. Your hand reaches for the handle. But before it can touch the knob, a voice resounds in the room: '*Stop!*' it warns, 'touch not that handle! For none may climb the spiral stairs save at the wish of the Superior One. Disobey and you shall pay with your life!' You look around, but see no one. The disembodied voice seems to have come from the walls themselves. Should you take heed of this warning? Is the door trapped? Decide whether you will try the door handle regardless (turn to **220**) or step back and consider your next move cautiously (turn to **265**).

471

The Birdmen want to know what you are doing in the Fortress, as there are few humans within its walls. Will you tell them of your mission (turn to **170**), or claim to be looking for an escort to take you further into the keep (turn to **89**)?

472

As you approach the double doors, you keep your eyes peeled for any signs of activity. Through the double doors, you can hear the early-morning sounds of the inhabitants preparing for the day ahead. But there is no sound coming from the short passageway in which you stand. You grasp the great brass handle and turn it. The doors are locked. Looking down the narrow slit between the doors, you can see that a heavy bolt holds them fastened. You will not get through this way. Turn to **493** to investigate the other door in the wall. Or, if you have another plan, turn to **193**.

473

Did you buy any of the other items for sale? If so, turn to the appropriate reference to find out what its properties are:

Rusty Cutlass	Turn to **85**
Candles	Turn to **303**
Spell Artefacts	Turn to **226**
Nest with Egg	Turn to **108**
Silver Pieces	Turn to **208**

If you have now investigated all of your purchases, leave the merchant and continue to the door at the end of the passageway. Turn to **310**.

474

You drop to the ground as quietly as possible and turn to step inside the door. *Aaaaahh!* You jump with fright, as you find yourself face to face with a guard in heavy armour! The guard is as surprised as you are and he bellows loudly. From outside and within, four guards come to surround you and you must now face all of them. If you attack them, turn to **40**. If you would rather try a spell, choose one:

DUM	WOK	DIM	FOG	TEL
718	636	656	766	599

475

Resolve your fight with the creature:

MUCALYTIC   SKILL 8   STAMINA 9

If it manages to score three wounds on you during the battle, turn to **576**. If you defeat it before it can score three hits, turn to **443**.

476

An hour or so later, a guard comes in through the door to give the two of you a meal. You may, if you wish, try attacking the guard (turn to **142**), or you may eat your meal and wait to see what happens – for surely someone will want to question you soon (turn to **177**).

477

You climb into the nest and start your search. Something glinting in the sunlight catches your attention. From underneath a small pile of twigs you pull a shimmering mirror with a golden back! Hastily, you place this in your backpack and look around for any more treasures.

But you are so preoccupied with your search that you do not notice the danger approaching. Finally, the flurry of flapping wings makes you spin round. Standing on the edge of the nest and casting a shadow across you are three man-sized creatures with long feathered wings. Their hair is wild, and sharp, hooked beaks project from their faces. Vicious talons protrude from their hands and feet. BIRDMEN! You curse silently; you should have recognized the signs. Xamen Birdmen are among the most hated and feared creatures known in the Zanzunus. One of them beats his wings and springs into the air. The others follow suit. Together they descend on you before you have a chance to react. Their sharp talons dig into your flesh and they lift you into the air. With a loud call, they drop you on to the path. From this height, your death is certain. And the pain from your shoulder makes it impossible for you to concentrate on a spell. Your journey has come to an end . . .

478

'*Thirteen* Gold Pieces, eh?' muses the Ogre, rubbing his stubbly chin. 'Now that's a fair amount of money. If you're offering me that much gold, then sure as Courga you're carrying more. I reckon your head will be worth more to me than 13 pieces of gold!' Turn to **270**.

479

You leave the room carefully, checking to make sure no one else is about. The way is clear. You creep quietly along the passageway until you reach a T-junction. To the left, the passage ends in a solid metal door. Over the door, almost as a trophy, is a rope tied in a noose. To the right, there are two doors to choose from. In the left-hand wall of the passage is a wooden door, while at the end of the passage is a half-open door with a bell-pull hanging next to it. Will you turn left and try the door at the end (turn to **6**)? Or will you turn right and try either the door on the left (turn to **517**) or the door straight ahead (turn to **319**)?

480

You hold up your hand and offer a word of greeting. The creature strains hard, pushing its ear with its hand. It seems not to be able to hear you. You shout the same message and it stops. From its expression, you would assume that it has heard you. But this creature must either be very deaf or very stupid, for your greeting was almost a bellow. A sound comes from its throat. You cock your head to one side. That sounded like a *sentence*, rather than an animal sound! The effect is immediate. If this creature is capable of speaking, you cannot help but sympathize with its being locked inside such a grotesque body. Again the faint sound comes from its mouth, but it is still too faint for you to hear. It motions that it would like to whisper in your ear. Will you allow it to come closer to give you its message (turn to **386**), or will you warn it to keep its distance, while you cross the room (turn to **515**)?

481

The game commences. To find out whether or not you win the game, you will have to actually play it. The illustration facing this page shows the Ten-up board. Place your left elbow firmly on a table and raise your hand as if you were about to start arm wrestling. Grasp your pen or pencil in your left hand like a dagger, as if you were about to stab someone. Place the book on the table in front of your arm. Keeping a tight grip on your pencil, and keeping your elbow firmly in place, *stab the book with your pencil*! The stabbing movement must be a quick strike. You are not allowed to do it slowly to make sure you hit where you want. Wherever your pencil lands on the illustration counts as the throw of the dart. If the throw misses the board, then there is no score. If the throw lands on the board, score that number of points. If it lands on a *black* number, increase the running score by that number of points. If it lands on a *white* number, deduct that number of points from the running total. You must 'throw' for each player in turn; you first, then the three guards. Whoever makes the throw which brings the running total exactly to ten or minus ten wins the game – and the 8 Gold Pieces in the kitty.

If you can afford it, you may play Ten-up twice before the guards must go. If you run out of money, or if you don't want to continue, you can stop after the first game. When you have finished playing, turn to **397**.

482

You threaten to strike the creature unless it will tell you truthfully what it has inside the room. Again, it shrugs its shoulders and looks at you pathetically. You are determined that your threat was no idle warning. Turn to **360**.

483

Without touching the door, you place your lips against the handle, as you saw the creature do before you. Nothing happens. You reach forwards and grasp the handle. You feel a tingle pass briefly through your body, but no other ill effects. You look at your hand. *What are you doing this for?* You step backwards and look around at the courtyard. *Where are you? What are you doing here? WHO are you?* You puzzle over these strange thoughts, trying desperately to find the answers. But you will never solve these mysteries. For the Throben Door you have just tried to enter has its own defence against intruders. Any unauthorized person trying to enter is subject to the same treatment. *Your mind has been wiped blank!* All knowledge of yourself and your mission has been erased for good. Your quest has ended . . .

484

A slight disturbance in the air catches your candle. The room goes dark, then flickers, as the candle struggles to to keep alight. Your foot is half-way through a step when this occurs, and the difficult light makes it impossible to judge your footing. It comes down on one of the blades! You yell out loud and instinctively withdraw your foot. But as you do this, you lose your balance completely and come crashing down . . . on top of the blades.

You have taken your last step in this adventure. And as the candle falls upon your broken and bleeding body, it seems to glow more brightly than before, as if it were fuelling itself on your misfortune. The blood candle earns its name not so much from its chief ingredient, but more from its lust for the life-blood of its victims.

485

You leave the pillory and carry on. Ahead, four guards are standing in a group against the wall. Every so often, one will step back and throw something at the wall. The others watch intently and grunt sounds of encouragement; sometimes the sounds are even laughter. If you want to head towards this group, turn to **532**. If you wish to avoid the guards, you must walk away from the wall into the open courtyard towards a ragged shape lying on the ground. To go this way, turn to **233**.

486

You set off down the stairs. Your morale has been reduced to an all-time low with the thought of having somehow to work your way back through the Fortress to get outside the walls. You open the Throben Doors at the foot of the staircase and step through . . .

Rough hands grab your shoulders and pull you through the doors. Shouts go up. You are surrounded by guards! Your lack of caution has now placed you in a dire situation. Turn to **430** to face the guards.

487

As his companion is keeping you engaged, the other guard lifts the horn from the wall and blows it loudly. Your heart sinks. An alarm call! Reinforcements will be sent immediately! You must dispatch these two and hide quickly. Continue the fight against the first guard and, if you win, attack the second:

Second GUARD   SKILL 8   STAMINA 6

If you defeat both the guards, turn to **577**.

488

You inch your way across the room. For your next few steps, choose either **52** or **341**.

489

'Ahhh, yes. I can feel something else in here, too. Something wicked taking hold of you from within. Something Javinne can help with.' Again she concentrates and her hands become warm. The disease is leaving your body and entering her hands! Javinne is a natural healer and her powers have cleansed you. Now turn to **436**.

490

The Skunkbear rises up on its hind legs and steps towards you, its sharp claws slashing the air. Resolve your fight with the creature:

SKUNKBEAR   SKILL 7   STAMINA 6

If you wish to leave the fight and run from the creature, you may do so only after your *first* successful attack, by turning to **469**. After your *second* successful attack (i.e. if you do not choose to escape), turn to **346**.

491

You quickly hurl the vial at the speeding creature before it can reach you. The glass shatters, spraying liquid all over the statue. But, to your dismay, it has no effect at all on it! Now the statue is almost upon you. Turn to **296**.

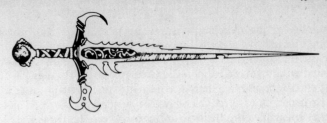

492

You follow the narrow path up to the door and listen carefully. The noises from within sound something like a busy kitchen in which a meal is being prepared. Will you enter this room (turn to **179**), or will you try the door on the left (turn to **565**)?

493

The timber door is a few centimetres ajar and, as you approach, you can hear gruff voices talking inside. *Guards!* As you creep closer, you hear a chair move as one of them stands up. You must decide quickly. Will you:

Burst into the room to surprise whoever is inside?	Turn to **553**
Stay to listen at the doorway?	Turn to **330**
Hide, by trying the doorway opposite?	Turn to **206**
Quickly go for the large double doors?	Turn to **253**

494

A number of the merchant's wares are interesting. You browse through his shelves and ask him about several items that take your fancy. He recommends a rusty cutlass, which he claims is an enchanted weapon and a bargain at 3 Gold Pieces. He also has a set of two candles, bound together. According to the merchant these will light to order. One is a red 'blood candle', made from the dried blood of a Firefox, while the other is an ordinary wax candle. These will cost you 2 Gold Pieces. He has a number of spell artefacts – some of the ones you might require for spells – but these are expensive, at 5 Gold Pieces each. A bird's-nest has a single golden egg inside: this will cost you 2 Gold Pieces. And a pouch hanging from one of the uppermost shelves contains ancient silver pieces. These will cost you 4 Gold Pieces, but he will not part with the pouch, which is not for sale.

If you wish to buy any of these, decide which you want, pay the price in Gold Pieces, and turn to the reference below:

Rusty Cutlass	Turn to **85**
Candles	Turn to **303**
Spell Artefacts	Turn to **226**
Nest with Egg	Turn to **108**
Silver Pieces	Turn to **208**

495

The guard falls to the ground, but another is ready to take his place. And if you defeat that one, there is another, then another. Your cause is hopeless. You cannot defeat *all* the guards – even if you carry a blessed hardwood spear – and it is simply a matter of time before your own strength runs out. Your attempt to rescue the Crown has been good, but not good enough . . .

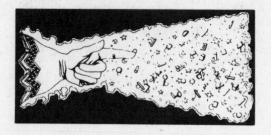

496

The guard beats the bushes with a sword, looking for some clue as to who or what has knocked on the door. He finds nothing. But the commotion has attracted the attention of another guard, and a second creature appears through the door. The two grunt at each other and look into the distance. Now is your chance. Will you drop quietly to the ground and step through the doorway (turn to **556**), or will you wait to see whether any more guards appear (turn to **364**)?

497

The other creatures watch in awe as their champion falls to the ground. Silence again falls over them and they watch you fearfully. You keep your weapon at the ready and step over to the door. Turn to **426**.

498

Do you know a password which will open the doors? Is it any of the following:

Alaralatanalara	Turn to **32**
Alaralamalatana	Turn to **312**
Alaralaramalana	Turn to **157**
None of these?	Turn to **379**

499

Slowly, the shape comes alive. Its scaly skin ripples and flexes as muscles crank it off the ground. You can do nothing but watch, your mouth agape, as the formidable shape takes form. It is a form that you recognize from legend rather than experience. For before your eyes, a great HYDRA is taking shape!

But its reptilian features are incomplete. Seven stumpy necks are flexing themselves, but its heads are *missing*! How can the creature live without heads? In the next instant, your question is answered. Materializing slowly on the creature's necks are seven heads. But these are not the snake-like heads you were expecting! Instead they are sinister human-like heads with grotesque faces. One bearded, stark-white face has great puffy cheeks. You swallow hard, for you recognize this face. It is Pangara, god of the air! A woman's face has sharp features and a shock of bright orange hair which glows in its own light. Burning red fireballs in her eyes confirm her identity: Glantanka, goddess of the sun! Other faces are beginning to form as the gods of Mampang appear before you on snake necks. If these are the gods, then you will have little chance against their powers unless you act quickly. Will you pull out your weapon and attack (turn to 65), or cast a spell:

GOD	ZEN	MUD	HOT	BIG
603	777	734	623	689

Or will you wait for the other heads to materialize (turn to 49)?

500

You are taken up by the spell and tossed like a feather in the air while, below you, visions of the world flash by. Eventually, the pace slows and you wait for a final bump as you return to earth. The spell is wearing off. *But where are you?* Turn to reference 254 of Book 2 of the *Sorcery!* series.

501

You wait for the mutation to take effect. You feel no physical change, but suddenly you wonder *why* you are waiting. Loss of memory is your mutation – and it is permanent. Although you may still be skilful with your weapons, you cannot remember any of your spells and may not use spells for the rest of the adventure. Consider yourself lucky that you can even remember what your purpose is at all! Eventually you wander off through the back door of the kitchen. Turn to **448**.

502

The pole is covered with ornate markings. All manner of faces and symbols are cast into it. Your eyes widen as you see, at the base of the pole, two swords and an axe! These may be useful weapons. But there is something strange about the way they are lying. Although arranged around the foot of the pole, they are leaning unnaturally, as if they were glued to it. Will you step forwards to investigate the weapons (turn to **383**), will you ignore them and instead head for the wooden double doors (turn to **397**), or will you cast a spell:

SUS	DOC	TEL	HUF	PEP
754	653	616	779	723

503

Your curiosity is aroused by the stoppered bottle. You ask what it is and begin to take out the stopper. 'Wait! No!' cries Sh'houri. 'You must not release the spirit!' You quickly put the bottle down. 'Do not be afraid, my friend,' continues Sh'houri. 'For the spirit must always advise, and it is not unfriendly. Inside that bottle is the genie of a long-dead human traveller like yourself. It will not speak to us, as we are not of your race. But if you wish to take this bottle, I am sure that the spirit will offer you advice at the right time. As the spirit is no use to us, you may have it without payment.' You may use this genie in the future at one time only and this time will be marked in the text by two asterisks (**). If you come across these two asterisks, then deduct 80 from the reference you are on and turn to the new reference.

When you have made the necessary adjustments to your Equipment List and thanked the She-Satyrs, you may leave the village by turning to **441**.

504

After five steps into the room you freeze! This may be a trick of the light, but you could *swear* that the shape in the centre of the room is moving! A creak confirms your suspicions. The sculpture is coming to life! It turns on its pedestal to face you as you move forwards. You take two more steps; its legs move, and it steps down from its plinth. There is something unnatural about its movements. They are abnormally quick. Stepping down on to the floor took the statue less than a second, but its bulk is considerable. Then, without warning, it charges!

Lowering its head, it races straight for you at tremendous speed. Its legs barely seem to move! *Test your Luck*. If you are Lucky, turn to **329**. If you are Unlucky, turn to **255**.

505

Roll two dice to determine whether your efforts are successful. If the number rolled is less than or equal to your SKILL score, the lock breaks open – turn to **348**. If the number rolled is higher than your SKILL, you have not been successful and you must try again. If you are unsuccessful twice in a row, you will damage your weapon and must deduct 1 SKILL point. If at any time you decide against continuing with your attempts to free this creature, turn to **485**.

506

You bellow back at the creature angrily and reach for your weapon. It steps back, shocked, and starts to mumble. Apparently, it is either impressed or terrified, and it is now bowing its head submissively and waiting for your next words. Will you order it to tell you the best way through into the inner keep (turn to **390**), will you order it to find you some nourishment (turn to **345**), or will you ask it what it has in its room (turn to **376**)?

507

There is plenty of room inside the cave. You step inside and glance around to satisfy yourself that there are no dangers about. It all seems safe enough. If you want to double-check by exploring the dark depths of the cave, turn to **268**. If you wish to settle down, perhaps to eat, turn to **366**. If you just want to stretch out and get some sleep, turn to **574**.

508

'The Analander!' exclaims the captain in a high-pitched voice. 'You have done well. This capture will be reported to the master.' The two guards shift their positions and grunt proudly at each other. The captain stares deep into your eyes and sits down at his desk. 'But now,' he says, 'we must question our prisoner.' You look round the room while he studies you. Turn to the illustration opposite reference **375** for a view of the room, and study it hard, for there may be a clue which can help you. The captain asks your intentions. Will you tell him that you have a private message for the Archmage (turn to **43**)? Will you tell him you have come to destroy the evil within the Fortress (turn to **122**)? Or will you offer him something from your backpack, perhaps as a bribe (turn to **232**)?

509

As your hand touches the axe, a faint humming sounds in the air and you feel an overwhelming force seize you. Turn to **451**.

510

You manage to wedge yourself into the doorway so that they may only attack you one at a time:

First BLACK ELF	SKILL 7	STAMINA 6
Second BLACK ELF	SKILL 7	STAMINA 7
Third BLACK ELF	SKILL 6	STAMINA 6

If you defeat all three Black Elves, you may leave the room by turning to **566**.

511

The room inside is empty and you breathe a sigh of relief as you lean back on the door. The clatter of the Birdmen's talons on the stone floor outside gets louder as they approach. Directly in front of you is another door which is a few centimetres ajar. High-pitched voices behind the door sound as if someone has heard you. A head pops round the door and your hopes fade. The eagle eyes of a tall BIRD-MAN glare at you! He caws to others and two more Birdmen appear at the door. Slowly they step towards you. You must think quickly. Will you turn and rush back out into the passageway to escape them (turn to **74**)? Will you try to lighten the atmosphere by making some quip about how their mothers must be proud of them (turn to **567**)? Or will you offer them something from your backpack (turn to **279**)?

512

The creature slams into you and knocks you sideways towards the middle of the room. You wince as you feel your ankle. It is seriously strained. Nevertheless, you must try to hobble across towards the doors. Deduct 4 STAMINA points. The statue is now ready to charge again, as you pick yourself up. *Test your Luck* again. If you are Lucky, turn to **25**. If you are Unlucky, turn to **296**.

513

Just in time you nip behind cover as the Birdman swoops down on you with talons flashing. It misses you by inches and shrieks loudly as it rises into the air and wheels round to attack again. You do not stand much of a chance hiding in the bush, and the thought occurs to you that other Birdmen may be in the area. Your best plan would be to attack this creature quickly and hope that none of its companions will see the disturbance. If you wish to fight with your weapon, turn to **450**. Otherwise you may cast a spell:

FIX	ZEN	HOT	SAP	YAP
701	778	598	716	661

514

Try as you might, you cannot work out how the machine works, nor what it is supposed to do. Eventually, you decide to leave it alone and continue with your mission. There does not seem to be a way through this room, so you had better return to the main hallway. Turn to 81.

515

As you step forwards, the creature lumbers towards you. It is not impressed with your manners and swipes at you with a large, blubbery arm. Will you draw your sword and attack it (turn to 475) or will you cast a spell?

KIN	DIM	DOZ	RAP	NIF
744	609	715	780	665

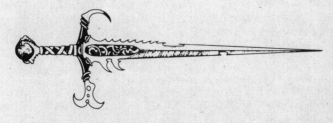

516

The creature shifts its weight around slowly as if it can sense that your intentions are hostile. Will you draw your weapon (turn to 442) or cast a spell?

DUD	PEP	ROK	SUN	SAP
633	606	675	740	762

517

The door is not locked, but you have some difficulty in turning the handle. It seems to turn easily, but the door will not open as it should. You try it several times before you discover its secret. A catch under the handle must be pressed at the same time as it is turned. Finally, the door opens, and your eyes widen as you see the scene of chaos inside . . .

A loud hubbub greets your ears as the door opens; inside the room are at least a dozen grotesque creatures. They are small, ugly creatures whose dark skins are pitted with warts. They resemble a group of Goblins, but they are cursed with horrendous mutations. One has two stumpy legs which hardly lift it off the ground. Another has a large, bulbous head, puffy like a sack of potatoes. Another sits in a corner making twittering noises like a bird, and flaps its arms. And yet another has no limbs, but its body is long and coiled like a serpent. The scene is frightening. A door is set in the wall across the room and this is the only way through. Will you draw your weapon and march across the room (turn to **56**), race for the far door as quickly as you can (turn to **571**), or cast a spell?

TEL	NIP	FOG	KID	SUN
728	622	677	698	799

518

Your feet once more touch the ground and you look around. The surroundings are not what you expect, but are nevertheless strangely familiar. The sky is darkening. Night is coming. You are in a dirty street outside a rowdy tavern. You spend a few moments getting your bearings, then enter the tavern. Turn to reference **110** of Book 2 of the *Sorcery!* series.

519

You follow the wall along to the corner of the courtyard. A small wooden door is set in the wall and you open it carefully. Suddenly, the door swings wide open! A short, stocky creature stands in the doorway and demands to know your business. 'Well?' he asks. 'What do you want in here? Come to torment the Mucalytics, I expect? Come on, then, where's your courage? I won't bite. Through there on the left. Hurry up.' You tell him you had no intention of 'tormenting the Mucalytics'. He raises an eyebrow. 'No? Then what in Throff's name do you want here? You can't be wanting to meet the Spiny Ones. What *do* you want?' Inside is a small room with two doorways. Will you tell him you want to pass through the door on the left (turn to **18**), or will you demand that he stand aside to let you pass through the door on the right (turn to **221**)?

520

You sit down beside him and start your meal. You may add 2 STAMINA points if this is your first meal of the day or 1 STAMINA point if you have already eaten. The two of you chat away, but the man in the pillory is curiously evasive each time you ask about the Fortress. You do manage to find out that something 'grand' is being planned by the Archmage and that some of his plans are being thwarted by a group called the 'Samaritans of Schinn'. But that is about all you can learn from him. When you are ready, turn to **485**.

521

Your mission, and your identity, are known to your host. Although you have concealed your journey thus far, it is now common knowledge that you have penetrated the Fortress's defences. Return to **561**.

522

One of the creatures calls out to you: 'Step forwards, puny human,' she scoffs. 'Step forwards where we can see you, you weak-bowelled cur! And tell us who gave you permission to pass through the domain of the SHE-SATYRS.' Will you do as she asks (turn to **244**), will you draw your weapon and hurl some equally offensive insults back at them (turn to **188**), or will you remain where you are and cast a spell?

PEP	DIM	GAK	JIG	SUS
746	772	685	760	620

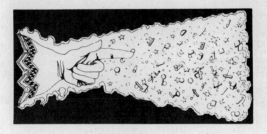

523

You must watch your step on the floor but otherwise the room appears to be quite safe. The oily smell becomes stronger in one corner of the room and your foot touches something soft and blubbery. The shape you have kicked twitches and begins to stir! Will you wait to see what you have disturbed (turn to **464**), or leave the room as quickly as you can (turn to **96**)?

524

You wait apprehensively for the mutation to take effect. You begin to grow. Your wrists become pudgy and your chest swells. You are gaining vast expanses of fat around your body! When the mutation is complete, you have more than doubled your previous weight. You will no longer be able to move quickly or nimbly: you must subtract 2 SKILL and 3 STAMINA points, and your *Initial* SKILL must be reduced permanently by 2 points. Eventually, you waddle out of the kitchen by a back door leading into the keep. Turn to 448.

525

Sh'houri looks at the parchment. 'Yes,' she nods, 'I can read this message. It is written in the hand of Sh'howna, an elder of our village, who disappeared some time ago.' The She-Satyr is engrossed in its contents; you have evidently made an important find. 'We must thank you, stranger, for bringing this to us,' says Sh'houri eventually. 'It describes matters which must remain known only to our kind, but suffice it to say you have found something which is of great import to us. We must reward you.' You accept her thanks and then the two of you converse about your travels. Turn to 371. After your conversation, she will reward you by *giving* you certain items which will be brought in a leather bag. For returning the parchment to her, you will not have to *exchange* items of your own for these items.

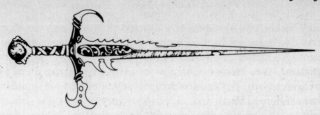

526

The old man's eyes start to flutter! Muscles twitch around his mouth and slowly life returns to the corpse. When he has recovered sufficiently to sit up, Farren Whyde looks at you. His expression is blank. He remembers nothing about the room or you, and you take some time to explain things to him.

'My friend, if all this is true,' he says finally, 'then I owe you my life. And more than that, every person in the Femphrey Alliance owes to you the prospect of future peace and prosperity. But all your efforts count for naught if you are unable to return the Crown to your own King. Perhaps here is a way I can repay you for your bravery.' He steps over to the desk and draws out a velvet bag from the lowest drawer. Inside the bag is a ball of clear crystal and the old man peers into it. 'If they are still alive,' he says, 'the Samaritans will help you. Ah, yes – there is Croo now.' You look into the ball. Clearly formed inside is the image of an angry Birdman, barking orders. 'This,' says Farren Whyde, 'is Peewit Croo, Chief Disciple of the Samaritans of Schinn. They will help you return to Analand, for they hate the power of Mampang as you do. You may summon the Samaritans with this.' He gives you a small silver whistle. Turn to **800**.

527

The Birdmen look at one another and squeak in a tone which indicates that they do not quite know what to make of the situation. You decide to take advantage of their confusion by leaving anyway. Turn to **479**.

528

They beckon you over excitedly and you quicken your pace. There are three Sightmasters in the group and you feel curiously at ease with them. At home, Sightmasters are stationed along the borders of Analand, their tremendous powers of vision making them perfect garrison troops. But caution returns as you once more wonder why they are here in Mampang. One of the Sightmasters pulls you into the group. 'We watched you come into the courtyard and we thought it best to warn you of the dangers in here,' he says. 'An outsider such as yourself could be in danger here. But we will do you no favours. We expect to be paid for our help. Our good advice will cost you 3 Gold Pieces.' Do you accept their offer (turn to **459**), or will you tell them that you have no need of their help (turn to **181**)?

529

Your struggles are to no avail. The guards tighten their grip on your wrists. When this gets painful, you give up struggling and face the captain. Turn to **508**.

530

There is no trail leading up to the great nest. You must climb up the rock-face, taking care not to let any of your belongings fall. A couple of times your foot slips and sends a cascade of small pebbles down to the path below, but eventually you reach the ledge. As it seemed earlier, the nest is like a huge eyrie, but with nooks and crannies where objects could be hidden. Do you want to investigate these possible hiding-places (turn to **477**)? Or do you feel it prudent to think not so much about possible treasures but more about what may live in this giant nest? If so, climb back down to the path and continue your journey (turn to **36**).

531

'Ten pieces of gold, eh?' The Ogre is quite interested in your offer. 'And what is it that you want to know for this reward?' Will you start by complimenting him on his fine torture-chamber and then ask him what he knows about the Throben Doors (turn to **215**), or will you ask him which torture he enjoyed the most and then see if he knows where to find the Archmage (turn to **143**)?

532

The guards are engrossed in their activities and, as you get closer, you can see they are playing a game of some sort. You wonder whether you aren't tempting fate by approaching the guards directly, but even if that were the case, a sudden change in direction would arouse suspicion anyway. So far, the guards have not noticed you. Their game consists of throwing darts at a target which is fixed to the wall. As you approach, one of the guards is preparing to leave, and the others seem to be trying to persuade him to stay. But he will not be persuaded. Noticing you, the other three guards beckon you over; they want you to join in to make up the numbers. Will you walk over to see what sort of game they are playing (turn to **461**), or will you tell them that you are too busy and walk past the game (turn to **294**)?

533

Hoping that whatever it is in the room will be unable to discern the real you, you draw your weapon out, in case it is hostile. Will your trick work? Turn to **15**.

534

You approach the cave with due caution, pausing by the entrance to check how fresh the hoof-marks are. To your relief, it seems that there are no recent prints. But whatever type of creature made the marks, two or three of them visited the cave, judging by the number of trails leading in and out. You peer into the entrance. The cave appears to be quite deep but empty, as far as you can make out. Clutching your weapon, you step inside.

Just inside the mouth of the cave, a shape makes you stop quickly! Sitting on a rock a little further back inside is a figure leaning against the wall! It is human-like and naked, but is making no movements. A long mane of hair sweeps down its back which is, thankfully, towards you – otherwise you would surely have been spotted by now. Will you call out to attract the attention of this creature (turn to **309**), will you rush in and attack before it has a chance to react (turn to **202**), or will you leave well alone and look for somewhere else to shelter (turn to **169**)?

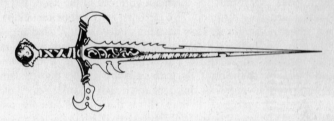

535

'There is only one way to enter the keep,' she says. 'But if you do not know about the Throben Doors, I fear you will never enter. For these gates have been protected by the magic of the Throben Necromancers' Guild. They are wizard-locked. Each has its own secret, be it key, password or whatever. But without knowledge of the secret, you will never pass through a Throben Door. And they are all protected with deadly traps.' You thank her for the information. She is anxious to hide with her new treasure and she leaves you. Turn to **8**.

536

You scoff that that was the sort of remark you would have expected from ignorant tar-poles such as themselves. Their reaction is immediate. The three of them spring to their feet to attack. You may either draw your sword and face them (turn to 510) or you may cast a spell:

NAP	MAG	HOW	NIF	POP
727	793	614	671	775

537

You step over to the old man's body. Sprinkling on the holy water, you wait anxiously to see what the effect will be on Farren Whyde. Turn to 526.

538

Slowly the door opens. As soon as it is open wide enough, you step inside. Behind the door is a short path leading up to the inner keep. It branches in two directions. To the left, it leads to a solid wooden door which looks as if it must be the main entrance to the keep. But this door is guarded by Birdmen! Two Birdmen by the door are talking to each other and laughing. They have not noticed you. A head appears at the door and beckons them inside. This could be your opportunity to nip inside if you are quick. But then anywhere you find Birdmen cannot be safe. To the right, the path leads to a smaller door. Steam is spouting from a window by this door and noises – clanking and voices – are coming from inside. Perhaps this is the tradesmen's entrance? Which way will you choose? Will you take the path to the left and risk the Birdmen (turn to 565), or will you investigate the other door in spite of the noises (turn to 492)?

539

You follow the path. It takes you downhill for a short distance, then across a rocky plateau. It disappears around a corner and you follow it through a short tunnel in the rock. When you come out of the other side of the tunnel you can see two ways onwards. The trail itself continues straight ahead. If you wish to follow it, turn to 59. To your left, another short trail leads down to a ledge. The ledge faces another similar ledge across a narrow crevasse. It is just too wide safely to jump across, but there is another way of crossing. A length of rope is hanging down above the ledge from a rock. Presumably this is for foot-travellers such as yourself to swing across. If you wish to investigate this, turn to 323.

540

Your spell takes effect slowly – too slowly. As you begin to rise in the air, the Demon completes its formation. It lunges forwards and swipes at you with a huge clawed hand. The claws slash your chest and you are knocked down to the ground! You cry out aloud as the blood seeps through your tunic. But your agony is short-lived. You look up to see the great beast's black foot descending on your face. You never hear the sickening crunch that follows . . .

541

You use the sapling once more to shove the door wide open. The roaring swells and the heat blasts your face. With stolid determination, you leap through the door. This leap is noble, but foolish. You land in the centre of the inferno, screaming wildly as your clothes, then your hair, catch fire, and your blood boils. Your death is mercifully quick.

542

The fat man's eyes light up as you open your pouch. You take out 1 Gold Piece and hand it to him. 'Thank you my friend, thank you. Now where were we?' You begin to question him about the Fortress, but he holds up his hand. 'Before we talk, perhaps a little tea?' Do you want to drink tea with him (turn to **238**) or will you tell him you are not thirsty (turn to **292**)?

543

As the creature dies, it lifts its head towards the sky and tries to emit a final distress-call. Realizing what the Birdman is doing, you swing your blade down through its neck. The beginnings of its cry gurgle and splutter, and it slumps backwards. You allow yourself a couple of minutes' rest after the battle and then set off again along the trail. Turn to **441**.

544

A thumping pain comes from your shoulder. To your horror, a protuberance starts to grow from your armpit. You wait for the pain to stop when the 'thing' has stopped growing. When it does, you have a fully formed third arm underneath your sword arm. The pain causes you 2 STAMINA points of damage, but with this extra arm, you may now use two weapons instead of one. From now on you may fight as two persons. Eventually, you leave the kitchen by a back door. Turn to 448.

545

After climbing for perhaps twenty minutes, the two She-Satyrs pause to allow you to catch up with them. With their goat-like legs, they are much more nimble than you are and they watch bemusedly as you arrive panting. One of them points forwards and you can see your goal. A wide ledge on the side of the mountain is evidently the centre of their village. Half a dozen other She-Satyrs are watching from the entrances to several caves which tunnel into the rock. In the centre of the rock-face is the largest cave, towards which your guardians are taking you.

As you approach the entrance, two She-Satyrs standing at their sentry-posts step forwards, but one of your own escorts, whom you have learned is called Sh'haarzha, waves her away. 'This is a nomad, a world-traveller who must see Sh'houri.' The guard allows you to pass and you enter a large cave which is well lit with torches. A number of smaller caves lead off from the main opening and from one of these an older-looking She-Satyr steps out. Will you tell her all she wants to know about your journey and the world outside of Xamen (turn to 371), tell her about Sh'himbli – which you may do only if you yourself know who Sh'himbli is (turn to 354), or will you wait to see what she might ask you (turn to 29)?

546

You feel around the bare stonework, looking for a clue as to where the secret doorway is. You can find nothing. You may try a password. Will you try:

Alaralatanalara?	Turn to 317
Ganthankamonta?	Turn to 343

If you don't want to try either of these, turn to 486.

547

The door is locked. You decide to leave it and try the other one. Turn to **263**.

548

The fat man snaps his fingers and barks a couple of words to the Jaguar. The creature bares its teeth when it recognizes the command. *Attack!* It leaps at you and you must fight it:

JAGUAR   SKILL 8   STAMINA 7

If you kill the creature, turn to **146**. If you decide to defend yourself from it without killing it, you may turn to **205** when you have reduced it to 2 STAMINA points.

549

'This is an insult!' screams your inquisitor. 'Not only does this fool lie to us – for if this fellow is from Kharé, then I am the Archmage himself – but the pig-brain dares to name the holy man of Slangg as a murderer!' Your guess was not a wise one. Turn to **12**.

550

You may either retrace your steps and try the door that you passed further back along the passageway (turn to **517**), or you may try a door that is just inside the creature's room in the wall adjacent to the entrance (turn to **573**). Meanwhile, the hairless creature keeps one shifty eye on you . . .

551

You follow the path back along the crevasse, but now you are on the Fortress side. A rumbling noise stops you in your tracks and you look around. There is nothing in front of you, nor anything behind. But your blood chills as you look up to your right. From somewhere on high further up the mountain, stones are breaking loose! You are directly beneath an imminent landslide! You will have to decide quickly what to do. Will you rush on ahead and try to beat the landslide (turn to 368), or will you pluck up courage and leap across the crevasse to your left, to return to the original trail (turn to 400)? You may, if you wish, cast a spell, but if you do so, you will not have time to escape should your spell fail:

NIF	HUF	ZIP	WAL	ROK
624	731	654	751	617

552

He stands up and shouts a single word: 'Guards!' As soon as he calls, a hidden doorway opens in the wall behind you. Three guards rush into the room and, before you can react, they hold you tight. They bundle you off through the door and up a narrow staircase to the top of the tower. Unlocking a heavy door at the top of the stairs, they fling you inside. Turn to 4.

553

You grab hold of your weapon and brace yourself. You throw yourself against the door and burst into the room. Two shaggy-haired, dirty GUARDS are seated at a table inside the room and your unexpected entrance has caught them by surprise. They stumble to their feet and clutch at swords. As the element of surprise is on your side, you have an advantage in this battle. If you and your chosen opponent roll equal Attack Strengths, you may treat this result as though you had rolled a higher Attack Strength. Now you must either turn to **453** to fight the guards, or cast a spell:

RAP	RES	YAZ	RAZ	GUM
738	641	688	765	756

554

You inch your way slowly across the room. For your next few steps, choose either **249**, **227** or **100**.

555

You sit down by the pillory and help him with his meal. Casually you ask him how he came to be pilloried like this. 'It wasn't my fault,' he sighs. 'It was my loose tongue. With a couple of jars of ale inside me, sometimes I just lose control. This isn't the first time a wagging tongue has brought me to grief.' You consider for a moment whether or not you may be able to learn anything of value from the man. 'And what of yourself?' he asks. 'You are certainly not from Mampang, as I am. What brings you to the Fortress? Are you another of the Archmage's warmongers?' His voice stops abruptly, as if he has suddenly realized he has said too much. He will not be persuaded to talk further. Will you try to coax him by offering to release his bonds (turn to **362**), or will you threaten him unless he tells you more about the Archmage's 'warmongers' (turn to **444**)?

556

You drop to the ground as quietly as possible and turn to step inside the door. *Aaaaahh!* You jump with fright as you find yourself face to face with a guard in heavy armour! The guard is as surprised as you are and he bellows loudly. From outside and within, four guards come to surround you and you must now face all of them. If you attack them, turn to **40**. If you would rather try a spell, choose one:

WOK	DUM	FOG	TEL	DIM
636	718	766	599	656

557

'But how can you refuse me?' chuckles the Ogre. 'What other choice do you have? Still, if that is the way you want it, so be it.' He cracks his whip in the air and steps forwards. You must either draw your weapon (turn to **270**) or cast a spell:

POP	ZIP	SUN	TEL	NIF
676	619	770	592	709

558

As your blow fells the creature, you step back out of the cave to catch a breath of fresh air. You rest for a few minutes and then return to your cave to finish your meal. Eventually, the onset of darkness makes you decide that you had better prepare your bed before you are unable to see at all. Turn to **384**.

559

Soon afterwards, the whimpering ceases and the creature slumps down into the corner, motionless. Will you risk searching the room (turn to **51**), or would you prefer to leave straight away (turn to **96**)?

560

A tinkling bell sounds just inside. Moments later, a strange face appears from behind the door. It is smooth-skinned and hairless, with broad shoulders and a mean-looking mouth. It snaps at you, wanting to know why you pulled the bell. Will you apologize for disturbing the creature (turn to **466**), or match its aggressive greeting by snarling back at it (turn to **506**)?

561

When you have calmed down from your close call with death, you sit up and look around. Straw lines the floor, but charts and maps are pinned to the walls. Some of these are charts of the heavens and a strange contraption is pointing from the window at the sky. Sitting behind the table across the room is a scrawny-looking fellow with spiky black hair. He looks up at you over half-moon glasses and smiles a sinister smile. Could this be the Archmage himself?

'And who is it that has been caught in our trap?' he asks. 'As if I did not know. *The Analander!* I wondered whether you would make it this far. My congratulations on your skill and courage, my friend. But here is where your luck comes to an end. For now you face no cowardly Black Elf, no brainless Klattaman.' You state defiantly that your journey will not end until the Crown of Kings has been returned to its rightful guardians in Analand. 'Ah yes,' he says. 'The Crown of Kings. What say I give it to you now and you be gone. I for one am anxious to remove the cursed thing from here.' This is a strange offer. Will you accept and ask him for the Crown (turn to **138**)? Would you prefer to draw your weapon and fight him (turn to **162**)? Or will you cast a spell?

GOB	MAG	FIX	KID	WOK
730	687	786	706	650

562

Your mutation is severe – a complete reorganization of the internal organs. It is one which no one could survive. You die in agony on the floor of Throg's larder.

563

As the guard slumps to the ground, you stand back to recover from the fight. But again the door opens, and *another* guard steps out towards you, sword in hand. You must fight this guard:

Second GUARD   SKILL 7   STAMINA 7

If you defeat this guard, you may either open the door and look around the room inside (turn to **44**), or you may decide it best to leave and head towards the double doors (turn to **176**).

564

There are a number of healing fruits within the bag. You may take up to four of these, and for each one you must leave behind 1 of your items of equipment (not food or gold). Each healing fruit will work only once, but will restore 4 STAMINA points if eaten. You may eat one at any time except in a battle. There is also a bottle with a stopper in it. If you want to exchange something for this item, turn to 503. If not, take what you want and bid farewell to the She-Satyrs. Turn to 441.

565

You creep up to the door, listening for any sounds which indicate the return of the Birdmen. You can hear voices – Birdmen voices – coming from somewhere inside, but the door seems safe enough. You open it and step through.

Inside is a wide hallway which stretches into the keep. Doors, some of them open, line both walls. There is also a weapon-stand by the side of the door where swords have been left. If you do not have a sword, you may take one from here. Your ears prick up at the sound of voices coming from further down the hallway. Someone is coming! You decide to hide quickly behind one of the doors leading from the hallway. Will you choose the nearest door on the left (turn to 161) or the nearest on the right (turn to 511)?

566

You continue along the passageway, through the door, and out into the archway. Will you turn left and approach the two double doors ahead (turn to 472), or will you instead try the door across the way (turn to 493)?

567

Your quip only serves to anger them further. 'Bah!' says one of them. 'Do not mention our mothers in our presence. We were taught how to hunt and defend ourselves by our fathers.' They advance. Do you want to continue a conversation with them (turn to 471)? If not, you may either draw your weapon and fight them (turn to 462) or cast a spell:

YAZ	MUD	DUM	GOD	NAP
758	605	790	707	647

568

They beckon you over excitedly and you quicken your pace. There are three Sightmasters in the group and you feel curiously at ease with them. At home, Sightmasters are stationed along the borders of Analand, their tremendous powers of vision making them perfect garrison troops. But caution returns as you once more wonder why they are here in Mampang. One of the Sightmasters pulls you into the group. 'We recognized you as you came through the Throben Door!' he says. 'Don't you know that you are expected here, Analander? Since the return of the first Serpent, the Archmage has been awaiting you. We can help disguise you. Here, put on this tunic.' He offers you a heavy-looking coat which is held together by thick ties. Will you accept his offer and put on the tunic (turn to 104), does your caution forbid you to accept this help (turn to 131), or will you attack them quickly (turn to 90)?

569

The Ogre's thoughts reach you. Mainly he is thinking of what he would like to do with you, and these ideas are not exactly pleasant. But you are also able to get an inkling of the Ogre's character. He is peculiarly houseproud, and this is reflected in the fact that his torture-chamber is quite tidy. Perhaps a little flattery will get you somewhere. You pay your respects. Turn to 215.

570

The Red-Eyes turn towards one another. 'As I suspected!' says the one who asked the question. 'You are not from Kharé at all! This impostor is asking for a seeing to. Well, let's cut some blood!' Your guess at the answer has been exposed. Turn to 12.

571
You rush for the door across the room. Your pace seems to communicate your fears to the Goblins and they move into action. One of them rises to its feet and steps towards you. This one has two arms of different sizes; its right arm is huge and muscular. This imbalance is mirrored by its legs; its left leg is twice the girth of its right. It stands directly in your path and bares its teeth. Turn to **332**.

572
You drop to the ground quietly and look towards the guards. They are still wrapped up in their investigation of the pass. The way ahead is clear and you step through the doorway into the Fortress. Turn to **129**.

573
The door opens into a short corridor. A window in the right-hand wall lights the passage and through it you can see the base of a tall tower across a courtyard. There is a door in the left-hand wall which you may try by turning to **517**. Otherwise you must head on to the end of the corridor and try another door (turn to **194**).

574

You find a soft area of ground well inside the cave, which would make a suitable place for you to lie down and get some sleep. Using your pack as a pillow, you make yourself comfortable. The day's events pass through your mind and you begin to feel quite exhausted. At any stage of fighting against the Archmage's messengers, the battle could have gone against you and your journey would have achieved nothing. How lucky you have been so far! These thoughts reassure you and you are soon drifting off to sleep.

But you are not destined to have an uninterrupted night's sleep. For, unknown to you, your choice of bedroom is a popular one, and a great SKUNKBEAR has already claimed this cave as his home. Waking in the night and catching a strange smell in the air, the beast has come to investigate and found an intruder in his lair! A split second before your death, your eyes flick open in time to see the creature's savage jaws fastening themselves around your neck . . .

575

Jann shakes his head but wishes you luck as you step up to the window. Placing your faith in the spell you have cast, you climb on to the ledge. Looking down, the height is frightening. But you pluck up all your courage – then leap outside!

Ordinarily, this would have been an excellent plan, and you would have floated down safely to the ground. But, unknown to you, your spell did not work. Minimites are protected from magic with a defensive aura which prevents all but the most powerful magic spells from working in their presence. Your courageous leap is to no avail. Your own screams are carried by the wind as you plummet down and down to your death.

576

While you nurse your last wound, the Mucalytic leans towards you. Its snout rises in front of its face and it blows a puff of breath at you. The smell is foul! You cough and hack as you take what will be your last breath. For the breath of a Mucalytic is a deadly poison to all but the Mucalytics themselves. The creature's expression is something like a smile as you drop to the ground.

577

The two guards lie dead at your feet, but you are desolate. They managed to sound the alarm! You look towards the Fortress and your heart sinks. From the uppermost battlements, large creatures are winging their way towards you! Birdmen! And you will not stand a chance against such numbers. You decide it best to hide, and run back out of the pass. But you cannot get far. As you turn, the ground in front of you rumbles, and a heavy portcullis rises out of the earth to seal off your exit! You turn to run the other way – into the plateau – and the same rumbling sound warns you back. The earth is parting and, as you leap over the crack, another portcullis rises. You shriek with pain as the portcullis catches your leg, impaling it on a metal spike.

Your future is hopeless. You are badly injured and the Birdmen will be on you within seconds. You have failed in your mission.

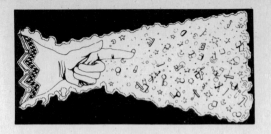

578

The three look at one another. 'From Analand, eh?' asks one, and they make little chirping noises quietly to one another. 'If you are from Analand, then you will no doubt have heard of the Crown of Kings. Have you any interest in this treasure?' Will you tell them that you have no interest in this 'Crown of Kings' and ask them instead for any news they might know of the Archmage and his henchmen (turn to **68**), or will you admit your interest and ask why they want to know (turn to **82**)?

579

The prison tower vanishes as you are whisked weightlessly through space. When the spell wears off, the rush of events in the world below slows down and your feet touch the ground once more. You curse silently as water seeps into your boots. For you have come back to earth in a muddy swamp, and your feet are under water! A crashing sound alerts you. Something is coming! Turn to reference **136** of Book 3 of the *Sorcery!* series.

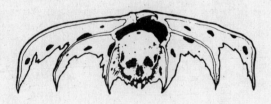

580

The door opens and you step into a large open chamber with dark alcoves around the walls. Torches, set into the wall, light the room with a flickering glow. The floor is marbled, as are the walls. Across the room you can see two large double doors.

Although there is no one about, there is some*thing* in the centre of the room. Standing on a pedestal, a few feet above the floor, is a large marble sculpture. It faces towards you, but in the dim light you can only just make out its shape. It is about the size of a large shaggy dog, or perhaps a sheep. But apart from this sculpture, the room is empty. Will you walk across the room towards the double doors, treading carefully (turn to **504**), or will you cast a spell?

SUN	FAL	SAP	MUD	ROK
705	595	659	719	771

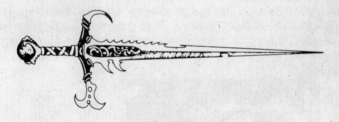

581

The Goblins rise up from where the teeth had been and wait for your instructions. You command them to capture the man behind the desk. While your Goblins have been forming, he has been watching intently. As they advance, he casts a spell of his own and, before the Goblins can take another step, his spell has created the same number of armoured HOBGOBLINS to intercept them! A furious battle rages as the two groups of magical troops attack each other. But your Goblins are no match for the Hobgoblins. Although they fight valiantly, they are defeated. The spiky-haired man smiles and looks up at you. Turn to **552**.

582

Deduct 4 STAMINA points. You cast your spell and conjure up a huge fireball which you hurl forcefully towards the creature, aiming straight for its chest. The Demon bellows loudly as the fireball finds its target, and its body catches fire. Luckily for you, the Demon has not been able to form itself fully for, if it had, even this powerful weapon would have been ineffective against it. But you now back off and watch it flailing about madly with burning arms, trying to swat out the fire which is consuming it. Eventually, it slows down. Turn to **351**.

583

The scraping noise stops and then swishes this way and that. Suddenly you hear a *ping* and something flashes through the air. You cannot make out what has happened as it is too dark for you to see. But one thing is for certain; you are in danger in this room. You decide to head for the door, covered by the illusion of your five doubles. You reach the door safely although another two similar sounds warn you that some*thing* is shooting at you. You close the door behind you, walk back through the entrance-room and try the other door. Turn to **18**.

584

Deduct 1 STAMINA point. Do you have a Ring of Green Metal with you? If not, the spell will not work – turn to **769**. If you have a Ring of Green Metal, you may place it on your finger and cast your spell. The spell works like a dream. To the amazement of your would-be aggressors, you disappear, and reappear in front of the fleeing Red-Eye! He knocks into you and the two of you fall to the ground. By this time, the others realize what has happened and rush over to help their comrade. Turn to **12**.

585

You wait for your spell to take effect. But nothing happens! You are sure you recited it correctly, but for some reason it has not worked. Return to **98** to choose your next action.

586

You must now choose your next course of action. Will you step towards the pole and investigate the weapons (turn to **383**)? Will you advance to the double doors (turn to **397**)? Or will you walk over to the corner of the wall to investigate the door there (turn to **519**)?

587

Deduct 1 STAMINA point. Do you have any Medicinal Potions or Blimberry Juice with you? If not, the spell will not work. If you have either of these, you may cast the spell to replenish your STAMINA. Restore your STAMINA score to its *Initial* level and turn to **245**.

588

Deduct 1 STAMINA point. Do you have a Cloth Skullcap with you? If not, your spell will not work and one of the Sightmasters steps in to score a quick hit: deduct 2 STAMINA points and turn to **110**. If you do have a Skullcap, turn to **787**.

589

You cast your spell and hold the mirror up to the cave entrance. Suddenly the howling sound starts again, followed closely by another. A vicious battle is about to take place! But then some*thing* comes scurrying past you out of the cave. It is a small ball of fur, about the size of a cabbage, running on two stumpy legs! It is hotly pursued by another identical creature. *Jib-Jibs!* The two of them disappear into the undergrowth. You climb inside the cave, which is quite shallow. Do you want to eat a meal (turn to **99**), will you get down on all fours and explore the back of the cave (turn to **14**), or will you just settle down and sleep for the night (turn to **384**)?

590

Deduct 1 STAMINA point. Do you have any small pebbles with you? If not, you cannot use this spell and the Red-Eyes attack – deduct 2 STAMINA points and turn to **225**. If you are able to cast your spell on some pebbles, you may do so on as many as you wish. Decide how many you will use and turn to **769**.

591

Deduct 1 STAMINA point. Do you have a Brass Pendulum with you? If not, this spell will not work. But even if you have a Brass Pendulum, there is nothing alive in the room which you may send to sleep! You have wasted your STAMINA. Return to **351** and make another choice.

592

Deduct 1 STAMINA point. Do you have a Cloth Skullcap with you? If not, your spell will fail and the Ogre attacks – lose 2 STAMINA points and turn to **270**. If you have a Skullcap, you may place it on your head and use your spell to probe the creature's mind. Turn to **569**.

593

Deduct 1 STAMINA point. Do you have a Ring of Green Metal with you? If not, the spell will not work and you will take 2 STAMINA points of damage as the guards attack – turn to **145**. If you have a Green Ring, you may slip it on your finger and use your spell to transport you. You disappear from the room, much to the bewilderment of the captain and his guards, and reappear just outside the door. Totally confused, the guards search the room, allowing you to leave. Turn to **463**.

594

Deduct 2 STAMINA points. You cast your spell and five identical images of yourself appear around you. Roll one die. If the result is a six, turn to **533**. Otherwise turn to **583**.

595

Deduct 2 STAMINA points. You are now protected against the chance of falling from a height. If there are any pits in this room, you will not be harmed. Turn to **504**.

596

Deduct 4 STAMINA points. You recite your spell and point your finger at the lock. A blast of lightning hits the lock dead centre – but fails to mark it! Return to **397** and make another choice.

597

You throw the sand on to the floor in front of the creature and cast your spell. A small pool of quicksand forms in front of it! You watch hopefully as the Hydra slithers towards you and into the pool. But it is no use. The Hydra is much too big to be caught in the quicksand; it is a tiny pool underneath its great bulk. Turn to **65**.

598

Deduct 4 STAMINA points. You cast your spell and create a burning fireball in your hand. You fling it towards the Birdman and, as it nears its target, it bursts into dozens of fiery balls! The creature cannot avoid them and the dry feathers of its wings burst into flames. It comes crashing to the ground a few metres from you. Turn to **543**.

599

Deduct 1 STAMINA point. Do you have a Cloth Skullcap with you? If not, your spell will not work and the guards inflict 2 STAMINA points of damage as they attack – turn to **40**. If you have a Cloth Skullcap, you place it on your head and cast your spell. You begin to be able to read the mind of whichever guard you focus your attention on. But their thoughts are simple. Each wants to be the first to run you through with his sword! By reading their minds, you are able to avoid their blows, but you soon decide that your spell is not helping you get inside the Fortress. You draw your weapon instead. Turn to **40**.

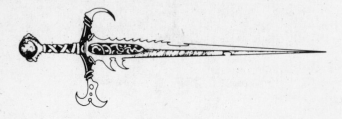

600

You place the Skullcap on your head and focus your attention on one of the creatures. It is thinking about using its deadly heat vision to attack, but there is also a feeling of fear which is preventing it from opening its eyes. Finally it has decided that it *will* use its powers and at that moment, you make your move. You fling yourself away from the creature just as it opens its eyes. The red jets of heat scorch the earth where you stood and follow you round. As you had hoped, the creature is concentrating on following you. You roll behind the other two and your plan has worked. The two other Red-Eyes squeal in agony as their comrade's heat vision sears their throats! They drop to the ground, dead. Seeing what it has done to the other two, the Red-Eye closes its eyes and begins to shudder in horror. Now you are able to close in to finish him off. When all three lie dead on the ground, you must choose your way onwards. Turn to **425**.

601

Deduct 2 STAMINA points. Whatever your reason for casting this spell, you are shocked to discover that it has no effect! Perhaps you have recited it incorrectly, or perhaps something is preventing it from working. Return to **427** and make another choice.

602

Deduct 1 STAMINA point. Do you have any Medicinal Potions with you? If not, your spell will not work and the Hobgoblin's cleaver cuts through your sleeve – deduct 2 STAMINA points and turn to **281**. If you have Medicinal Potions, you may cast your spell as you begin to drink them. The Hobgoblin, however, is not going to just watch you drink in front of her. She grabs the bottle from you and finishes it off! You may add 2 STAMINA points for the effect on you, but now you must turn to **281**. The Hobgoblin's STAMINA has been increased by 4 points for the magical healing potion she has been drinking.

603

Deduct 1 STAMINA point. Whether or not you have the Jewel of Gold you need to cast this spell, it will do you no good: the spell will not work against a creature such as this. Turn to **65**.

604

Deduct 2 STAMINA points. You cast your spell to protect you from the effects of a fall. Do you now wish to try jumping out of the window (turn to **575**) or will you consider another option (return to **98** and make another choice)?

605

Deduct 1 STAMINA point. Do you have any sand with you? If not, you cannot use this spell and the Birdmen attack – deduct 2 STAMINA points and turn to **462**. If you have some sand, you may throw it on the floor and cast your spell, to create a pool of quicksand in front of the Birdmen. One of the creatures steps forwards into the pool and begins to sink! He squawks loudly to his companions and, alas, it is a simple matter for them to haul him out of the trap by flapping their wings and rising into the air. Your plan has been foiled! But worse than that, the Birdmen are now extremely angry. They cross the room and grab you with powerful talons which dig into your flesh. But your pain is short-lived. Their plan is to drop you into your own pool of quicksand! And with the three of them holding you tightly, there is nothing you can do to prevent them . . .

606

Deduct 1 STAMINA point. Do you have a Potion of Fire Water with you? If not, you cannot use this spell and you must return to **516** to choose again. If you have any Fire Water you may use it to increase your strength dramatically. Turn to **442** to fight the creature. But you will find your extra strength offers no advantage against the creature's massive blubbery body.

607

Deduct 1 STAMINA point. Are you carrying an Orb of Crystal? If not, your spell will not work – return to **123** and make another choice. If you have such an Orb, turn to **796**.

608

The Demon bellows loudly as the Holy Water burns its skin. Steam rises from the splashes you have made. You watch hopefully as the creature writhes in agony. Will your plan work? Have you used an effective spell? Turn to **172**.

609

Deduct 2 STAMINA points. You cast your spell at the creature. At first, you can notice no difference in its actions, but eventually you realize that it is not coordinating its movements properly. The great hulk is acting as though it is thoroughly confused! It shuffles towards the corner, throwing its long snout into the air as if it is trying to flail the ceiling. You decide to use the opportunity to try to sneak past. But suddenly, it springs to life and an arm crashes into your chest! Lose 1 STAMINA point and turn to **386**.

610

You raise your Flute to your lips and begin to play. But before a note can come out, the captain knocks it from your hands and the guards attack. Turn to **145** to resolve the battle. During the fracas, one of the guards steps on the Flute, and it cracks and breaks under his heavy feet. You have lost this artefact.

611

Deduct 1 STAMINA point. Do you have a Gold-Backed Mirror with you? If not, your spell does not work and the Skunkbear clouts you with its claws – deduct 2 STAMINA points and turn to **490**. If you do have a Gold-Backed Mirror, turn to **663**.

612

Deduct 1 STAMINA point. Do you have a Potion of Fire Water with you? If not, nothing happens; return to **323** and choose another course of action. If you have any Fire Water, turn to **678**.

613

Deduct 2 STAMINA points. You cast your spell and wait for the darkness to descend over the courtyard. But your wait is in vain. This spell will not work in open spaces. Meanwhile, the first guard is upon you and catches you with a blow. Deduct another 2 STAMINA points and turn to **449**.

614

Deduct 2 STAMINA points. You cast your spell and wait for an indication of how you may escape from this situation. As you find from your spell, there is no easy escape. You will have to fight, and run at the first opportunity! Turn to **510**.

615

You pull the Orb from your pack and cast your spell into it. A milky-white cloud seems to swell up inside the Orb and, when it clears, you can see a wide open courtyard. Figures around the edge of your view are going about their business, but in the centre is a tall metal pole, with weapons around its base. A guard approaches the pole, holding his sword towards it. When he is a few feet from it, his sword starts to move in the air. The guard struggles; he is evidently putting a lot of effort into holding the sword. With one great tug, he pulls his sword away from the pole and falls to the floor, laughing. His companions, also laughing, gather round him. What can this mean? One thing is certain: it can be of little help to you outside this door. Will you turn round and try either the door on the left (turn to 493) or the door on the right (turn to 206), or will you try something else from your backpack to see if it can get you through the doors (turn to 31)?

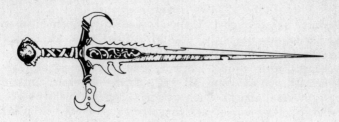

616

Deduct 1 STAMINA point. Whether or not you have the Cloth Skullcap it requires, this spell will do you no good, as there is no one about to focus its effect on. You decide instead to step up to investigate the weapons. Turn to 383.

617

Deduct 1 STAMINA point. Whether or not you have any stone dust with you, there is nothing you can do with this spell to halt the mounting landslide. Deduct a further 2 STAMINA points of damage as the rocks fall around you. You decide to risk all by running ahead along the trail. Turn to 368.

618

Deduct 1 STAMINA point. Do you have a Galehorn with you? If not, you cannot use this spell. But even if you have a Galehorn, the tremendous blast that it is capable of producing will not be strong enough to budge the doors! You may now either step up to the doors and copy the creature's actions (turn to 483), or head for the door in the corner of the courtyard (turn to 519).

619

Deduct 1 STAMINA point. Do you have a Ring of Green Metal with you? If not, you may not use this spell and the Ogre attacks – deduct 2 STAMINA points and turn to 270. If you have a Ring of Green Metal, you may place it on your finger and use the spell to transport yourself. Where will you wind up? This spell is not terribly reliable and in this case, the result is not as you would have hoped. You disappear and wind up only a couple of yards from where you were before; but in the direction of the Ogre! Your magic has angered him, and he approaches. Turn to 270.

620

Deduct 2 STAMINA points. You cast your spell while the creatures watch, bemused. You wait for an indication of the trap you suspect, but you receive no such warning. Now they are becoming impatient, and one is poised ready with her spear. Will you step forwards with your hands raised (turn to 244), or will you try a little bluff and courage (turn to 188)?

621

Deduct 1 STAMINA point. Do you have a Brass Pendulum with you? If not, your spell will not work and the fat man is becoming impatient with your dawdling: return to **160** and choose again. If you have a Brass Pendulum, you may draw it out and begin to cast your spell. The man watches it intently. It seems that he has mistaken it for gold! Turn to **759**.

622

Deduct 1 STAMINA point. Do you have any Yellow Powder with you? If not, turn to **571**. If you have any Yellow Powder, you may sniff some and cast your spell over yourself. As it takes effect, you can feel the power surging through your body; you feel as if your legs could carry you faster than the wind! You race across the room heading for the far door. But the Goblins are scattered about the room. There is no clear way through. You trip over a strange-looking creature with huge arms. Turn to **332**.

623

Deduct 4 STAMINA points. You create a huge fireball between your hands and wait for your moment. As the Hydra slithers forwards, you fling the ball into the centre of its body, scoring a direct hit! The creature roars and hisses, its body twisting in agony. As it does so, its tail whips round towards you. Turn to **305**.

624

Deduct 1 STAMINA point. You cast your spell and a terrible stink begins to surround you. Do you have a pair of nose plugs? If not, the smell makes you feel ill and you must run away from it. Deduct 2 STAMINA points and turn to **400**. If you have nose plugs, you may use them to avoid the smell. But this was still not a particularly wise choice. You will have to run ahead quickly to avoid the rock-fall. Turn to **368**.

625

You place the Wig on your head and cast your spell. Again, the howling comes from inside the cave, but this time its tones form sounds which take on their own meanings. Something inside is protecting its home! You talk to it and discover that it is a JIB-JIB. These creatures are small and harmless, but their defence is a powerful voice which makes them sound ferocious. You tell the little beast that you intend to enter his cave to spend the night. A scurrying is followed by a rush as a small ball of fur, the size of a cabbage, races out of the cave into the undergrowth. You climb inside the cave, which is quite shallow. Do you want to eat a meal (turn to **99**), will you get down on all fours and explore the back of the cave (turn to **14**), or will you just settle down and sleep for the night (turn to **384**)?

626

Deduct 1 STAMINA point. Do you have a Giant's Tooth with you? If not, your spell will not work – return to **79** and make another choice. If you have a Giant's Tooth, you may cast your spell on it to create a burly Giant. But the room has not been made to accommodate a Giant! As the creature appears, it cracks its skull against the low ceiling and drops unconscious to the floor. A short time later it disappears. Turn to **245**.

627

Deduct 1 STAMINA point. Do you have any Yellow Powder with you? If not, the spell will not work and the leading Sightmaster lands the first blow – deduct 2 STAMINA points and turn to **110**. If you have any Yellow Powder, you may sniff a little before you cast your spell. The effect is to enable you to move at an incredible speed! You may use this either to escape from the Sightmasters (turn to **135**), or to fight. If you choose the latter, turn to **110**, but you may add 3 points to your Attack Strength for the duration of the battle.

628

Deduct 1 STAMINA point. Do you have any Holy Water with you? If not, this spell will not work: draw your weapon and turn to **172**. If you have any Holy Water, you may throw this on to the creature and cast your spell – turn to **608**.

629

You hold up the Mirror and begin to cast your spell. The Hobgoblin is not completely stupid; she realizes something is afoot. And her suspicions are doubly aroused when her own reflection in the mirror starts to move out of time with her own movements. Instinctively, she hurls the cleaver at the Mirror and it shatters, destroying the image forming inside. The shattering glass flies around the room. You try to shield yourself, but it is too late. Fragments have already showered your face and pierced your eyes! You drop to the ground in agony. Here, in Throg's larder, you have come to the end of your journey. For without your sight, your mission is hopeless.

630

Deduct 1 STAMINA point. Do you have any beeswax with you? If not, this spell will not work. If you have some beeswax, you may rub it on to your weapon to enhance its powers. During the next battle in which you use this weapon, it will do double damage – that is, 4 STAMINA points instead of 3. Now return to **221** and choose your next course of action.

631

As quickly as it started, the spell wears off and you are returned to earth in new surroundings. The prison tower has disappeared and, as your feet touch the ground, you must fight to keep your balance. For you are on a spiral stairway. Behind and beneath you is a large set of double doors. Ahead of you, at the top of the stairs, is another heavy door. You climb the stairs and try the handle. It turns! Turn to **321**.

632

Deduct 2 STAMINA points. You cast your spell on the lock and wait to hear the familiar click of the tumblers turning to open the doors. But you hear nothing. Has your spell worked or not? If you wish to try turning the handle, turn to 344. Otherwise return to 397 and make another choice.

633

Deduct 2 STAMINA points. Choose something from your pack (not gold or Provisions) and cast your spell on it. Instantly, it changes from its real self into an illusory pile of glinting treasure. You offer it to the creature. It seems to be not at all interested, but you cannot be sure it can even *see* your offering. A soft noise comes from its head. Perhaps it *has* seen your treasure after all. Do you want to give up with your gift (return to 516 and choose again), or will you listen to what it has to say (turn to 405)?

634

The guards grab your hands again, but the captain orders them to release you. Your spell is working! 'We must treat such a worthy opponent with more respect,' he announces. 'You may leave us, guards.' The two creatures release your hands and shrug their shoulders. As they leave the room, the captain begins to talk to you freely. 'My apologies for your rough treatment,' he starts. You stop him and tell him you have no time for pleasantries; you must make your way into the inner keep. The captain nods and agrees to escort you. This is a nuisance, but he may be useful. The two of you leave the room and head towards a large door on the far side of the chamber. Turn to 301.

635

Deduct 1 STAMINA point. Do you have any Medicinal Potions with you? If not, your spell will not work – return to **123** and make another choice. If you have Medicinal Potions, you may use them on yourself and cast your spell. The healing effect will restore your STAMINA to full strength. Return to **123** to choose your next action.

636

Deduct 1 STAMINA point. Do you have a Gold Coin? If not, the guards attack for 2 STAMINA points of damage and you must face them – turn to **40**. If you have a Gold Coin, you may place it on your wrist and cast the spell. An invisible shield forms around your arm. Turn to **40** to attack the guards, but you may deduct 2 points from each of their Attack Strength rolls because of the defensive effect of your shield.

637

Deduct 1 STAMINA point. Do you have any stone dust with you? If not, this spell will not work. If you have some stone dust, you may choose your target and turn this target to stone. But what good has this done you? Whether or not you used this spell, return to **351** and make another choice.

638

Deduct 2 STAMINA points. You cast your spell and watch as it takes effect. The Skunkbear looks a little off balance, then steps forwards slowly . . . very slowly. Will you use this as an opportunity to escape from the creature (turn to **469**), or will you fight it? If you wish to fight it, turn to **490** but, under the effects of your spell, deduct 3 from its SKILL.

639

Deduct 1 STAMINA point. Do you have a Cloth Skullcap with you? If not, your spell will not work and the Red-Eyes attack – deduct 2 STAMINA points and turn to **769**. If you have a Skullcap, turn to **600**.

640

Deduct 1 STAMINA point. Do you have an Orb of Crystal with you? If not, you cannot cast this spell – you must return to **193** and choose again. If you have an Orb of Crystal, turn to **615**.

641

Deduct 1 STAMINA point. Whether or not you have any of the Holy Water necessary to complete this spell, it will do you no good, for it is entirely inappropriate here! Meanwhile, the guards attack. Deduct 3 STAMINA points and turn to **453**.

642

Deduct 1 STAMINA point. Do you have a Bamboo Flute with you? If not, the spell will not work and the guards attack – deduct 2 STAMINA points and turn to **145**. If you have a Flute, turn to **610**.

643

Deduct 2 STAMINA points. Focusing your spell on the gate, you cast it and wait for the door to open. Nothing happens. Your spell is not powerful enough to open the entrance to the Mampang Fortress. Turn to **304**.

644

Deduct 1 STAMINA point. Whether or not you have the Bracelet of Bone this spell requires, it will do you no good. You are guessing at whether your unseen companion even *has* a mind to be susceptible to your illusion at all! To play it safe, you decide to draw out your weapon. Turn to **15**.

645

Deduct 1 STAMINA point. Do you have an Orb of Crystal with you? If not, you cannot cast this spell. Return to **362** and make another choice. If you have a Crystal Orb, turn to **792**.

646

Do you have any Goblin Teeth with you? If not, the spell will not work and the first guard catches you with its sword: deduct 2 STAMINA points and turn to 394. If you have any Goblin Teeth, you may throw as many as you want on to the ground and cast your spell on them. Each will form into a fighting Goblin (SKILL 5, STAMINA 5) and you may order them to attack the guard standing before you. Turn to 394.

647

Deduct 1 STAMINA point. Do you have a Brass Pendulum with you? If not, you cannot use this spell and, in your embarrassment, you turn to run quickly from the room – turn to 74. If you have a Brass Pendulum, you may hold it up before them and start it swinging, as you cast the spell. But the creatures are not in the least concerned by the Pendulum and they leap at you to attack. Turn to 462.

648

As you cast the spell, you blow deeply on the Galehorn. A tremendous wind gushes from it towards the pole. The metal post is firmly set and the blast hardly moves it at all. But surprisingly enough, the weapons resting against the pole do not move either. What can this mean? Turn to 586.

649

Deduct 2 STAMINA points. You cast your spell and wait for its effects to help you. Sure enough, you get an inclination against tampering with the doors in front of you. When you wonder how you might best get through the doors, a mental trail leads you towards one of the doors behind you. If you will follow the spell's advice, turn to **493**. Otherwise you may either hold something up against the door (turn to **31**), or try the other door (turn to **206**).

650

Deduct 1 STAMINA point. Do you have a Gold Piece with you? If not, the spell will not work. If you have a Gold Piece, you may place it on your wrist and cast the spell. It remains fixed in place as an invisible shield. If you fight any battles within this room, you may deduct 2 points from any attacking creature's Attack Strength. Whether or not your spell has worked, draw your weapon and turn to **162**.

651

Deduct 1 STAMINA point. Do you have any small pebbles with you? If not, then you are wasting your time with this spell – return to **452** and make another choice. If you have some pebbles, choose how many you want to use and cast the spell. Turn to **270**. You may throw these pebbles at the Ogre, but for each one, you must roll a number equal to or less than your SKILL score in order to score a successful hit. Each successful hit will inflict 1 STAMINA point of damage. If you miss with two throws, the Ogre will step in to attack and you may throw no more pebbles.

652

Deduct 2 STAMINA points. You reach into your backpack and draw out one of your artefacts (your choice). Secretly casting your spell over it, you turn round to present the fat man with what appears to be a handful of treasure. His eyes light up. Put he is more interested in the gold than the other treasures you have created. You strike a bargain with him. You will give him the gold if he will give you information which will help penetrate the inner keep. He agrees. Turn to **20**.

653

Deduct 1 STAMINA point. Do you have any Medicinal Potions with you? If not, you cannot cast this spell. If you have any Potions, you may swallow them and cast the spell. Its revitalizing effect begins immediately. You may restore your STAMINA to its *Initial* level. Return to **502** to decide what to do next.

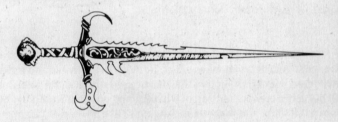

654

Deduct 1 STAMINA point. Do you have a Ring of Green Metal with you? If not, you are showered with rocks and stones and you must try to escape – lose 3 STAMINA points and turn to **368**. If you have such a ring, you may place it on your finger and cast your spell. As it takes effect, you quickly fade and reappear a short distance away. The spell has worked, but to your horror, you have been transported even *nearer* to the path of the landslide! Your only means of escape is to leap over the crevasse. Turn to **400**.

655

Deduct 1 STAMINA point. Do you have a Staff of Oak Sapling with you? If not, your spell will not work and the guard attacks: deduct 2 STAMINA points and turn to 394. If you have an Oak Staff, then you may hold it and cast your spell to stop the guard in his tracks. As he stands immobilized, you may leap forwards with your weapon to finish him off. Turn to 495.

656

Deduct 2 STAMINA points. You cast your spell on to one of the advancing guards. As it takes effect, he stops in his tracks and looks bewildered. He stares out into the distance, then back at the gate. It is as if he has no comprehension of what is going on at all! Suddenly, he drops to all fours and makes a roaring noise like Snattacat! You must now turn to 40 to face the other guards, but you need fight only three, not four (you choose which you have cast your spell on). But there is one danger which you did not foresee: this spell can make creatures act irrationally. In this case, your victim will get in a lucky hit on you with its weapon during the fight. Deduct 2 STAMINA points after four Attack Rounds.

657

Deduct 2 STAMINA points. You cast your spell and images of yourself surround you. As one, you step into battle with the creatures, hoping that they will be fooled into attacking the illusions. But, alas, they are not! Perhaps this is a feature of their powerful vision. One of them steps in and grazes your arm with a blow. Deduct 2 STAMINA points and turn to 110.

658

Deduct 1 STAMINA point. Do you have a Galehorn with you? If not, you cannot use this spell: return to 79 and choose again. If you have a Galehorn, you may use it to create a blast of wind, which you may aim at anything you like. The tremendous force will have its effect, but will do nothing to help you in this situation. Turn to 245.

659

Deduct 2 STAMINA points. You cast the spell towards the centre of the room. Any living creatures within the room will be affected by this spell and, thus demoralized, they should be easy for you to defeat. Turn to 504.

660

Deduct 4 STAMINA points. You cast your spell and create an invisible shield around yourself. Protected by this shield, you are safe to pass through the Red-Eyes without being harmed. Seeing that their weapons do no good, they both open their eyes. Blasts of heat vision sear towards you, but they cannot penetrate your defence. Seeing how easily you are able to protect yourself, the creatures decide to leave you alone. Turn to 425.

661

Deduct 1 STAMINA point. Do you have a Green-Haired Wig with you? If not, the spell will not work, and the Birdman seizes its opportunity to attack while you are undefended – deduct 3 STAMINA points and turn to 450. If you have such a Wig, you may place it on your head and cast the spell, which will allow you to converse with the Birdman. But he is not interested in conversation; you are trespassing in his territory! Draw out your weapon quickly and turn to 450 before he attacks!

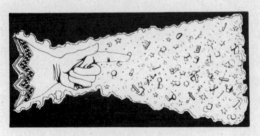

662

Deduct 4 STAMINA points. You summon up a lightning-blast and focus it on the door's lock. The lock shatters and the door yawns open. Inside, the room is unlit. You step forwards cautiously. But as you cross the threshold, you lose your balance! You have missed the two steps just inside the door leading down into the room. Turn to 112.

663

You hold up your Mirror and cast the spell. The creature roars as its double materializes in the Mirror and springs towards it. But instead of fighting, the Skunkbear turns and lifts its tail. Its double does likewise. Suddenly, the air is filled with the most nauseating smell you have ever come across – and a double dose! You turn to the corner and retch violently. Deduct 4 STAMINA points. You race from the cave as quickly as possible. Turn to 469.

664

Deduct 1 STAMINA point. Do you have a Pearl Ring with you? If not, your spell will not work and the Red-Eyes mount their attack – deduct 2 STAMINA points and turn to 769. If you have a Pearl Ring, you can place it on your finger and cast your spell. You immediately disappear from view. Confident that you cannot be seen, you try to advance around the back of the Red-Eyes with your weapon drawn. But something is not right. They are following your steps! You bring your weapon down to strike one of the creatures and it parries the blow perfectly! Then the answer dawns and you want to kick yourself for wasting your STAMINA. These creatures keep their eyes permanently closed. *They don't need to see you!* But your fight has already begun. Turn to 159.

665

Deduct 1 STAMINA point. You cast your spell and wait, as a horren-dous stink fills the room. Do you have any nose plugs with you? If so, you must put them on quickly, or you will be affected. If you don't have any nose plugs, then you *are* affected by the spell, which makes you vomit violently – deduct 3 STAMINA points. But whatever you think of the smell, the creature's reaction is worse. Unable to avoid the stench, the creature has fallen to the ground in the corner of the room and seems to be having a fit of some sort! Its convulsions finally stop and it settles back motionless. It is dead! Turn to **443**.

666

Deduct 1 STAMINA point. Do you have any Yellow Powder with you? If not, you may not cast this spell – return to **427** and make another choice. If you have some Yellow Powder, you may sniff it and cast your spell – turn to **714**.

667

Deduct 1 STAMINA point. Do you have a Pearl Ring with you? If not, you cannot use this spell – turn to **304**. But even if you have a Pearl Ring, this spell will do you no good. You may be able to make yourself invisible, but you will not be able to walk through the door! Turn to **304**.

668

Deduct 1 STAMINA point. Do you have a Bracelet of Bone with you? If not, you cannot use this spell and the Hobgoblin launches her attack: deduct 2 STAMINA points and turn to **281**. If you have a Bracelet of Bone, you may place it on your wrist and cast your spell. In her eyes, your image changes. Instead of being a stranger, your face becomes familiar to her – the familiar face of the Archmage himself! She drops her weapon and bows low before you. You bid her rise. For you were merely making an incognito tour of the Fortress, and you are satisfied that all is well in the kitchens. She thanks you and backs off, still with her head bowed, to allow you to pass out of her kitchen. Turn to **448**.

669

Deduct 1 STAMINA point. Do you have a Gold-Backed Mirror with you? If not, you cannot cast this spell and must return to **123** to choose again. If you have such a Mirror, turn to **589**.

670

Deduct 1 STAMINA point. Do you have a Cloth Skullcap with you? If not, the spell won't work and the guards attack, causing 2 STAMINA points of damage – turn to **449**. If you have a Skullcap, you may place it on your head and cast your spell. The images within the mind of the leading guard become clear, but they are not surprising: he means to capture you! Turn to **449** and battle the creatures.

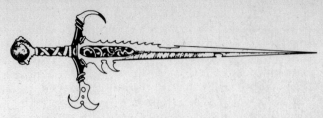

671

Deduct 1 STAMINA point. You cast your spell and, within moments, a horrible stink fills the room. The Black Elves, unsavoury creatures at the best of times, sniff the air and grip their stomachs. Do you have any nose plugs with you? If not, the smell makes you feel just as ill – deduct 3 STAMINA points and turn to **510**: when the smell wears off, the battle will commence. If you have nose plugs, you may use them and the stench will not affect you. You may leave the room by turning to **566**.

672

Deduct 1 STAMINA point. Whether or not you have the stone dust necessary for this spell, it will do you no good as you have no opponent to cast the spell on! Not one you can see, at any rate. You decide instead to draw your weapon. Turn to **15**.

673

Deduct 1 STAMINA point. Do you have any Yellow Powder with you? If not, you cannot cast this spell; return to **98** and choose again. If you have some Yellow Powder, you may sniff some and then cast your spell – turn to **585**.

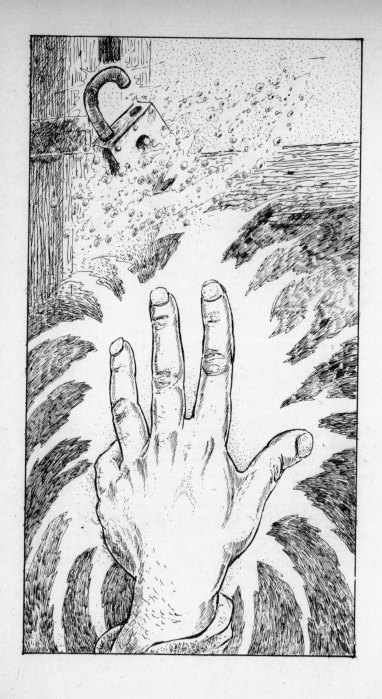

674

Deduct 4 STAMINA points. You cast your spell, pointing your finger at the lock. A bolt of lightning shoots from your finger and cracks the lock, which springs open. Turn to **348**.

675

Deduct 1 STAMINA point. Do you have any stone dust? If not, you may not use this spell: draw your weapon and turn to **442**. If you have some, you may throw it over the creature and cast your spell. Within moments, the lumpy, shapeless creature is beginning to solidify. A short time after that, it has turned into stone. Will you risk searching the room (turn to **51**), or will you just leave quickly (turn to **96**)?

676

Deduct 1 STAMINA point. Do you have any pebbles with you? If not, then you are wasting your time with this spell – return to **557** and make another choice. If you have some pebbles, choose how many you will use and and cast your spell. Turn to **270**. You may throw these pebbles at the Ogre, but for each one, you must roll a number equal to or less than your SKILL score in order to score a successful hit. Each successful hit will inflict 1 STAMINA point of damage. If you miss with two throws, the Ogre will step in to attack and you may throw no more pebbles.

677

Deduct 2 STAMINA points. You cast your spell into the room while the Goblins look on curiously. Darkness suddenly fills the room! The creatures cannot understand what has happened and they shriek and call, rushing around the room and bumping into one another. Meanwhile, you are able to make your way across to the door on the far side. You take a few knocks from the creatures on the way, but otherwise arrive unhurt. Turn to 426.

678

You swallow the potion and cast your spell. A surge of power runs through your body and you step up to the rope. You give it a firm tug to test its strength. But with your enhanced powers, the rope merely snaps in your hand! You have destroyed this way of crossing the chasm. Continue along the trail by turning to 59.

679

Deduct 2 STAMINA points. You cast your spell over one of your captors (your choice) and it takes effect. Turn to 145 and fight your battle. During the fight, the victim of your spell will be confused and unable to join in.

680

You gaze into your Orb. 'What is that?' demands the fat man. But for the moment you ignore him; a vision is clearing in the Orb. You can see a dark room, lit by a single white candle held in a hand; there are sharp blades set in the floor. You are watching the scene as if through the eyes of whoever is holding the candle. The way forwards is precarious, but the candle-bearer makes his way safely to a door at the other end of the room. Then the vision disappears. Again the fat man demands to know what you are doing. You stuff the Orb back into your pack. It is much too valuable a treasure to let him get his hands on! Will you offer him something from your backpack (turn to **66**), or will you draw your weapon and leap across the table at him (turn to **205**)?

681

You throw the sand in front of the statue and cast your spell. A small pool of quicksand appears on the floor. You may now make your way across the room. Turn to **504**. But your trap will only slow down your opponent, not prevent it from reaching you. When you are told to *Test your Luck*, you may ignore this and turn to **329** instead, as if you had been Lucky.

682

Deduct 2 STAMINA points. You cast your spell hopelessly in the dark. Unable to focus it on any particular target, it has no effect. Draw your weapon and turn to **15**.

683

Deduct 4 STAMINA points. You aim your finger at the creature's head and unleash your lightning-blast. Unable to complete its transformation, the Demon can do nothing to prevent this attack. The blast hits the creature on target, and its head seems to explode from inside, spraying its gory vital juices around the room. Turn to 351.

684

The Goblin's thoughts begin to reach you, but they are confused and meaningless. Little did you know it, but you have chosen to read the mindless head of a Goblin imbecile! You learn nothing. You step across the room; turn to 56.

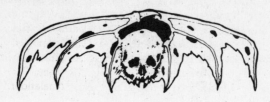

685

Deduct 1 STAMINA point. Do you have a Black Facemask with you? If not, you cannot use this spell. And while you are delaying with your futile attempts, the She-Satyrs hurl another spear at you which grazes your leg: deduct 2 STAMINA points and return to 522 to choose a non-spell option. If you have a Black Facemask, you may hold it before your face and cast the spell. The sight terrifies the creatures, who race off to hide behind a large rock. You may continue your journey. Turn to 441.

686

Deduct 1 STAMINA point. Do you have a Jewel-Studded Medallion with you? If not, your spell does not work and the Skunkbear catches you off guard with a blow: deduct 3 STAMINA points and turn to 490. If you have a Medallion, you place it round your neck and cast your spell. Slowly you rise in the air! The Skunkbear, however, is not impressed. And you cannot rise out of its reach as the cave is not high enough. It swipes at you and catches your leg with its claw. Deduct 2 STAMINA points and turn to 469.

687

Deduct 2 STAMINA points. Your host watches as you cast the spell. 'Magic!' he exclaims. 'Do we have a fellow magician with us? Let's see how strong the Analander's magic really is!' He mumbles a few words and points a finger towards a rope lying on the floor. Immediately, the rope flies into the air like a serpent and darts towards you. It is attempting to bind your hands! But your spell has protected you, and the rope halts a couple of feet away, unable to penetrate your defence. The Sorcerer smiles. 'A magical protection spell. I see. Then we will have to use less impressive means to capture the Analander.' Turn to 552.

688

Deduct 1 STAMINA point. Do you have a Pearl Ring with you? If not, you cannot use this spell and you must lose 2 STAMINA points as one of the guards gets in a first blow – turn to 453. If you have a Pearl Ring, you place it on your finger and wait for the right moment. One of the guards swings his sword and you release the spell. Before their mystified eyes, you vanish! They are confused, but come to the conclusion that the blow must have been more powerful than they had thought. Meanwhile, you quietly head for the double doors. Turn to 176.

689

Deduct 2 STAMINA points. You cast your spell quickly, before the Hydra can attack. Immediately, you begin to feel its effects. Your body grows rapidly to three times its normal size and you stand like a Giant before the creature. But you are nearing the height of the ceiling; this spell is not fully effective in confined spaces. Nevertheless, it will give you an advantage in your battle with the Hydra. Turn to 65 to fight the creature. While enhanced by your spell, you may add 4 SKILL points during the battle.

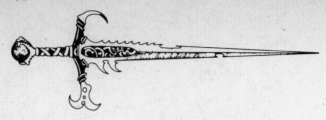

690

Deduct 2 STAMINA points. You cast your spell quickly to protect yourself from any magic that might try to harm you. Turn to **281** and, if you are attacked by magic, you may ignore the effects.

691

Deduct 1 STAMINA point. Do you have a Sun Jewel with you? If not, you cannot cast the spell and the Ogre attacks you for 2 STAMINA points of damage – turn to **270**. If you have a Sun Jewel, your spell will temporarily blind the Ogre, but will do him no harm. Return to **452** and make another choice.

692

You hold the Mask up over your face and cast the spell. But you were foolish to think that such a weak spell could affect a Demon from the Netherworld. Turn to **172**.

693

Deduct 2 STAMINA points. Secretly you cast your spell at the fat man. He sits quietly watching you and you have no clue as to whether or not your spell has worked. Return to **160** and make another choice.

694

Deduct 2 STAMINA points. You cast your spell to protect you from the effects of a fall. Do you now wish to try jumping out of the window (turn to **575**), or will you consider another option (return to **427** and make another choice)?

695

Deduct 4 STAMINA points. You concentrate on your spell and point your finger towards the fleeing Red-Eye. The others realize what you are doing. Turn to 769.

696

Deduct 1 STAMINA point. Do you have a Jewel-Studded Medallion with you? If not, you cannot cast this spell: return to 98 and make another choice. If you have such a Medallion, you may place it round your neck and recite the spell – turn to 585.

697

Deduct 1 STAMINA point. Do you have a Green-Haired Wig with you? If not, your spell will not work: return to 123 and choose another course of action. If you have a Green-Haired Wig, turn to 625.

698

Deduct 1 STAMINA point. Whether or not you have the Bracelet of Bone necessary to use this spell, it will do you no good, as the Goblins are far too stupid to understand any illusion you may create. A Goblin in the centre of the room closes in as you fuss with your spell. It is a grotesque creature with two arms of different sizes. Its right arm is huge and muscular; its left is fairly puny. Its legs are proportioned in the opposite way: its left leg is twice the size of its right. At first, you think it is taking an interest in your illusion. But it is not. It bares its teeth and attacks. Turn to 332.

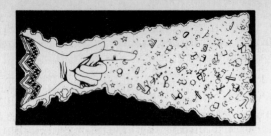

699

Deduct 2 STAMINA points. You cast your spell and step forwards to fight the Sightmasters. You are protected from magical attacks, but these creatures are not using magic! One of them catches you unawares with a blow. Deduct 2 STAMINA points and turn to 110.

700

Deduct 1 STAMINA point. Do you have a Potion of Fire Water with you? If not, you cannot use this spell and you will have to try smashing the lock – turn to 505. If you have some Fire Water, you may drink it and cast the spell on yourself. Power begins to surge through your body. When you feel you are fully charged, you grasp the lock and twist it between your hands. It breaks. Turn to 348.

701

Deduct 1 STAMINA point. Do you have a Staff of Oak Sapling with you? If not, this spell will not work and you must deduct 2 STAMINA points as the Birdman slashes at you with its talons – turn to 450. If you have a Staff, you hold it out and cast the spell at the creature. Ordinarily, this spell would work, but as fate would have it, the creature chooses that very moment to dart down from the sky. Your spell misses, and the creature is upon you. Turn to 450.

702

Deduct 2 STAMINA points. You focus your spell on to the locked door. When you have completed it, you hear a small click come from the lock. The door opens into a lightless room. But before you can take anything in, you lurch forwards! You have not seen the two steps just inside the entrance which you have now fallen down. Turn to **112**.

703

Deduct 2 STAMINA points. You cast your spell to create six different images of yourself in the room. But you have wasted your STAMINA. There is nothing alive in the room to be taken in by your illusion. Return to **351** to make another choice.

704

Deduct 1 STAMINA point. Do you have any Medicinal Potions with you? If not, the spell will not work – return to **323** and make another choice. If you have any Medicinal Potions or Blimberry Juice, you may swallow some and cast your spell. The healing effects will be magically enhanced. You may restore your STAMINA to its *Initial* level. Now return to **323** and choose your next course of action.

705

Deduct 1 STAMINA point. Do you have a Sun Jewel with you? If not, the spell does not work – return to **580** and choose again. If you have a Sun Jewel, the spell makes it glow brilliantly, filling the room with light. But you can see nothing particularly unusual about the room. Turn to **504**.

706

Deduct 1 STAMINA point. Do you have a Bracelet of Bone with you? If not, you cannot use this spell – turn to 552. If you have a Bracelet of Bone, you may place it on your wrist and cast your spell. You have thought of your illusion well. The desk at which he is sitting begins to heave and crack. He jumps back, startled, and watches as the wood becomes alive and forms itself into a gnarled Wood Golem in front of him! A scrawny arm reaches towards him. But his reaction is immediate: a ball of fire swells up in his hand and he flings it at the Golem. The creature shrieks as it catches fire and a sly smile spreads across the man's face. Holding his hand high in the air, he swirls it in a circular motion above the blazing Golem. Drops of water form in thin air and, moments later, the fire is out. You watch in amazement and your concentration lapses. The blackened Golem reforms once more into the burnt-out desk it really is.

Realizing how he has been tricked, the man's temper bursts. 'Trickery!' he screams. 'I have had enough of these games!' Turn to 552.

707

Deduct 1 STAMINA point. Do you have a Jewel of Gold with you? If not, you cannot use this spell and the Birdmen attack – deduct 3 STAMINA points and turn to 462. If you have a Jewel of Gold, you may hold it up and cast your spell. The Birdmen stop their advance and watch you bemusedly. You explain that, to be totally honest with them, you are hiding from the Captain of the Guards and you would appreciate a little help. The Birdmen burst out laughing and agree that you may shelter in their room. They have taken quite a liking to you! When the coast is clear, you may leave – turn to 479.

708

Deduct 1 STAMINA point. Whether or not you have the Holy Water necessary to cast this spell, it will do you no good as it is not appropriate here. Turn to **769**.

709

Deduct 1 STAMINA point. Your spell creates an awful stink in the room. The Ogre curls his nose up, horrified. He thinks that it is you who smells so bad! Do you have any nose plugs? If not, the stink will make you ill and you must lose 3 STAMINA points. If you have nose plugs, you may use them to protect yourself. The Ogre asks that you leave straight away, for he cannot stand the smell. But you will leave only if he will tell you what he knows about the Throben Doors. 'Yes, yes,' he agrees. 'Anything. Only get that smell out of here! Leave through the door in the corner. When you eventually come to a pair of double doors, you will find they open into a flaming hell-fire. Ignore this, for it is only an illusion. Now go!' This is useful information. If you follow his advice and come across a large double door, when you step through it into the fire beyond, turn to reference **399** instead of the one you are instructed. You may leave the Ogre by turning to **230**.

710

Deduct 1 STAMINA point. Do you have a Jewel-Studded Medallion with you? If not, you cannot use this spell – return to **427** and make another choice. If you have a Jewel-Studded Medallion, you may place it round your neck and cast your spell – turn to **714**.

711

Deduct 2 STAMINA points. You cast your spell and wait for an indication of your safest way of escape. Nothing happens. Either your spell is not working correctly, or there just is no safe way of escape. The guards are now almost upon you. Turn to **449**.

712

Deduct 2 STAMINA points. You cast your spell on yourself. You are protected from falling, but so far you have not fallen! Meanwhile, you must face the first guard. Turn to **394**.

713

You cast your spell and look into the Orb. It turns from clear to cloudy, then an image begins to form. Guards! A number of shaggy-haired guards are involved in a battle of some kind, against a human. Eventually, the image fades and you must decide what to do next. Turn to **245**.

714

You wait for your spell to take effect. But nothing happens! You are reasonably sure you recited it correctly, but for some reason it has not worked. You consider your other options. You may either plan an ambush on the guard when he arrives with food (turn to **476**), or you may simply wait to see whether anyone will summon you (turn to **214**).

715

Deduct 2 STAMINA points. You cast your spell on to the creature and wait for it to take effect. But the brute is so slow anyway that you cannot really tell whether the spell has worked or not. In fact the spell *has* affected the creature. You may now draw your weapon and fight it. Its reactions have been slowed considerably:

MUCALYTIC   SKILL 4   STAMINA 9

If it manages to score three wounds on you during the battle, turn to **576**. If you defeat it before it can score three hits, turn to **443**.

716

Deduct 2 STAMINA points. You cast your spell and the Birdman stops in mid-attack. It looks at you, then looks around complacently. It seems to have lost its desire to continue the battle. If you could reach it, now would be a good time to finish it off, but it hangs in the air as if wondering what to do next. Eventually, it flies off and you may continue along the trail. Turn to **441**.

717

Deduct 1 STAMINA point. Do you have a Black Facemask with you? If not, your spell will not work – turn to **172**. If you have a Black Facemask, you may cast your spell. Turn to **692**.

718

Deduct 4 STAMINA points. You cast your spell at one of the guards. Immediately, this guard seems to trip over his own feet and falls flat on his face on the ground. He stands up, picks up his sword and swings it in the air. It flies out of his hands! The guard has been well and truly incapacitated by your spell. But there are still three more advancing towards you! Turn to **40** to face them, but you may ignore one of the guards (your choice). If you manage to defeat the other three, you will easily be able to kill the last one afterwards.

719

Deduct 1 STAMINA point. Do you have any sand with you? If not, your spell will not work – return to **580** and make another choice. If you have any sand, turn to **681**.

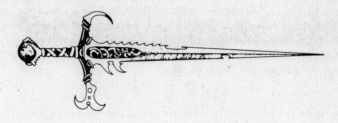

720

Deduct 2 STAMINA points. Your spell has its effect on its target. The Red-Eye's movements slow down dramatically, so that it seems to be moving in a dream. The other two have noticed that their comrade has been gripped by magic, and their response is deadly for you. Fearing that you may use magic on them, they unleash their most powerful weapon – heat vision. Opening their eyelids, four searing beams of heat shoot towards you and hit your chest before you have time to react. Your last memory is the smell of burning flesh – your own.

721

Deduct 1 STAMINA point. Do you have a Pearl Ring? If not, your spell will not work and the guard attacks: deduct 2 STAMINA points and turn to **394**. If you have a Pearl Ring, you may place it on your finger and cast the spell. To the amazement of the guard standing before you, you disappear instantly! The guard shifts nervously. He can hear your footsteps coming towards him, but he cannot see where you are. He slashes the air desperately with his sword, but misses. While under the influence of this spell, it will be an easy matter for you to kill this guard. A swift blow to the neck ends his life. But now the spell is beginning to wear off! Turn to **495**.

722

Deduct 1 STAMINA point. Whether or not you have the Crystal Orb this spell requires, you have no time to use it. The guards grab you again. You manage to break free of their hold just long enough to grab your weapon. Turn to **145**.

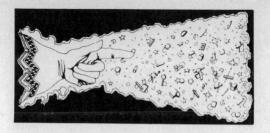

723

Deduct 1 STAMINA point. Do you have a Potion of Fire Water with you? If not, you cannot cast this spell – turn to **383**. If you can drink a Potion of Fire Water, you may do so and then cast your spell. As it takes effect, your body surges with power. You may perform an act of strength – but what good will it do you? Turn to **586**.

724

Deduct 1 STAMINA point. Do you have a Galehorn with you? If not, this spell will not work – turn to **165**. If you have a Galehorn, you may cast your spell and blow through it. A tremendous blast breaks from the instrument and catches the rope. It blows out across the crevasse. When the blast ceases, the rope swings back towards you. It seems safe enough. Do you want to try swinging across on the rope (turn to **165**), or will you instead continue down the path (turn to **59**)?

725

Deduct 1 STAMINA point. Do you have a Ring of Green Metal with you? If not, you cannot use this spell and you must return to **98** to make another choice. If you have a Green Ring, you may place it on your finger and cast your spell. Turn to **585**.

726

Deduct 2 STAMINA points. You reach into your backpack and choose something on which to cast your spell (cross 1 item off your Adventure Sheet). The spell turns this into a handful of illusory treasure, which you hold out towards the Hobgoblin. But your peace offering has no effect. You have deeply insulted her! Her cleaver comes down, narrowly missing your hand. Turn to **281**.

727

Deduct 1 STAMINA point. Whether or not you have the Brass Pendulum required for this spell, it will do you no good, as you need time to concentrate your victim's attention on the Pendulum as it swings. In this situation you do not have time to put the Black Elves to sleep, and they attack you. Deduct 2 STAMINA points, as they strike the first blow, and turn to **510**.

728

Deduct 1 STAMINA point. Do you have a Cloth Skullcap with you? If not, you wait for the spell to take effect, but nothing happens, and you cross the room hurriedly (turn to **571**). If you have a Cloth Skullcap, you may place it on your head and concentrate on one of the Goblins. Turn to **684**.

729

Deduct 1 STAMINA point. Do you have a Bracelet of Bone with you? If not, your spell will not work: return to **362** and make another choice. If you have a Bracelet of Bone, this will still not do you much good. Even if you create the illusion that the prisoner is free of the pillory, the illusion will soon be shattered when he finds he cannot move about. Return to **362** and make another choice.

730

Do you have any Goblin's Teeth with you? If not, you cannot cast this spell – turn to **552**. If you have any Goblin's Teeth, you may throw them on the ground and cast your spell over them. Deduct as many STAMINA points as Goblin's Teeth you use and turn to **581**.

731

Deduct 1 STAMINA point. Do you have a Galehorn with you? If not, your spell will not work and the rocks fall around and on you – deduct 2 STAMINA points and turn to 368 to escape the landslide. If you have a Galehorn, you cast your spell and blow, creating a raging gale which blows up against the falling rocks. The force is tremendous, but it cannot hold back the landslide. Your only means of escape now is to leap across the crevasse (turn to 400).

732

Deduct 1 STAMINA point. Do you have any beeswax with you? If not, you cannot use this spell and the first guard attacks: deduct 2 STAMINA points and turn to 449. If you have some beeswax, you may rub it on your weapon to enhance its effect. Turn to 449 to fight the guards, but each wound that you inflict in this fight will cause 4 STAMINA points of damage instead of the normal 2.

733

As the spell wears off, your feet once more touch solid ground. The confusion clears and you take in your surroundings. They are strangely familiar. You are far from the prison tower, that's for sure. But where are you? You are alone on a wide plain, standing on a path. The featureless landscape offers no encouragement. You choose your direction and set off along the path. Turn to reference 48 of Book 3 of the *Sorcery!* series.

734

Deduct 1 STAMINA point. Do you have any grains of sand with you? If not, you cannot use this spell – return to 499 and make another choice. If you have some sand, turn to 597.

735

Deduct 1 STAMINA point. Do you have a Crystal Orb with you? If not, you cannot cast this spell – return to 160 and choose again. If you have a Crystal Orb, turn to 680.

736

Deduct 1 STAMINA point. Do you have a Jewel-Studded Medallion with you? If not, the spell will not work – turn to **304**. If you have such a Medallion, you may place it round your neck and cast your spell. You begin to rise in the air towards the top of the Fortress wall. But as you float upwards, a sight makes you stop in mid-flight. Birdmen, patrolling the parapets! So far, they have not seen you, but if you rise any further, you will surely be discovered. You decide against trying to enter this way and return to the ground. Turn to **304**.

737

Deduct 1 STAMINA point. Do you have any small pebbles with you? If not, you cannot use this spell and must decide to copy the creature – turn to **483**. If you have any pebbles, you may cast your spell on them to charge them with explosive power. But even throwing them against the lock has no effect. And the noise attracts the attention of a group of guards! You decide to leave and hide in the corner of the courtyard. Turn to **519**.

738

Deduct 1 STAMINA point. Do you have a Green-Haired Wig with you? If not, your spell will not work and the guards get in the first blow: deduct 2 STAMINA points and turn to 453. If you have a Wig, you may place it on your head and talk to the guards. They stop in their tracks, amazed at hearing someone talk to them in the language of their homelands, the Tinpang Valley. But they have little to say, except that you are not allowed in the area. As a special privilege, they will allow you to leave them peacefully and approach the double doors. If you decide to do this, turn to 176. If you don't want to do this, you will have to fight them (turn to 453).

739

Deduct 2 STAMINA points. You wait for the area around you to go dark, but nothing happens! This spell will work only indoors. Meanwhile the Sightmasters attack quickly, landing the first blow. Deduct 2 STAMINA points and turn to 110.

740

Deduct 1 STAMINA point. Do you have a Sun Jewel with you? If not, your spell will not work and you must draw your weapon – turn to 442. If you have a Sun Jewel, you may hold it up and cast your spell into it. It begins to glow with a throbbing light which becomes brighter and brighter. Suddenly, it bursts into brilliance and the creature shrieks with a pitiful cry! It backs off into the corner of the room and you cannot help but take pity on it. It is whimpering with a sound that could be a sentence, if only you could hear it properly. Will you step over and listen to it (turn to 405), or will you remain still, holding up the Jewel (turn to 559)?

741

Deduct 1 STAMINA point. Do you have a Ring of Green Metal with you? If not, this spell will have no effect and you decide to try something from your backpack against the doors – turn to **31**. If you have such a ring, you may place it on your finger and concentrate on your spell. Whereas the spell can take you short distances instantaneously, it cannot take you through solid wood. In an instant, you are standing at a different spot, carried by the spell. You are standing in front of a door which you recognize as the one you have just passed on the left. Will you open the door and enter (turn to **206**), or will you head back for the doors you have just come from (turn to **253**)?

742

Deduct 1 STAMINA point. Do you have a Crystal Orb with you? If not, the spell will not work – return to **79** and make another choice. If you have a Crystal Orb, turn to **713**.

743

Do you have any Holy Water with you? If not, you cannot cast this spell – return to **351** and choose another course of action. If you have any Holy Water, you may cast your spell on the body of Farren Whyde. Turn to **537**.

744

Deduct 1 STAMINA point. Do you have a Gold-Backed Mirror with you? If not, you cannot cast the spell and the creature swipes again, this time smacking you in the side: deduct 2 STAMINA points and return to **515** to make another choice. If you have a Gold-Backed Mirror, you may hold it up to the creature and cast your spell. But the poor light and the sheer size of the blubbery hulk are affecting your spell; it is taking a long time to work. Meanwhile, the creature lumbers forwards and swings its arm. Your Mirror is knocked from your hand and smashes on the floor! Turn to **475**.

745

Deduct 1 STAMINA point. Do you have a Sun Jewel with you? If not, you cannot cast this spell – turn to **769**. If you have a Sun Jewel, you pull it out and cast your spell. The Red-Eyes laugh at your efforts. For how can you blind them with a Sun Jewel if their eyes are already closed? Draw your weapon and turn to **225**.

746

Deduct 1 STAMINA point. Do you have a Potion of Fire Water with you? If not, you cannot use this spell. The She-Satyrs become annoyed at your futile efforts and one throws a spear which grazes your arm: deduct 2 STAMINA points and return to **522** to choose again. If you have a Potion of Fire Water, you may drink it and cast your spell. A surge of strength runs through your body. You grab a huge boulder and hurl it at the She-Satyrs. Although it misses them, they look nervously at each other and decide you are a little too powerful for them to capture. They allow you to leave the area unharmed. Turn to **441**.

747

Deduct 1 STAMINA point. Do you have a Jewel of Gold with you? If not, you cannot use this spell – turn to **145**. If you have a Jewel of Gold you may cast your spell quickly on the captain. Turn to **634**.

748

Deduct 1 STAMINA point. Do you have a Gold-Backed Mirror with you? If not, you cannot use this spell and the Red-Eyes attack as you are trying to make it work. Turn to **769**. If you have a Gold-Backed Mirror, you cast your spell on to it and turn it towards one of the creatures. A double of this creature crawls out of the mirror and stands in front of them. The three Red-Eyes are astonished! You may command this creation to attack its model. But before you do this, you may cast the spell twice more to create duplicates of all three Red-Eyes (casting each spell will drain 1 STAMINA point). Decide how many you will create and turn to **159**. Each replica will battle its model to the death. It will have the same SKILL and STAMINA scores as its original and will also have the same powers of heat vision. You may join in the battle and help your creations to win if you wish.

749

Deduct 1 STAMINA point. Whether or not you have a Green-Haired Wig with you, this spell will do you no good. There is no one around for you to talk to! Turn to **304**.

750

Deduct 1 STAMINA point. Whether or not you have the Green-Haired Wig you need to complete this spell, it will do you no good, as there is no one around who can hear you. Turn to **53**.

751

Deduct 4 STAMINA points. You cast your spell and create an invisible barrier along the side of the trail, such that the falling rocks smash into it and pile up. Your creation shudders as the weight builds up, and you decide it best to run ahead quickly before the spell wears off. You pass the landslide safely. Further along the trail, you come to a wide crack in the rock, which is spanned by a narrow bridge. Turn to **411**.

752

Deduct 1 STAMINA point. Do you have a Sun Jewel with you? If not, you cannot cast the spell and the Ogre attacks you for 2 STAMINA points of damage – turn to **270**. If you have a Sun Jewel, your spell will temporarily blind the Ogre, but will do him no harm. Return to **251** and make another choice.

753

Deduct 7 STAMINA points. Your body trembles as you cast the spell. What lies in store? You have no idea what the spell will do. The first sound you hear is a squeaky scream from the Minimite. You look towards him and find he is in great pain, lying down on the floor and clutching his stomach. *Magic!* The spell has broken the little creature's defences and it is writhing in agony on the floor! Suddenly, Jann falls still. The strain has been too much. He is dead.

But what about yourself? As the Minimite dies, it seems to have the effect of triggering your spell. The room swirls. A rush of sound, like the sea in a large shell, comes to your ears. Your sense of balance falters . . . and is lost, as you tumble over and over in a magical void. You can see the world below you flashing past. People, places, creatures . . . all swirl past you – *travelling backwards!* The secret of the spell! That must be it! Your are travelling backwards through time! But, the question is – and here you realize the folly of your actions – *where to?* Turn to **438**.

754

Deduct 2 STAMINA points. You cast your spell and wait for an indication as to whether or not this strange structure is safe. Sure enough, your spell signals a warning. Turn to **586**.

755

Deduct 1 STAMINA point. Do you have a Gold-Backed Mirror with you? If not, you cannot use this spell and the Hobgoblin attacks with the cleaver – deduct 2 STAMINA points and turn to **281**. If you have a Gold-Backed Mirror, turn to **629**.

756

Deduct 1 STAMINA point. Do you have a vial of glue? If not, the spell will not work and the guards attack: deduct 2 STAMINA points and turn to 453. If you have a vial of glue, you throw it on to the floor in front of the leading guard and cast your spell. Your aim is good but, as luck would have it, the guard changes his pace as he reaches your trap and his stride takes him over it! Turn to 453 and face the guards.

757

Deduct 1 STAMINA point. Do you have a Green-Haired Wig with you? If not, your spell does not work and the creature catches you off guard with a blow: deduct 2 STAMINA points and turn to 490. If you have the Wig, you put it on and cast the spell. You find you are able to converse with the creature. But it is not interested in conversation; it simply wants you out of its home! Will you leave it in peace (turn to 469), or will you fight it (turn to 490)?

758

Deduct 1 STAMINA point. Do you have a Pearl Ring with you? If not, you cannot use this spell and while you try in vain to complete it, the Birdmen attack – deduct 2 STAMINA points and turn to 462. If you have a Pearl Ring, you may cast your spell to make yourself invisible. But this is not an ideal spell to cast in this situation. You are in a small room, so there is not much chance of avoiding the Birdmen, and your opponents have a sharp sense of hearing. *Test your Luck*. If you are Lucky, you may slip out of the room (turn to 479). If you are Unlucky, the Birdmen locate you (turn to 462).

759

The Pendulum swings slowly backwards and forwards as his attention becomes more and more focused on it. Under the influence of your spell, he is soon asleep and you are able to look through his room. It seems that he keeps his gold well hidden, for all you can find is a pouch on the desk containing 10 Gold Pieces. You may keep these. But under his table is a drawer containing a book which you find most interesting. On one page is a diagram that you recognize as the courtyard. Written next to the double doors is the word 'Alaralata-nalara'. *The password!* You memorize the word, snap the book shut and leave the room. Turn to 141.

760

Deduct 1 STAMINA point. Do you have a Bamboo Flute with you? If not, you cannot cast this spell and your futile efforts serve only to anger the creatures. Another spear comes flying towards you, and this one catches your leg – deduct 3 STAMINA points and return to 522 to choose a non-magical option. If you have a Bamboo Flute, you may cast your spell and start playing. As the spell takes hold, the effect is comical. The two She-Satyrs begin dancing uncontrollably in time to your music! They step awkwardly on their clumsy hooves, and are unable to prevent you continuing along the trail. Turn to 441.

761

Deduct 1 STAMINA point. Whether or not you have the Green-Haired Wig that this spell requires, it will do you no good: there is nothing around for you to talk to. You decide instead to try something from your pack. Turn to 31.

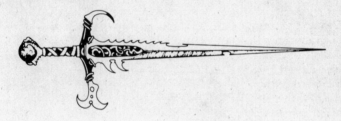

762

Deduct 2 STAMINA points. You cast your spell on the creature and wait for some indication that it has worked. You get no such indication. You draw your weapon. Turn to 442.

763

Deduct 1 STAMINA point. You cast your spell. Almost immediately, an invisible cloud, which smells like a thousand rotting dungheaps, swells up in the room. Do you have any nose plugs with you? If not, then the smell will make you feel ill and you must deduct 3 STAMINA points as you are sick in the corner. You turn towards the fat man. He looks towards you smiling, holding a scented handkerchief to his nose. The spell is not affecting him at all! Do you want to leap across the table and attack (turn to 205), or will you instead offer him something from your backpack (turn to 66)?

764

You cast your spell into the Jewel. It starts by glowing dully, then suddenly a brilliant light bursts from it and fills the room. Gasps go up all round and the Goblins cringe away from you into the corners of the room, shielding their eyes from the light. You have a clear path across the room to the door on the far side. Turn to **426**.

765

Deduct 1 STAMINA point. Do you have any beeswax with you? If not, you cannot use this spell and you take a first blow from one of the guards: deduct 2 STAMINA points and turn to **453**. If you have some beeswax, you may quickly rub it on to your weapon to enhance its abilities. Turn to **453** and fight the guards, but your weapon will do double damage – 4 STAMINA points of damage instead of the normal 2.

766

Deduct 2 STAMINA points. As the guards approach, you cast your spell. *But nothing happens!* This spell can only be used within the confines of a windowless room, not outside as you are now. The guards are approaching fast and one strikes you with his sword. Deduct 2 STAMINA points and turn to **40**.

767

Deduct 4 STAMINA points. You cast your spell to create a magical defensive barrier. But nothing happens! Perhaps you have not cast it properly. Return to **98** and choose an alternative course of action.

768

Deduct 1 STAMINA point. Do you have any Medicinal Potions with you? If not, you cannot use this spell. If you have any such Potions, you may swallow them and cast your spell. Your wounds begin to heal and you start to feel revitalized. You may restore your STAMINA score to its *Initial* level. Whether or not you have been able to cast the spell, return to **362** to choose your next move.

769

The Red-Eyes watch you go through the motions of casting your spell. It is obvious to them that you are summoning up magic and that they must act quickly. Their best defence is attack. And their best means of attack is their deadly power of heat vision. The Red-Eyes open their eyelids and stare directly into your face. Your last memory is of burning beams of heat from the eyes of the creatures heading directly for your own. Your mission has ended.

770

Deduct 1 STAMINA point. Do you have a Sun Jewel with you? If not, you cannot cast the spell and the Ogre attacks you for 2 STAMINA points of damage – turn to **270**. If you have a Sun Jewel, your spell will temporarily blind the Ogre, but will do him no harm. Return to **557** and make another choice.

771

Deduct 1 STAMINA point. Do you have any stone dust with you? If not, you cannot use this spell – return to 580 and make another choice. If you have some stone dust, you may throw it over anything that you wish in the room and use your spell to petrify it. Turn to 504.

772

Deduct 2 STAMINA points. You concentrate on one of the creatures and cast your spell. The She-Satyr shakes her head and looks first at you, then at her companion. Her expression is one of bewilderment! The other creature begins to shift uneasily; she had no wish to confront a magician. 'Release my companion from this spell,' she shouts, in a voice more fearful than threatening, 'and we will let you pass.' This seems a fair deal to you, and you pick up your belongings to leave. Suddenly, the confused She-Satyr grabs a handful of pebbles and hurls them at you! Before you can react, they shower you painfully. You must deduct 2 STAMINA points, but then you may leave the area. Turn to 441.

773

Deduct 2 STAMINA points. You cast your spell and, almost immediately, you begin to grow until you are Giant-sized. You step up to the doors. With your extra strength, you hope you can smash them open. Do you want to grip the handle and give the door a shove (turn to 344), or will you first try imitating the creature you saw earlier (turn to 483)?

774

Deduct 2 STAMINA points. You cast your spell over Farren Whyde. He begins to protest, but it is too late. He slumps miserably on to the floor. You try talking to him, but he is not interested. The old man's spirit has been broken. There is now nothing you can do. You will have to leave, work your way back through the Fortress and head for the tower outside. Turn to **486**.

775

Deduct 1 STAMINA point. Do you have any pebbles with you? If not, you cannot use this spell and the Elves will attack: deduct 2 STAMINA points and turn to **510**. If you have any pebbles, you may cast your spell on them and use them as exploding missiles against the Black Elves. You may throw as many of your pebbles as you want and, during this time, the Black Elves will not dare approach you too quickly. Turn to **510**. Choose your target and roll two dice. If the number rolled is equal to or less than your SKILL score, deduct 3 STAMINA points from your target. If the roll is higher, the pebble misses. When you have finished throwing your pebbles, you must finish the battle off with your weapon.

776

Deduct 1 STAMINA point. Do you have any Medicinal Potions with you? If not, you cannot cast this spell – return to **193** and choose again. If you have Medicinal Potions, you may swallow them and cast your spell. Within moments, the spell will take effect. You may restore your STAMINA to its *Initial* level. Now return to **193** to choose your next course of action.

777

Deduct 1 STAMINA point. Do you have a Jewel-Studded Medallion with you? If not, you cannot cast this spell – return to **499** and make another choice. If you have such a Medallion, you may place it round your neck and cast the spell. Almost immediately, you begin to rise into the air. But the ceiling is low and you cannot gain any advantage of height on the creature: you cannot rise out of its reach! As it closes in, you decide to return to the ground where you will be able to fight more easily. Turn to **65**.

778

Deduct 1 STAMINA point. Do you have a Jewel-Studded Medallion with you? If not, the spell will not work and you must deduct 2 STAMINA points as the Birdman darts down from the air to attack – turn to **450**. If you have such a Medallion, you may place it round your neck and cast your spell. As it takes effect, your body begins to rise in the air. The Birdman stops his attack and watches, incredulous, as you float towards him. You may now draw your weapon and attack. Turn to **450**.

779

Deduct 1 STAMINA point. Do you have a Galehorn with you? If not, you cannot cast this spell – turn to **383**. If you have a Galehorn, turn to **648**.

780

Deduct 1 STAMINA point. Do you have a Green-Haired Wig with you? If not, your spell will not work and you will not avoid the creature's next blow: deduct 2 STAMINA points and return to **515** to make another choice. If you have such a Wig, you may place it on your head and cast your spell, to try to talk to the blubbery hulk. Recognizing something of your message, it cocks its head to one side and stares at you intently. Turn to **386**.

781

Deduct 4 STAMINA points. You cast your spell over the fallen Demon and command it to rise, under your control. But nothing happens. The creature is dead and cannot obey you. You have wasted your STAMINA. Return to **351** and make another choice.

782

Deduct 2 STAMINA points. You cast your spell and wait for an indication of any traps or danger ahead. Something is not quite right. Although you are sure you are about to face danger, no indication is given by the spell. Return to **123** to choose your next course of action.

783

Deduct 4 STAMINA points. Unsure of what you are facing in this room, you decide to try a powerful spell. As it takes effect, the shuffling stops. You approach the general direction of the shuffling noise. But in the blackness you bump into a prickly bush! Or was it a bush at all? Whatever it was, you are now bleeding and must deduct 2 more STAMINA points. Rather than wait around to find out what it was, you decide to give up on this room. You leave, heading through the entrance-room, to try the other way onwards. Turn to **18**.

784

Deduct 1 STAMINA point. Do you have any small pebbles? If not, you cannot use this spell and the first guard clouts you with the flat of his sword – turn to **449**. If you have some pebbles, you may cast your spell on to as many as you want (but not more than you have). The guards are a cowardly lot. As you throw the pebbles at them, they explode and frighten them off. Once you have decided how many pebbles you will enchant, you must then determine how many of the guards you will frighten. Roll two dice and compare the total with your SKILL score for each of the pebbles. If the roll is equal to or less than your SKILL, then that pebble has frightened off one of the guards. If you manage to frighten off all three guards, turn to **397**. If you frighten off two of the guards, turn to **401**. If you frighten off none, or one of the guards, you will have to draw your weapon and face the others – turn to **449** (but ignore the first guard, if you have frightened him off).

785

Deduct 2 STAMINA points. You cast your spell and wait for some indication of whether the rope is safe or not. You begin to feel a strange sensation. The hand which is gripping the rope begins to glow with a peculiar heat! At first you think you may be imagining things, but eventually, you are certain that the spell is trying to tell you something. But what? If you wish to swing across on the rope, turn to **165**. If you leave it and continue along the trail, turn to **59**.

786

Deduct 1 STAMINA point. Do you have a Staff of Oak Sapling? If not, you cannot use this spell; instead draw your weapon and turn to **162**. If you have an Oak Staff, you may hold it up and cast your spell. The strange man raises an eyebrow and then grimaces as the spell takes effect. 'A Holding Spell!' he grunts, evidently struggling against its power. He reaches into his desk and pulls out a small glass vial. Before you can stop him, he drinks the potion within it and slumps back in the chair. You step forwards to take advantage of his weakness, but not before he can call out loudly. Turn to **552**.

787

By wearing the Skullcap and casting your spell, you are able to reach out and focus on the mind of the leading Sightmaster. But now you must face the creatures. Being able to read the mind of the first Sightmaster, he will not be able to hit you. Turn to **110** to battle the group. You must follow the combat instructions, but you will not suffer any hits from an opponent whose mind you are reading, even if its Attack Strength is higher. Thus you may dispatch the first Sightmaster in two successful rounds, but you must still follow the instructions in case one of the other Sightmasters lands a hit. When the first is defeated, you may cast the spell again on the second (this will cost another 1 STAMINA point), and then the third when the second is defeated.

788

Deduct 2 STAMINA points. You draw something from your backpack (you choose what) and cast your spell on it. It immediately turns into a gleaming pile of treasure! But the Skunkbear is not interested in these apparent riches. He wants you out of his cave! The creature hits you with a paw. Deduct 1 STAMINA point and decide whether you want to draw your weapon and face it (turn to **490**), or run from the cave (turn to **469**).

789

Deduct 1 STAMINA point. Do you have a Giant's Tooth with you? If not, the spell will not work and the first guard attacks: deduct 2 STAMINA points and turn to **394**. If you have a Giant's Tooth, you may throw it on the ground and cast your spell to create a large, burly Giant (SKILL 8, STAMINA 9) which will attack the first guard. Turn to **394** to conduct this battle. The Giant will disappear as soon as the fight is over.

790

Deduct 4 STAMINA points. You cast your spell towards the strongest-looking Birdman. There is a *clang* as the creature's sword drops to the ground. It looks surprised, and bends down to retrieve the blade. This time, the Birdman smacks its head against the table on the way down and it collapses in a heap on the floor. It has knocked itself out! Turn to **462** to fight the remaining two Birdmen (ignore the first Birdman).

791

Deduct 1 STAMINA point. This spell will do you no good here. Although you may be able to create a pool of quicksand, there are no creatures around that you could trap in it! Turn to **304**.

792

You cast your spell into the Orb and watch to see what happens. A milky cloud spreads through it and eventually begins to clear. An image takes shape. An old man, dressed in long undergarments, is in a room, standing behind the door. Apparently he is waiting for someone to enter, as he holds a brass pot above his head, ready to attack. What can this mean? Does it mean anything? This revelation is not helping you to break the lock of the pillory. Return to **362** and make another choice.

793

Deduct 2 STAMINA points. You cast your spell and it takes effect immediately. You are protected from any magic that may be used against you. But these Black Elves will not be using magic. Turn to **510**.

794

Deduct 1 STAMINA point. Do you have any pebbles with you? If not, then you are wasting your time with this spell; return to **251** and make another choice. If you have any pebbles, choose how many you will use and cast your spell. Turn to **270**. You may throw these pebbles at the Ogre, but for each one, you must roll a number equal to or less than your SKILL score in order to make a successful hit. Each successful hit will inflict 1 STAMINA point of damage. If you miss with two throws, the Ogre will step in to attack and you may throw no more pebbles.

795

Deduct 1 STAMINA point. Whether or not you have the Green-Haired Wig you need to complete this spell, it will do you no good, as there is nothing around to hear you. Turn to **53**.

796

You cast your spell and stare into the Orb. Images form within the glass and shortly you are looking at a scene, in which nothing is moving. A narrow trail leads down towards a crevasse in a rocky mountainside. What can this mean? Not a great deal at the moment. Return to **123** to choose your next course of action.

797

Deduct 1 STAMINA point. Whether or not you have the Gold-Backed Mirror that this spell requires, it will do you no good: this spell is not appropriate here. Frustrated at the poor choice you have made, you step up to the rope. Turn to **165**.

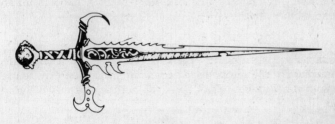

798

Deduct 1 STAMINA point. Do you have a Jewel-Studded Medallion with you? If not, your spell will not work and you have now wasted time – draw your weapon and turn to **172**. If you have such a Medallion, turn to **540**.

799

Deduct 1 STAMINA point. Do you have a Sun Jewel with you? If not, the spell will not work and you must try to pick your way through the Goblins – turn to **56**. If you have a Sun Jewel, turn to **764**.

You step over to the window and blow your whistle. A shrill, warbling sound comes from the silver piece and you wait for it to summon its masters. A short while later, nothing has happened and you begin to get anxious. But, sure enough, your call has been heard. A fluttering of wings can be heard at the window, followed by a familiar face. The head of Peewit Croo appears. 'Do you have the Crown?' he asks. You nod, and tell him of the struggle, patting your backpack to indicate that the Crown is safe. 'Then let us go!' he cries. 'For both our missions are now done. Without the Crown, Mampang is powerless. Give me your hands, friend.' The Birdmen take you and fly you away from the Fortress and across the peaks of High Xamen.

You have succeeded in your mission. The Crown of Kings will be returned to Analand. The Archmage is dead. Perhaps sometime soon another warlord will seize power in Mampang and your country will once again be threatened. But for the time being, you hold your head high in pride. Yours has been the most difficult task ever completed by a native of your country. You have firmly written yourself into the history books of Analand. And your adventures will become legends, passed on through generations of your people.

Your journey is over. You have earned your rest.

THE SORCERY SPELL BOOK

RULES FOR USING MAGIC

During your training you have been taught a number of spells and incantations which you use to aid you on your quest. The full list of spells follows these instructions.

Spells are identified by a three-letter word. Throughout the book you will be given the option of using spells to overcome problems and opponents. *The spells will be identified only by these three-letter words, so it is important that you memorize at least some of the codes.*

Thus, before you can start using your powers of sorcery, you will need to spend some time memorizing spells, as would a real wizard learning the magic arts. Obviously, you will not be able to memorize all forty-eight spells at once, but the more you use the book, the more familiar you will become with the most useful spells.

Try starting by memorizing between six and ten spells (the best ones to start with are given below) and relying on your swordsmanship to fight some of the creatures you encounter. It is possible, with a little luck, to complete your quest with these spells, but your task will become easier when you are capable of using more spells.

Some spells also require the use of an artefact, such as a piece of jewellery or a magic ring. If you try to use a spell without possessing the correct artefact, you will be wasting your STAMINA as the spell will not work.

Each time you use a spell – whether it is successful or not – it will draw on your reserves of energy and concentration. A cost, in STAMINA points, is given for each spell. Each time you use a spell, you must deduct the cost from your STAMINA score.

You may study the Book of Spells for as long as you want before embarking on an adventure, *but once you have set off, you may never again refer to it and must rely purely on your memory until your adventure is over*. Nor may you write the spells down for easy reference. In a real situation where you may be surprised by a creature, you would not have time to start flicking through your Spell Book trying to work out the best spell to cast!

The Six Most Useful Spells

Code	Effect	Stamina Cost
ZAP	Creates a lightning bolt which shoots from the fingertip	4
FOF	Creates a protective force-field	4
LAW	Enables creatures to be controlled	4
DUM	Makes creatures extremely clumsy	4
HOT	Creates a fireball which can be aimed at enemies	4
WAL	Creates a magic wall to defend against physical objects	4

ZAP and HOT are strong attacking spells, FOF and WAL are good general-purpose defensive spells, while LAW and DUM will be useful if you get into a tricky situation.

Note that these spells will often be more powerful than you need in a given situation – they are not cheap in terms of STAMINA points – but they are good all-rounders. As you get to know more spells from the Spell Book, you will be able to choose more economical spells which will be equally effective against certain perils.

Read through the list again, then cover up the 'Effect' column with your hand. How many can you remember? When you can remember them by heart, you can begin your quest.

HINTS ON USING SPELLS

As you familiarize yourself with the spells in this Spell Book, your skill and abilities in the adventure will improve.

Learning the six basic spells will allow you to start playing with minimal delay. These spells will get you out of most difficulties, but they are expensive (in terms of STAMINA points) and you will often find it necessary to rely on your limited powers of swordsmanship, particularly with weaker creatures, in order to avoid running dangerously short of STAMINA.

Other spells are more economical but will be given less often as options, thus relying more on your memory and skill as a wizard. The most economical spells of all are those which require magical artefacts, which must be found on your adventure.

Remember that there are heavy penalties for guessing spells! If you choose a spell code which does not represent a spell, or if you choose a spell for which you do not have the required artefact, you will lose extra STAMINA points. In some cases, death will be your penalty!

Not all the spells are used in this adventure.

You will soon begin to make your own discoveries about the spells themselves. There is a certain logic to the way they are arranged, the options that are given and their codes. But these discoveries you must make for yourself. Experience will make you more skilful with magic. All this is part of the art of sorcery.

ZAP

An extremely powerful weapon, this spell creates a blast of lightning which shoots from the caster's hand, which must be pointed in the desired direction. It is effective against virtually all living creatures which have no magical defences. But it takes great strength and concentration to use.

Cost 4 STAMINA points

HOT

The caster may direct this spell with his hands in any direction desired. As it is cast, a burning fireball shoots from the hands towards its target. It will be effective against any creature, whether magical or not, unless that creature cannot be harmed by fire. The fireball so created causes severe burns on impact, but extinguishes soon after hitting its target.

Cost 4 STAMINA points

FOF

This powerful spell creates a magical and physical barrier in front of the caster which is capable of keeping out all physical intruders and most magical ones. Its creation takes excessive mental concentration but the resulting force-field is both extremely strong and is under the control of its creator's will, who can allow one-way penetration, or can position it as desired.

Cost 4 STAMINA points

WAL

The casting of this spell creates an invisible wall in front of the caster. This wall is impervious to all missiles, creatures, etc. It is a very useful defensive spell.

Cost 4 STAMINA points

LAW

Casting this spell at an attacking creature allows the caster to take control of the attacker's will. The attack will cease and the creature will immediately come under the control of the caster. However, this spell works only on non-intelligent creatures and lasts only for a short time.

Cost 4 STAMINA points

DUM

When cast at a creature holding an object of some sort (e.g. a weapon), this spell will make the creature clumsy and uncoordinated. It will drop the object, fumble to pick it up, drop it again – in short the creature is unlikely to do the caster any harm with any objects while under the influence of this spell.

Cost 4 STAMINA points

BIG

When this spell is cast on the caster's own body, it will inflate the body to three times normal size. This increases the power of the caster and is especially useful against large opponents, but must be used with caution in confined spaces!

Cost 2 STAMINA points

WOK

A coin of some sort is necessary for this spell. The caster places the coin on the wrist and casts the spell on it. The coin becomes magically fixed on the wrist and acts as an invisible metal shield with an effective protection circle of just under three feet across. This will shield the user against all normal weapons. Afterwards, the coin is no longer usable as a coin.

Cost 1 STAMINA point

DOP

This spell may be used to open any locked door. Casting the spell works directly on the lock tumblers and the door may be opened freely. If the door is bolted from the inside, the bolts will be undone. The spell will not work on doors sealed by magic.

Cost 2 STAMINA points

RAZ

To perform this spell, beeswax is required. By rubbing the wax on any *edged* weapon (sword, axe, dagger, etc.) and casting this spell, the blade will become razor-sharp and do double its normal damage. Thus, if it normally inflicts 2 STAMINA points' worth of damage, it will now inflict 4.

Cost 1 STAMINA point

SUS

This spell may be cast when the caster suspects a trap of some kind. Once cast it will indicate telepathically to the caster whether or not to beware of a trap and, if so, the best protective action. If caught in a trap, this spell may also be used to minimize its effects in certain cases.

Cost 2 STAMINA points

SIX

This spell is cast on to the caster's own body. Its effect is to create multiple images of the caster, all identical and all capable of casting spells and/or attacking, although each will perform identical actions as if reflected in a mirror. Most creatures faced with these replicas will be unable to tell which is the real one and will fight all six.

Cost 2 STAMINA points

JIG

When this spell is cast, the recipient gets the uncontrollable urge to dance. The caster can make any creature dance merry jigs by playing a small Bamboo Flute. If this flute has been found, the affected creature will dance for as long as it is played. This will normally give the caster time to escape – or he may continue playing and watch the show!

Cost 1 STAMINA point

GOB

This creation spell requires any number of teeth of Goblins. The spell may be cast on to these teeth to create one, two, or an army of Goblins. These Goblins can then be commanded to fight an enemy or perform any duties they are instructed to carry out. They will disappear as soon as their duties have been performed.

Cost 1 STAMINA point per Goblin created

YOB

Casting this spell requires the tooth of a Giant. When this spell is cast upon the tooth correctly, a Giant, some twelve feet tall, will be created instantly. The caster has control over the Giant and may command him to fight an opponent, perform some feat of strength, etc. The Giant will disappear when his duty is done.

Cost 1 STAMINA point

GUM

Casting this spell, together with using the contents of a vial of glue, will cause the glue to become super-sticky, bonding in less than a second. Using the spell, the caster will be able to stick creatures to the floor or walls, although it is necessary to get the victim into contact with the glue from the vial. This can be done, for instance, by throwing it at the creature's feet, or by resting it on top of a slightly opened door, so that it falls when the door is opened.

Cost 1 STAMINA point

HOW

This spell is to be used in perilous situations when information about the safest way of escape is desired. When it has been cast, the caster will get an inclination towards one exit or, if a means of defence is present near by, will be directed towards it by a strange psychic force.

Cost 2 STAMINA points

DOC

Medicinal potions carried and used by the caster will, under this spell, have their effects increased so that they will heal any wounded human or creature who drinks them. The potions may be used on the caster – the spell must be cast as potion is being administered – but they will not bring a being who has actually died back to life.

Cost 1 STAMINA point

DOZ

This spell may be cast upon any creature, reducing its movements and reactions to about a sixth of its normal speed. Thus the creature appears to move as in a dream sequence, making it much easier to evade or defeat.

Cost 2 STAMINA points

DUD

By casting this spell, the caster can create an illusion of treasure in its many forms. Gold pieces, silver coins, gems and jewels can be created at will and these can be used to distract, pay off or bribe creatures. The illusory riches will disappear as soon as the caster is out of sight.

Cost 2 STAMINA points

MAG

This spell protects its caster from most magical spells. It must be cast quickly, before the attacking spell takes effect. It works by neutralizing the attacking spell which disperses harmlessly. This spell is thus a very powerful protective weapon, but it does not work against every spell.

Cost 2 STAMINA points

POP

A potent little spell, but one which calls for great mental concentration, this spell must be cast on small pebbles. Once charged with magic, these pebbles can be thrown and will explode on impact. Apart from being dangerous to anything within shatter distance, the pebbles make a loud bang when they explode.

Cost 1 STAMINA point

FAL

This spell is useful if the caster is caught in a pit trap or falls from a considerable height. When cast, it makes the caster's body as light as a feather. The caster will float down through the air and land gently on the ground.

Cost 2 STAMINA points

DIM

A good defensive spell, this can be cast at any creature attacking the caster. Its effect is to muddle the mind of its victim, temporarily confusing the creature. However, it must be handled with caution, as a creature so deranged may act irrationally and unpredictably.

Cost 2 STAMINA points

FOG

This spell may only be cast in a closed room with no windows. Once cast, the room turns pitch black in the eyes of all but the caster – even though torches and candles may still be burning. It renders blind any creatures within the room. Its effects are only temporary.

Cost 2 STAMINA points

MUD

As this spell is cast, the caster must sprinkle grains of sand on to the floor as desired (e.g. in front of a creature). The spell takes effect on the sand and the floor, creating a pool of quicksand. Any creature stepping on this quicksand will slowly be drowned in it.

Cost 1 STAMINA point

NIF

As this spell is cast, the air surrounding the caster becomes filled with a nauseating stench. This smell is so horrible that it will cause any creature which catches a whiff of it to vomit violently. It will thus weaken any adversary with a sense of smell. This includes the caster unless he is wearing a pair of nose plugs. The effect will be more pronounced in creatures with large noses.

Cost 1 STAMINA point

TEL

To activate this spell, the caster must wear a cloth skullcap. With the aid of this cap, the spell will allow the user to read the mind of any intelligent creature encountered, learning about its strengths, weaknesses, the contents of nearby rooms, etc.

Cost 1 STAMINA point

GAK

In order to use this spell, the caster must be in possession of a Black Facemask, which must be worn while the spell is being cast. It can be cast directly on to an opponent and has the effect of creating a terrible fear within his mind. Brave creatures will be less affected than cowardly ones, so the effect varies from a cold sweat and loss of nerve to the creature's being reduced to a quivering jelly cowering in the corner of a room.

Cost 1 STAMINA point

SAP

The effect of this spell, which is only useful in combat, is to demoralize an opponent so that his will to win is lost. Any creature so demoralized will be easier to defeat – though victory is still not certain.

Cost 2 STAMINA points

GOD

This is a form of illusion which can only be performed if the caster is wearing a Jewel of Gold. When this spell is cast, any creatures or humans in the vicinity will take an immediate liking to the caster. This does *not* mean that they will not fight, if such is their duty, but they will be more likely to give information that they would not normally give. They may even help the caster in spite of their normally being hostile.

Cost 1 STAMINA point

KIN

This creation spell is useful in battles. It requires the use of a Gold-Backed Mirror, which must be pointed at a creature as the spell is cast. It creates an exact replica of any creature being fought and his double is under the control of the caster, who can instruct it to fight the original creature. Both will fight with the same strengths and weaknesses – only luck will separate their fates. If the original creature dies, its double will disappear. It will also disappear if it is defeated.

Cost 1 STAMINA point

PEP

A Potion of Fire Water must be taken by the caster for this spell to be used. It will enhance the effects of the Fire Water to give the caster double or treble his or her own normal strength. Although the effects are temporary, they will normally be enough to aid in battle or to perform some feat of super-strength.

Cost 1 STAMINA point

ROK

Stone dust is required for this spell. The dust must be thrown at a creature as the spell is being cast. Within seconds, the victim will start to petrify. As its movements become slower and eventually cease, it will start to turn grey. Some moments after the spell is cast, it will have solidified into a grey stone statue.

Cost 1 STAMINA point

NIP

The caster must cast this spell on his or her own body. Under the influence of this spell, the caster becomes exceedingly quick and may run, speak, think or fight at three times normal speed. However, this spell will only take effect if the caster sniffs Yellow Powder before using the spell.

Cost 1 STAMINA point

HUF

In order to use this spell, the caster must possess the Galehorn, a trumpet-like instrument which plays a discordant note. The spell is cast on to the horn and it is blown in a particular direction. As the spell takes effect, a tremendous wind rushes from the trumpet. This wind is capable of blowing over man-sized creatures, or it can be used to blow things off shelves, over ledges, etc.

Cost 1 STAMINA point

FIX

Applicable to both animate and inanimate objects, this spell has the effect of holding an opponent or object where it stands, unable to move even if in mid-air. In order to cast this spell, however, the caster must be holding a Staff of Oak Sapling. Anything held fast by this spell will remain frozen until the caster leaves the vicinity.

Cost 1 STAMINA point

NAP

Effective only against living creatures, this spell causes them to become drowsy and, within several seconds, to fall fast asleep. It is used in conjunction with a Brass Pendulum. The spell concentrates the creature's attention on the Pendulum, which the caster must swing slowly to and fro before the creature, in order to hypnotize it.

Cost 1 STAMINA point

ZEN

In order to cast this spell, the caster must wear a Jewel-Studded Medallion around the neck. Casting this spell will then allow the caster to float in the air at any height desired. A magician hovering thus will remain suspended for as long as desired and may float around at will.

Cost 1 STAMINA point

YAZ

This spell will not work unless the caster is wearing a fine Pearl Ring. Casting the spell while wearing this ring renders the caster's body invisible to any reasonably intelligent creature. It may be used to give considerable advantage in battle or to escape from a dangerous situation. Any creature with ears will be able to hear the caster as he moves around the room. Less intelligent creatures will only be partially convinced, as this is a form of illusion spell.

Cost 1 STAMINA point

SUN

This spell may only be cast upon the yellow Sun Jewel. Once cast, the Jewel begins to glow brightly. Its intensity is under the control of the caster, who can make it brilliant – in order to blind attacking creatures – or just light enough to act as a torch to see in dark rooms.

Cost 1 STAMINA point

KID

In order to use this spell, the caster must be wearing a Bracelet of Bone. Once the spell is cast, the caster must concentrate on a particular illusion (e.g. the floor is made of hot coals, the caster has turned into a Demon, etc.) and this illusion will appear real in the eyes of its intended victim. This may allow time for escape or lower a creature's defences. The spell will not work on non-intelligent creatures. If the caster acts in such a way as to destroy the illusion (e.g. turns into a mouse and then goes on to strike the creature with a sword), its effect will be lost immediately.

Cost 1 STAMINA point

RAP

To use this spell, the caster must be wearing a Green-Haired Wig. In conjunction with this wig, the spell will allow the caster to understand the language of, and communicate with, creatures speaking a non-human tongue (e.g. Goblins, Orcs, etc.).

Cost 1 STAMINA point

YAP

This spell allows the caster to understand the language of, and communicate with, most animals. It will be ineffective unless the caster is wearing a Green-Haired Wig.

Cost 1 STAMINA point

ZIP

An invaluable aid in close battle, this spell is only usable when the caster is wearing a Ring of Green Metal, such metal having been mined from the Craggen Rock. When the spell is cast on to his ring, it enables the wearer to disappear, and reappear a short distance away. The transportation can be through some soft materials such as wood and clay, but is blocked by stone, metal and the like. It is a rather unreliable spell, though – occasionally it has disastrous results.

Cost 1 STAMINA point

FAR

In conjunction with an Orb of Crystal, this spell will enable its caster to see, with certain limitations, into the future. The Orb must be held in the hands and the spell is recited while concentrating on the Orb. Very little control can be exercised on exactly what will be seen, but the normal tendency is to see near-future events.

Cost 1 STAMINA point

RES

When cast upon a dead human or humanoid creature (i.e. one with two arms, two legs, a head, etc.) while Holy Water is being sprinkled on the corpse, this spell brings it back to life. The resurrection takes some time to work – the body does not simply spring back on its feet – and the ex-corpse can be killed again as normal. For some time after this spell has taken effect, the resurrected creature is dull and dozy, but it may answer questions asked of it by the caster.

Cost 1 STAMINA point

ZED

Casting this spell is beyond the means of most minor conjurors because of the great powers of concentration necessary. In fact, in all known history, this spell has been cast only once. Its caster, a powerful Necromancer from Throben, was never seen again and thus its effects are unknown. The Necromancer's notes were subsequently found, but only indications as to its effects could be assumed. Suffice it to say that this is perhaps *the* most formidable spell in known magic lore – but no living magician knows its true effect.

Cost 7 STAMINA points